OPEN.

D.M. Pickersgill

OPEN

ISBN: 978-1-0684280-4-3

Cover Design by More Visual / bookartwork.com

PROLOGUE

He comes at me before I'm even fully through the doorway — a blur of fists and fury. No warning. No words. Just impact.

My back hits the floor hard, the breath punched out of me, and suddenly we're rolling.

He's on top of me, swinging wildly, one punch catching the side of my jaw so hard my vision whites out. Another lands. My head cracks against the tiles. He's stronger than he looks. Desperate. Like this is the last thing he'll ever do.

I grab at anything — shirt, skin, air. My hand hits metal. Small. Cold. A knife. I don't think. I just move.

I drive it up into him.

The sound he makes isn't a scream. It's a choke. A wet gasp.

His hand flies to his throat and comes away red. He blinks at me like he can't believe it.

I pull the blade back and strike again.

Again.

Again.

Hot blood hits my face, my clothes. His body jerks, then slackens, collapsing over me with dead weight.

I shove him off, choking on the smell. My heart is hammering so hard I can hear it in my skull.

Silence settles. No shouting. No footsteps. Nothing but the drip of blood on tile.

And then… I feel it.

The sense of being watched.

Not by him.

By something else.

Somewhere in the room, a tiny red light glows.

Chapter 1

TOM

I'm sweating. Not a subtle shimmer across the forehead. Not a dignified glow. Sweating in that full-bodied, damp-shirt, regretting-my-life-choices way.

It's the middle of July, thirty degrees outside, and somehow even hotter inside the sauna that is Revolution on Baldwin Street. Whoever thought to host a speed dating night upstairs on the balcony should be charged with crimes against humanity. Bristol's early evening might be glittering outside, the bars humming with life on a sunny Thursday, but I'm trapped in a steam-bath-cum-enforced-small-talk-nightmare that serves overpriced cocktails in jam jars.

Yanking at my shirt collar, I silently curse myself for wearing pale blue cotton.

Idiot.

The sweat patches are practically performance art by this point. I can feel the damp vertical line extending down my back, essentially waving at those behind me.

The long balcony bar has been transformed tonight into speed-dating central. Fairy lights droop overhead, looking borderline whimsical, while tiny round tables dot the space, each with a lit candle in an attempt to add romance.

A number card is propped at each table. I've been positioned at table four, where I'm pretending to read the "rules" sheet in front of me as if it contains spoilers for the end of Stranger Things.

I already know the rules: five minutes per person, rotate when the bell rings, give them a tick if you fancy seeing them again.

Nothing complicated.

Except the dating itself, which is very complicated indeed. Complicated, gruelling, exhausting. Like actively trying to find love during a fire drill.

I scratch the stubble on my chin. It's "deliberately rugged," something I thought I'd try out for in a desperate attempt to add sex appeal, but I lack the confidence to pull that one off. My brown hair is flecked with grey that arrived uninvited and now refuses to leave.

I've been here twelve minutes, avoiding eye contact with the other gentlemen as much as feasibly possible, while also taking in every inch of them without being clocked.

I scan the room, doing the mathematics nobody admits to doing.

Ten men.

I am, generously, attracted to three.

One is wearing a waistcoat without irony. Another looks like he might be here because he got lost on his way to a Wetherspoons curry club. And then there's the wild card: a Chinese student who can't be older than eighteen, to which no one has explained that it's "30s & 40s night" while equally sidestepping the safeguarding concern.

I check my reflection in the blacked-out window. Average is all I see shining back at me. Average height, average build, a little soft around the middle since the sabbatical became a lifestyle. I'm the kind of man people used to call "boy next door," although not since Britney last had a top ten hit. But I've been told I have warm eyes. Strangers tell me things in queues. A woman in Greggs once told me about sleeping with her boss's wife while lining up for a vegan lattice.

Unfortunately, this is speed dating, not confessional, and what I mostly want right now is industrial air-con and a shirt the colour of camouflage.

I sigh and glance at the event host, a relentlessly chipper drag queen named Mercedes Bends, dressed head to toe in leopard print, with matching Bette Lynch hair, who looks like she runs on vodka Red Bull and healing crystals. She claps her hands together.

"Okay, everyone, places! Let's make some magic!"

Magic. Sure.

I came tonight with the sort of optimism normally reserved for lottery winners and labradors. In my head, speed dating was going to be a glittering carousel of possibility, like some wonderful human pick-and-mix where somewhere between "semi-professional magician" and "accountant with a good pension plan" I'd stumble upon The One.

Last night, while lying in bed, my optimistic brain tried to convince me this was going to be all fireworks and violins. A night of easy laughter, natural chemistry and that electricity when your hands touch for the first time. Maybe even a romantic story we could one day tell at our wedding:

We only had five minutes, but that's all we needed to find true love.

A wealth of rom-com cliches.

In reality, of course, I'm wedged into a sticky chair on an overheated balcony, praying my deodorant has more stamina than I do.

But still, I live in hope. I came prepared to meet my Disney prince, even if destiny had only packed me ten dwarves.

I look over the edge of the balcony to the bar below. At least there's a practical escape route if it all gets too uncomfortable. Extreme, but a legitimate option.

My first date is an IT Consultant called Gareth, 37.

"So, what do you do?" Gareth asks, leaning forward with the zeal of a man who probably has very strong opinions about HDMI cables.

Here it comes.

The part where I have to explain my life in thirty-second soundbites, as if condensing forty-two years of awkwardness and mild trauma into a LinkedIn summary.

"I, um, work in finance," I say automatically, though that's not true anymore. "Well, I did. Took a step back recently. Bit of time off."

"Burnout?" Gareth asks.

"Death of my father, actually," I reply. Because why not drop a conversational anvil in the first thirty seconds?

Gareth looks uncomfortable. "Right. Sure. OK. Sorry."

I force a smile. "Oh, it's fine. I'm doing the whole self-care thing. Yoga, journaling, meditation. You know. Wellness."

Gareth nods like a man who has never meditated in his life.

Much like me, to be fair. Same with journaling. It's just one of those things you say to sound like you're into personal growth, when really you're spending your evenings watching Netflix murder-documentaries while scrolling PornHub.

"And do you like gerbils?" he asks, as if it's a perfectly sensible segue from parental death response.

"Gerbils?" I ask, my forehead turning into a scrunchy.

"Well, I have gerbils," Gareth says, with the expression of a serious gerbil owner.

"Gerbils? Like plural?" I ask, wondering why I need this clarity.

"Yes, I have fourteen of them. But they're all very friendly."

"Oh, good," I faux-engage.

"Apart from Betty, but she can get anxiety during the winter months."

I consider the over-the-balcony escape route, settling for mentally scrubbing Gareth off the list with three and a half minutes left to go.

Date two is Marcus, a 40-year-old property developer, originally from Windsor. He spends at least four and a half minutes talking about his buy-to-let portfolio and how "Brexit was actually a good thing if you knew how to play it right." I spend four and a half minutes imagining Marcus being chased through the streets of Stokes Croft by his tenants with rolling pins, in response to the latest rent hike.

Bell rings. Mercifully.

Date three: Alex, 40, nurse.

Finally. Someone I actually find attractive. Alex has glorious eyes and a soothing smile. I feel my face reddening and my chest tightening like it's 2002 and I'm buying condoms and lube in Boots.

I can barely make eye contact. I tug my shirt away from my chest and vow never again to trust a weather app that says *feels like 25°C.*

It feels like an air fryer.

"So, what's your story?" Alex asks, eyes twinkling.

Here it comes again. My story. I have so many versions of it, depending on who's asking. Tonight's version: "Forty-two, Bristol-born, divorced, currently on a sabbatical. Bit of a hopeless romantic."

"Divorced?" Alex raises an eyebrow.

"Yes. We were together for ten years. Married at thirty, divorced at forty. But all very amicable."

That's a lie. It wasn't amicable.

It was Daniel.

Daniel, who controlled the money, the holidays, the thermostat. Daniel, who called me "too sensitive" so often that I started to believe it was stamped on my DNA.

But I don't say that here.

Instead, I shrug. "We're still friends."

Another lie. I haven't spoken to Daniel in months. But it's easier to pretend, in five-minute chunks, that I'm a functional adult with healthy breakups.

Alex smiles. "At least you know what you want now, right?"

I want to say *Yes. I want Disney-princess love. I want a grand sweeping romance with fireworks and orchestras and the kind of sex that makes the neighbours complain.*

Instead, I say, "Yes. Something like that."

Bell rings. Alex squeezes my hand like he's consoling my whole existence, before moving on. I'm left staring at the sweat marks on my notepad from where my palm was rested.

The dates blur together after that.

A man who talks exclusively about CrossFit. Another who calls himself "sapiosexual" and makes it sound like a medical condition. One who is actually quite nice but looks disturbingly like my uncle.

By the end of round ten, I feel like I've run a marathon in conversational small talk. My smile muscles ache. My shirt could be wrung out over a houseplant.

Mercedes Bends bounces past, sequins around her deep eye makeup sparkling. "Well, how did we do tonight?"

I muster a grin. "I think my soulmate might have been at Wagamama instead."

She laughs sympathetically and hands me my scorecard. "Fill it in anyway. You never know."

But I do know. I know I'll tick maybe one or two names, they won't tick me back, and I'll get the dreaded "Thanks for coming!" email tomorrow.

I stare at the scorecard, then tick Alex, because those eyes. I hesitate over the nice one who looks like Uncle Stephen, but, decide incest-adjacent is not a kink I need to unlock today.

After the dates, the evening should continue with all the guys coming together to chat some more, but after pretending to go to the bathroom, I bolt out the door like I've just nicked a mug from Starbucks.

Walking through the city, I find myself by the harbourside. The place is alive with laughter, music, and the clink of glasses. Life is carrying on elsewhere while I marinate in my own mediocrity.

I catch my reflection again in a dark shop window: the kind eyes, the fluffed-out hair, the sweat halo. Not unhandsome, I decide, in the way a mid-renovation kitchen is not unlivable.

Me. Tom: a good man, a little dented, a little anxious, funny on a good day. The sort you could bring home, and I'd do your washing up without being asked.

A couple brushes past, laughing into each other's shoulders. I want that. Shoulder laughter, the nose-snorting kind. I want a kiss I can hear. I want a hand to take without a seminar on terms and conditions.

And then, for some reason, I'm thinking of Daniel.

Ten years married. Ten years of subtle control.

I had mistaken it for love, once. Mistaken being managed for being cherished.

By the time I left, I was in pieces. Two years later, the pieces still don't fit back together.

My dating life since has been a depressing parade of men with exit strategies. The ghoster who said, "I'm just so busy," but I still see him on Grindr every time I log in. The one who cried at dessert because he wasn't over his ex (I paid. Of course, I paid). The man who brought his mother to the third date because "she has great instincts about people" and whose mother referred to me as "nice."

Nice. Jesus. The worst word in dating. You may as well just write BEIGE on my forehead with a Sharpie.

I laugh bitterly to myself. If there's a god of romance, he must have me on some kind of watchlist.

Love, it seems, is still on back order.

Chapter 2

TOM

My house looks cosy in the shine of the Clifton streetlights. It's a three-storey Georgian terrace, all cream stone and sash windows. The kind of house that estate agents describe as "full of period charm."

I remind myself of this every time the boiler breaks when the temperature falls below zero.

I fumble the key in the lock and push open the door into silence. Except not silence, because here comes Buster, my tabby cat, tail upright like a feather duster.

Buster doesn't so much greet as judge. His narrow eyes scream *give me tuna.*

"Evening," I say, bending down to scratch him behind the ears. "Did you find a cure for loneliness while I was out?"

He meows in the tone of a cat who has already filed for emancipation.

Inside, the house is lovely in a way that it absolutely should be for the fortune it costs. High ceilings, cornices, wooden floors polished enough for me to slide across in white socks. The walls are painted tasteful shades with ridiculous names like "Urban Pigeon" and "Elephant's Breath." There are plants. Well, there were plants. What remains is an arrangement of terracotta pots full of dried-up spider plants cursing my name.

I toss my keys into the bowl by the door, shrug off the sweat-stained shirt, and head for the kitchen. It's sleek and expensive, all granite counters and integrated appliances I ignore in favour of my air fryer. The wine fridge whirs quietly, its contents a selection of impulse buys made after watching one too many reruns of *Food and Drink* on iPlayer.

I select a bottle of red, pour a glass the size of a swimming pool, and sink into the sofa.

Buster leaps up and kneads at my lap with claws that could perforate steel. I wince. "Yes, you're the only consistent relationship in my life. Do you have to puncture me to prove it?"

I take a long sip of wine and stare at the bookshelves across the room. Instead of books, my father's old cricket trophies sit there instead. They look out of place up there, but I can't put them in storage. That feels like betrayal. So they stay, passing judgement on the son who never once bowled a ball.

Twelve months have passed since the funeral.

Twelve months since I stood by the grave in a hired black suit, wondering why I felt empty instead of heartbroken.

People had said, *You must be devastated, losing your dad.*

And I was. But not the way they imagined.

I grieve the idea of my father more than the man himself. The idea of Sunday kickabouts, shared pints, conversations that weren't about weather or work.

Instead, our relationship had been a polite cold war.

He wanted a son he could talk cricket with, a son who didn't come out as gay at twenty-five and move to the city to work in finance.

I wanted a dad who would ask me how I was without it sounding like a job interview.

We missed each other constantly. Not literally, but mentally, emotionally. Just never connected. Ships in the night, except one ship was captained by stoicism and the other by sarcasm.

And yet, I miss him. Or maybe more miss the possibility of what could have been.

Guilt soaks everything: that I didn't try harder, that the last conversation was about an overdue MOT, that I will never now fix what was broken.

I take another gulp of wine.

It was his death, in the end, that shook me awake. The high-paying finance job, the long nights at the office. Work had consumed my life. And for what? To end up like him: respected, comfortable, emotionally unavailable?

No. I walked away. Or at least, drifted. The inheritance gave me freedom. The house, the money, the security. His only gift, really, was the means to stop becoming him.

So here I am. Sabbatical. Time off. Focus on mental health, they call it.

I call it not-working.

Either way, it's my chance to find meaning in my life, move on from the past I've been wed to for so long, and find love.

Buster purrs, loud and demanding, and I stroke him absently.

I open my phone. No new matches on the dating apps, but I do a few courtesy swipes for the dopamine hit, like a man shaking an empty vending machine, before opening my photos.

Scrolling through, despite being divorced for nearly two years, there are still plenty of pictures of Daniel and me: Barcelona, Australia, Japan.

Daniel.

Ten years of marriage. Ten years of being told I was too much or not enough, depending on the day.

Ten years spent overthinking everything I did to pacify Daniel's volatile mood.

Daniel, who made me believe that control was love. Who had a love for gambling, but not the debts that came with it. The divorce should have freed me, but it only left me guarded and scarred.

I close the photo app and place the phone by my side.

As if on cue, my phone vibrates.

A message: Daniel.

I stare at the notification on the lock screen. Just his name. This isn't unusual. He texts sporadically. Sometimes just to say hi. Always Daniel, never me, but something I always find uncomfortable. Even now, I feel the obligation to acknowledge and reply.

But not tonight.

I should open it. I should see what the man who once held ten years of my life in his hands has to say.

But I don't. I place the phone face down on the coffee table, heart beating louder than the cat's purr.

Outside, a car door slams.

Buster lifts his head, his ears twitching, and I do the same.

The phone vibrates once more on the table.

I don't reach for it.

Instead, I turn my head and glance toward the window.

For the briefest moment, I swear I see movement in the darkness outside, like a figure at the edge of the lamplight, standing motionless.

Watching.

I blink, and it's gone.

Just a shadow.

Probably.

Chapter 3

TOM

Saturday morning, and Tesco is already auditioning for Dante's next circle of hell.

The automatic doors swoosh open, unleashing an attack on my senses. Trolleys clatter, children shriek, while the man at the entrance is attempting to hand out leaflets for "Tesco Mobile" with the same enthusiasm as a hostage reading a ransom note.

I throw a basket over my shoulder and head into the madness.

As I drifted off to sleep last night, I had envisioned the morning differently: maybe some brunch, a little flat white action, some quiet self-reflection.

Instead, my inbox delivered a cheery email over porridge:

Thank you for attending Bristol Speed Dating! We're sorry to inform you that you had no mutual matches this time. But don't give up, love is just around the corner!

They may as well have added: Please try again once you've grown a personality.

So now, here I am. A man on a mission to buy salad and distract myself from the fact I'm statistically less appealing than a CrossFit obsessive and a man with fourteen gerbils.

I push past a display of doughnuts, their sugar-glazed eyes begging me to adopt them, but I resist and head into the fray.

The supermarket is chaos.

Walking down the first aisle, I side-step a toddler who's wailing, while parents look like exhausted zombies. Hitting the cereal aisle, an old man blocks the way with his trolley, his eyes focused on a box of Shreddies like it's a new Harry Potter manuscript. I step around a dropped strawberry yoghurt pot that has splattered across the floor, resulting in an anonymous pink footprint treading up the aisle.

I weave through it all, narrating to myself. "This is fine. Civilisation is intact."

I toss items into my basket: olives, hummus, sourdough bread. God, when did my inheritance turn me into a middle-class cliché?

I reach for a bottle of wine, think better of it.

Too early. Even for me.

I take two.

My phone vibrates, this time with the familiar pop of Grindr. Against my own better judgment, I open it.

A new message: *Hey, how's your morning going?*

The profile picture is disarmingly wholesome, stopping me dead: a strong jawline, striking blue eyes, the sort of smile that looks like it could comfortably put up an IKEA shelf and still ask about my day. There are other pictures: walking in the forest, laughing at a coffee shop. And ot an ounce of flesh on display.

Even the position field is empty.

This feels unique. I read the profile.

Dog dad. Cooks a mean Sunday roast. Loves a 90s teen slasher marathon.

I love all these things.

For a moment, my chest lifts. A man who doesn't open with anatomy shots? Revolutionary. I start to type a reply, something a bit light, a touch of wit, but then my eyes flick to the fine print beneath the profile.

In an open relationship.

Of course. The wholesome ones are always attached, like a limited-edition collectable you can admire but never actually own.

Why is everyone in an open relationship these days? Monogamy must be retro.

I drop the phone back in my pocket and round the corner into the fruit and veg section.

As I'm looking around for a bag of spinach, a voice comes from my side.

"Any idea how to tell if these are ripe?"

I look up and jolt at the sight of an extremely handsome man holding up a green grenade.

No, wait. It's an avocado.

He has dark hair, stubble, and a light blue jacket thrown over a white T-shirt. Effortlessly attractive in a way that says I woke up like this without the Beyoncé irony.

I blink. My brain shuts down.

Words. I know words. I just have to pick some.

"Um, I think it's something about earlobes," I respond as if I'm talking in cryptic code.

"Earlobes?"

"I mean…" *God, what do I mean? Think of normal person words.* "… If it feels like your earlobe, apparently. That's what Nigella said once."

He laughs, warm and easy. "Any earlobe in particular?"

I feel my heart rate picking up pace. The internal panic or a handsome stranger starting avocado-based small talk with me sends me into a spiral. I make an odd laughing sound, kind of like a startled donkey clearing its throat, then try to disguise it with a cough.

Like James Bond levels of smooth.

"Yes. Though, ideally, don't test against a random stranger without asking them first." I finally say. "That gets you looks."

"Well, consent is sexy," he says. His eyes twinkle as he talks, although arguably that could be in my head.

I laugh nervously at the mention of the word sexy from this delightful stranger. This is immediately followed by me choking on my own saliva.

Nothing says date me like mild asphyxiation over avocado chat.

"Well… yes…" I manage to say.

He chuckles, presses the avocado gently, then holds it to his ear like he's trying to hear it tick. "This one's saying I'm in luck."

I aggressively smile, kind of akin to Jack Nicholson's Joker, before reeling it in. "Well, the avocado support hotline is always available," I reply.

"Excellent, it's just what I needed this morning," he says with a grin.

Is this flirting? It feels like flirting. In Tesco. Am I in an alternate dimension?

He tosses the avocado into his basket. I pretend to need tomatoes and grab a packet in front of me, along with a bag of lettuce.

He gestures to my basket. "Spinach, lettuce, tomatoes… are you one of those people who actually enjoys salad?"

And he's extending the conversation.

Various parts of my anatomy flutter.

My anxiety levels are through the roof. I laugh again. Too hard, again. So much so that a passing toddler turns and stares at me.

"I'm…one of those people who buys salad and then throws it out two weeks later because it liquefies in the fridge," I say.

He laughs again. His laugh calms me somewhat. God, it's a nice laugh. I feel it in places salad has never reached.

"Ah, well, the good intention is there. I had to use all available willpower to walk calmly past the doughnuts."

"The pink ones with the white sprinkles?" I fire back.

"Yes!"

"I had the same exact thought. All I want is to murder a six-pack of those over a cup of tea."

"Sounds like heaven."

Our eyes catch. For a moment, the chaos of Tesco fades: no screaming toddler, no squeaky wheels, just us and the smell of fresh pastries.

"I'm Pete," he says, holding out a hand.

"Tom." I shake it, noticing the rainbow flag image on his Apple Watch's display.

My chest feels like it's been intravenously hit with eight espresso shots.

I may even have audibly gasped as my eyes lock on the watch.

As our hands release, I think about asking.

Ask for his number, my brain screams.

My throat goes dry, my hand still warm from the handshake. The words almost tumble out: How about coffee sometime?

But nerves clamp down. My face feels bright red, even my ears feel hot.

It's Tesco, for God's sake.

So instead, I smile, too quickly, and say, "Well, good luck with the avocado surgery."

Pete grins. "Thanks. Enjoy the liquefied salad."

And just like that, we part. He heads down the aisle, basket swinging. I loiter, watching him disappear around the corner.

I kick myself immediately. The moment was there. An organic, romantic connection. Served up on a platter, and I bottled it.

By the time I leave the store, Pete is gone. I scan the car park instinctively, just in case he's heading to his car, but no luck.

I stand there, dazed by the whole experience, clutching onto my shopping like it's evidence of our conversation.

Did that just happen? Did I just flirt in Tesco? Meet someone organically, in the wild?

I thought my romantic life had been reduced to awful dating apps and rejection emails. But no. A random handsome stranger somewhere on the LGBTQ+ spectrum has approached me and made pleasant, borderline-flirty small talk.

For the first time in years, albeit fleeting, a real organic connection seems possible.

My phone vibrates. Heart leaping, I stare at it, only to freeze.

Daniel.

A short, sharp message: *I need to see you.*

The unexpected opportunity of Tesco, the warmth of Pete's grin: it all feels a million miles away.

I stare at the screen, chest tight. I don't reply.

Not yet.

Chapter 4

PETE

Pete takes the long way home.

The M32 would be quicker, but today he doesn't want quick. He wants to delay the inevitable return home while he replays the morning in his head on a loop.

Tesco, of all places. He's still half-laughing at the ridiculousness of it. Out of the thousands of forgettable shopping trips in his life, this one gave him Tom.

Tom.

The name sounds comfortable already, like something he's said a hundred times before. There was something about him, something unpolished and natural. Not the artificial smiles Pete usually encounters.

Tom seemed… real.

Pete parks outside the house but doesn't go in straight away. He kills the engine, sits on the drive and watches the quiet street in his mirror.

It's a nice house, on paper. Bigger than anything he grew up in. A beautiful façade of comfort, neat hedges, white shutters. But Pete knows better than to trust appearances. Houses can be prisons as easily as sanctuaries.

He leans back, closing his eyes as a memory slips through. One where he's lying awake in a damp bedroom, listening to arguments through thin walls, plates crashing, drunken footsteps coming closer.

He learned early that safety is never guaranteed.

Inside, the house is dim. The curtains are drawn even though it's still daylight. Pete drops his keys in the bowl by the door and kicks off his boots, careful not to make too much noise.

The silence is uneasy, one he doesn't want to break.

He moves through the rooms quietly, like a guest in his own home. In the kitchen, he fills a glass of water, trying to ignore the knot tightening in his stomach.

Pete runs a hand over his face. He doesn't usually feel this restless after meeting someone. But Tom won't leave his head.

At home, things are strained. Tense. He never knows if today will be calm or explosive. Sometimes he wonders how much longer he can keep juggling everything before it all topples.

Pete leans back against the kitchen counter and stares out at the garden.

Meeting Tom makes him think about the cracks in his life, the ones that get wider by the day. Thinking about Tom brings him comfort from all that.

Comforting, but dangerous.

Pete lets out a slow breath.

On the countertop next to him, he notices a flash of red.

Blood.

Dried. From last night's incident.

He must have missed a bit when he was frantically cleaning. The smear is thin but unmistakable, a rusty line against the light stone. Grabbing a cloth and the strongest spray he can find, he scrubs hard until the cloth turns pink, the sharp smell of chemicals filling the kitchen. He keeps going long after it's gone, polishing until the stone shines, until there's no trace left.

Not of blood, not of last night, not of anything.

Because that's the point. No traces.

Upstairs, a voice calls his name. Sharp. Cutting.

Pete stiffens. The knot in his stomach coils tighter. He pushes himself upright and pockets his phone.

"Coming," he says, forcing his tone to stay light.

But his hand is still slightly damp from the cloth, and when he looks down, he swears he can see a smear of red along his skin.

He rubs it against his jeans, hard.

And then he climbs the stairs.

Chapter 5

TOM

I lie sprawled on my bed, one arm folded beneath my head, my phone resting in my chest. My bedroom is dim except for the golden shine of the bedside lamp, casting long shadows across my wall.

My phone vibrates. It's Craig calling. I answer immediately, grateful for the distraction.

"Alright, lover boy," Craig teases. "You've been quiet all day."

I grin despite myself. "You make me sound like I've got some sordid secret."

"You do. It's called a crush. Now come on, give me everything."

So, I do. Staring up at the ceiling, I recount the whole strange, wonderful encounter with Pete at Tesco. Craig interrupts constantly with questions, gasps, and exaggerated noises of approval.

"You met in Tesco? Tesco?" Craig cackles. "I thought you were a Waitrose boy these days since you became a middle-class Clifton snob."

"Well, yes, normally I would, but thank God, I went back to my roots. Who knew Tesco was the new Love Island?" I say, laughing. "Organic too, not matching on some stupid app. Like a real-world connection. It honestly felt like I was in some kind of '90s Hugh Grant film."

Craig hums approvingly. "Real is good. Real is rare. And he's handsome, right?"

"So handsome." I bite my lip, the memory of Pete's smile making my chest fizz. "Like cheek dimples kind of handsome."

Craig groans dramatically. "Well, thank God. I was starting to worry you'd end up alone forever with just Buster the cat for company."

"Buster's already planning the wedding," I shoot back.

"Don't pretend that Buster gives a fuck about anything other than the tuna in your cupboards."

"True."

We fall into easy laughter, the kind that's carried us through years of friendship. It still amazes me, sometimes, that Craig and I made it through. We'd dated briefly in our early twenties for two weeks. A collection of drunken dinners, ill-advised kisses, and one particularly awkward fumble in Craig's old student flat. By mutual, silent agreement, we'd decided we were better off as friends. Over twenty years later, that decision felt like the smartest thing I'd ever done.

"So, you're already very healthily planning the wedding in your head?" Craig asks.

"Yes."

"Based on a conversation in the fruit and veg aisle."

"Yes."

"With someone you've not even swapped numbers with."

"That's right, yes."

"Excellent, can I have front-row seats at the ceremony? I need an excuse to dress up."

"Of course you can. Your husband not wining and dining you this week?"

Craig snorts. "Don't make me laugh, the most excitement we had was watching the final of *The Traitors New Zealand* on Tuesday night."

"Wow, that sounds about as fun as my speed dating rejection email."

"Actually, it was exceptional television. That said, we have a busy weekend ahead of us."

"A busy weekend as in a DIY project in the spare room, or a busy weekend as in you'll need two days and a vitamin B injection to recover from it?" I ask.

"Definitely the second one," Craig admits.

I shake my head. "You dirty dogs. I don't care what you say, your sex lives are far more exciting than mine."

There's a pause, just long enough for my phone to vibrate again. I pull it away from my ear and glance at the screen. It's Daniel.

Craig picks up on the silence. "What is it?"

I pause, hesitant to answer. "Daniel."

There's a groan from Craig. "Oh, for God's sake. What does he want?"

I open the message:

We need to meet.

Just that. My chest tightens.

"He says he wants to meet," I murmur.

"Of course he does," Craig snaps. "That's what he does. He dangles you, reels you back in, just to keep control. Ignore it."

I chew the inside of my cheek. Daniel. The name still stings.

"He sounds serious," I say.

Craig's voice sharpens. "Serious? Tom, he was serious about controlling what you wore to dinner. And making you doubt yourself every five minutes. You spent most of your relationship walking on eggshells. He doesn't get another chance."

I nod, though he can't see me. "You're right."

"I'm always right."

The warmth returns to Craig's tone. "Forget Daniel. You've got something good starting here with your new imaginary husband Pete. Don't let that bastard ruin it before it's even begun."

I swallow. "Okay. I'll try."

Craig exhales, satisfied. "Good. Now, enough drama. Come over for dinner this week. Thursday? I'll cook. We can make plans about how you're going to live in Tesco for the next month until you bump into this guy again."

I grin. "Deal. As long as it's not that lentil stew again."

"Excuse me," Craig protests, "my lentil stew is legendary."

"It's legendary for giving me wind."

By the time we say our goodnights, my chest aches with affection for my best friend.

But when the line goes dead, silence creeps back in. I stare at Daniel's message. Craig's voice echoes in my head: *ignore it.*

I should. I know I should.

Instead, I type: *About what?* I hit send before I can stop myself.

The second it goes, regret prickles at my skin. Too late now.

I set the phone down on my chest and close my eyes. I listen to the faint hum of traffic outside, the purr of Buster curled on the chair. I tell myself I won't look at the screen again, not until morning.

Another buzz.

I don't want to look. But I have to. Just to know. I reach for my phone.

The message is not from Daniel.

There's a momentary sigh of relief, which swiftly disappears as I recognise the name on the screen.

Another name that sends a shiver down my spine.

Another message I don't want to read, but know I have to.

I can't stop thinking about the blood, the message reads.

Chapter 6

DANIEL

The phone glows in Daniel's hand, lighting up his face in the darkness. A simple message sits on the screen. Two words: *About what?*

That's it. No warmth, no enthusiasm. No remorse either. Just cold, clipped letters that make his jaw tighten.

He hasn't replied. Not yet. He's been staring at it for over three hours, while thoughts whip around his brain. He had expected Tom to agree instantly. *We need to meet.* That should have been enough. After everything they'd been through. After a decade together. Ten years of marriage that Tom has apparently discarded like an old jumper.

Daniel mutters under his breath. "About what? About us. About everything you threw away."

The words feel basic, ordinary. He needs much more from Tom.

Crouched down in the dark, Daniel brushes the cold gravel aside with anxious fingers.

Where the fuck is it?

It's 2am. Despite the weather being tropical for the last few days, it's starting to get chilly.

Now he searches for it more frantically, the frustration building. The gravel disperses under his hands, sharp edges scraping his skin. He swears softly, while the night air bites at his cheeks.

But Tom is still very much the centre of his thoughts.

How dare Tom move on, as though those years meant nothing? As though the dinners, the trips, the arguments, the reconciliations, the vows — their marriage — were just a phase?

“You don’t get to erase me,” he whispers. “You don’t get to forget.”

It should have been simple. Tom should have read his message and agreed, instantly, naturally, the way it always was.

Daniel speaks, Tom follows.

That’s the rhythm they had perfected. That’s the way it worked.

He thinks back over the last year, how quickly Tom has slotted into this new version of his life, all smiles and friends and freedom. Like Daniel was never there. Like he never mattered.

Daniel refuses to make peace with the unfairness of it. No one else ever loved Tom like he has. No one else knows him that deeply. Tom belongs with him. Always has.

“I need you back,” he mutters.

And he means it. He’ll say whatever he has to. He’ll promise anything.

As long as Tom lets him in again.

Just one more time.

About what?

He rehearses replies in his head. *About us*. Too soft. *About how you still love me.* Too hopeful. *About how you owe me ten years of your life.* Closer. That one has weight. That one might pierce through Tom’s arrogance, his newfound independence, and drag him back where he belongs.

Where the fuck is this rock?

Daniel continues to look through the flower beds, wiping his brow with his arm, his legs starting to ache as he stays crouched.

He clenches his teeth. Tom never understood what Daniel gave up for him, how much of himself he poured into that marriage. He never appreciated the rules that kept them steady, the order Daniel imposed to stop everything falling apart.

He needs that back.

He must have it, before it’s too late.

Daniel’s fingers rest on the rock that he’s been looking for.

Bingo.

The night is so quiet that even his own breathing feels loud.

Standing up, he palms the rock in his hand. That familiar rock. The same one they had during their marriage, Tom never got rid of it.

Daniel opens the fake rock to find the spare key reflecting in the moonlight.

For the first time all night, Daniel smiles.

He slowly slides the key into Tom's side door, and it turns easily, like it belongs to him.

The door yields with a gentle click.

Daniel steps inside.

Chapter 7

TOM

The next morning, I'm back doing the harbourside circuit, which is basically my version of therapy, but with more steps and opportunity for alcohol. It's the same loop I've done hundreds of times: start at the M Shed, then head up to the SS Great Britain, while dodging joggers, and smiling politely at the smug couples holding hands.

This used to be mine and Guy's loop.

Guy, my work wife, amongst other things.

Lunchtimes, back when we both worked in finance. Guy was one of the rare ones in the office who didn't make me want to fake my own death during meetings. We'd grab sandwiches, walk the harbour, and moan. I'd complain about Daniel, he'd complain about his partner, and somehow we'd both end up laughing by the time we got back. A friendship built entirely on shared grievances and ham sandwiches.

I miss that. I miss him. And now I've left my job, and he's not around, the walk feels quieter.

I pass a group of tourists taking selfies by the cranes. The backdrop of industrial history on one side and the Coyote Ugly Saloon on the other.

What a time to be alive.

My phone vibrates in my pocket. Grindr. Again. Of course.

I swipe it open like the masochist I am: the same faces, the same men who've been "online now" since 2013, with the same pictures, the same "hey" from people I ignored yesterday. Then the Lazarus accounts: the ones I've blocked, who miraculously rise from the dead with a new profile picture and slightly tweaked bio.

Sometimes Grindr is basically The Walking Dead but with more poppers.

A cock pic arrives without preamble. Looking angry and tragic. It's draining. I'm not shocked anymore. Not surprised. Just numb. Scrolling for connection on an app where ninety per cent of people think "connection" means "can you host?"

Grindr is kind of like waiting for a train: the promise of a brand new destination, the anxious excitement of a fresh start, but forty minutes later you're still standing on the platform, wet, frustrated and now you've switched to Uber for a taxi.

Profiles screaming "No timewasters," while actively wasting your time. Endless face, stating they're "Into fun," which could mean literally anything from Monopoly to fisting.

Half of them say "Discreet" or "Open" like it's a selling point, while the other half are blank profiles still demanding an immediate reply.

It's the same old story, and it's exhausting.

Honestly, it's like the world's worst job interview process, except the HR department is a headless torso and overly eager to show you their bumhole.

I went on a date with a guy called Dan a few years back, who said he would never write off Grindr because he'd made some "wonderful lasting connections" and "close friends" through it.

The only lasting connection it's helped me make is the Unity sexual health clinic on Tower Hill.

My experience? Not so much lifelong friendship as lifelong therapy bills. Clearly, Dan was living in some kind of delusional Narnia where dick pics are ice-breakers, and Mr Tumnus is discreet, into fun, no timewasters.

Well, maybe I'm just jealous. Congrats, Dan, on your wholesome, Disney Channel Grindr experience.

Although last I heard, I think he got stabbed on holiday.

I use my walk 'n' scroll Grindr time to do something productive. I try to find Pete. Not that I know where he lives, or whether he even has a Grindr account. But I set a reasonable age range and scroll anyway, hoping.

Nothing.

Which, annoyingly, makes me like him more. There's something attractive about him not being there. About not being another thumbnail on the block.

Guy used to love listening to my Grindr rants. He'd lean over in the office, stealing my crisps, and say, "Why don't they just put what they actually want? Saves everyone the drama." I told him: if gay men actually wrote what they wanted, Grindr would combust and take the entire internet down with it. He laughed, and Diet Coke came out of his nose, over his monitor.

I think about that now and smile like an idiot.

But then the smile fades. Maybe I made the whole Pete thing up. Maybe it wasn't flirting, just politeness. Maybe he looked at me and thought poor sweaty man in the fruit and veg aisle, better humour him before he cries into the prepared salad bags.

That's the thing about loneliness: it's a gaslighter.

Even when you have good friends like Craig, who'd drag me over hot coals before letting me spiral, it still creeps in and whispers: you're imagining things, no one actually likes you, stop embarrassing yourself.

I just want someone to share life with. Someone to laugh at stupid telly with. Someone to bring to Sunday lunch who isn't my cat.

Speaking of which: Buster. I make a mental note to buy more tuna on the way home or face his furry wrath.

I stop by the water's edge and watch a boat trundle past with what looks like a stag do. The chorus of straight-bloke howls sound like they're already on their third round of pints. The groom is dressed as a lobster. Life is cruelly unfair: he's meeting his soul mate by the altar next week, and I'm here, alone, desperately searching for my mystery man on a Grindr grid like it's my last hope.

I unlock my phone again and scroll back through my texts.

Daniel.

I'd replied *About what?* when he first messaged. Shouldn't have, but I did.

Then he came back with: *I'm in a difficult place. Could really do with some friendly advice.*

Friendly advice. That's what you ask a colleague about broadband providers, not your ex-husband you spent ten years trapped under.

I didn't reply. I couldn't.

But now, standing here, watching couples glide past on paddleboards like some smug Noah's ark, I feel its weight.

I start typing: *Okay. We can meet.*

My thumb pauses, then hits send before I can stop myself, where I'm immediately hit with regret.

Guy would have told me not to. He was always blunt like that. Once, when I was still married, I moaned about Daniel's silent treatments, and Guy just said, "Sounds exhausting. My other half's obsessed with scatter cushions, but at least I can switch off without getting frostbite." He had a point. He always did. I wish I still had his voice in my ear now.

As I come to the circuit, I tuck my phone away, sigh and keep walking. Past the Arnolfini, past the busker murdering Ed Sheeran on an acoustic guitar. The air carries the smell of chips and canal water, which is less romantic than it sounds.

And then, I look up.

And there he is.

Pete.

Walking towards me. Just him. Dark hair, stubble, jacket unzipped against the breeze.

For a split second, my brain panics. Should I smile? Should I say hello? Should I turn away? Almost like the anxiety and self-doubt are talking me out of approaching him.

But then he lifts a hand in recognition, smiling, and my chest does this ridiculous flip that could probably be measured on the Richter scale.

"Hey," he says when he's close enough. "Tom, right?"

And just like that, the harbour doesn't feel lonely anymore. It feels… electric.

Of course, my brain's contribution to the moment is: *Don't trip over a bollard.*

Chapter 8

TOM

He says my name and everything in me starts fizzing, like someone's tipped a can of Coke and a Berocca into my bloodstream. I try to walk toward him at a normal-human pace, rather than standard "gay spede."

"Hi," I say, aiming for suave. Although it comes out more breathy.

"Hi," he echoes, his smile easy, eyes crinkling. "Fancy seeing you here and not by the avocados."

"Uh, yes, well, I've branched out," I say. "I'm testing a new diet plan. Less healthy fats, more tripping hazards."

He laughs. "Well, it's a pleasant surprise. I'm just here for a walk while the sun is out, before it no doubt turns to torrential rainfall next week."

"Yeah, same here."

He gestures down the harbourside. "You fancy carrying on the walk with me?"

"Yes!" I say, far too quickly and with uncomfortable levels of enthusiasm. "Absolutely. Yes. Walking. Love… walking."

Inside, I'm screaming.

Oh God. He wants to walk with me. Act normal. Do not do that weird arm swing you do when you overthink walking. Just… be human. A human who walks. Normally.

Pete holds out a hand, guiding me forward, and we fall into step. The water is slap-slap against the boats, while seagulls wheel overhead, plotting crimes.

"I do this loop when my brain's noisy," I say. "Less therapy, more sea breeze and passive-aggressive seagulls."

"Same," Pete says. "Although I tend to find it's the pigeons who are really out to get me."

"Well, they can be particularly devious."

It's stupid, how quickly the conversation loosens. I had worried that Tesco was a one-off. This feels like… a sequel. The good kind. The Paddington 2 kind.

"So," Pete says, stuffing his hands in his jacket pockets. "What do you do when you're not consulting on avocado ripeness for the community?"

"Currently? Not a lot. Sabbatical. Life administration. Long walks. Arguing with my cat."

"Ah, a cat person."

"Don't put me in a box," I say. "He won't allow it."

Pete grins. "How long's the sabbatical?"

"Undefined," I start. "I used to work in finance, which was all long hours and very sexy spreadsheets. My dad died and it sort of… reoriented me. I'm figuring out what I want to be when I grow up."

"Sorry about your dad," he says. Simple, no pity, which I appreciate.

"Thanks." I clear my throat. "What about you?"

"I do a lot of project stuff," he says. He goes on to describe work in classic corporate buzzwords that mean everything and nothing: stakeholders, deliverables, timelines. "Basically, I use magic and mind games to manipulate people into doing what I need them to do to get the work done on time."

"So, you're a wizard."

"Yes! I'll put that on my LinkedIn," he says, and we both snort.

We keep walking, swapping Bristol notes. Our favourite coffee spots (we both say Ahh Toots by the Christmas Steps and then argue over our favourite cakes), favourite place for a roast (I admit my booking at the Bank Tavern for October made over ten months ago better be the most wondrous roast in existence), the Balloon Fiesta (we both pretend it's whimsical while quietly admitting watching balloons rise is only so much fun and the traffic is post-apocalyptic).

He asks if I grew up here. I nod. "Bristol-born, yes. Redland. Mum died when I was young. So, I was just mainly me and Dad…"

"And how was that?"

"Um, well he was…complicated."

"Oh, complicated how?" he asks gently.

"Um, well…we never quite… connected," I say. "He wasn't the most emotional man, kind of like having a relationship with your school headmaster. We loved each other, we just never really knew each other."

Pete nods. "Yes, family can be like that," he says. "Like you have everything and nothing in common."

"Exactly. What about you?"

"I grew up all over," he says. "Before here, I moved from place to place. Bristol's the first one that felt like home." He looks out at the water. "I like that it's lovely without trying too hard. Like…scruffy-pretty."

"Like me," I say as a reflex, then die inside. "I mean…not that I—"

He laughs. "Scruffy-pretty works for you."

My face flushes with crimson. But then I smile.

We loop by the water taxis, and I, in a moment of overzealous eye contact, nearly walk into a bench. Pete catches my elbow. His touch is light, anchoring.

"Careful," he says.

"Thank you," I say. "It would be very on-brand of me to be felled by street furniture on a first… non-date."

"I'm sure there's a plaque for that."

We keep talking. The easy stuff. The little hooks you throw out to see if someone will catch them: favourite films, the worst gig we've ever been to, our takes on the proper ratio of crisp to sandwich.

But then, he tells me about nights when he can't sleep, and how walking the harbour calms his brain. I tell him about needing a break from life after my dad's funeral.

It's all relatively light, but the light has roots.

At the bridge, we pause and lean on the rail, watching the water traffic glide its way through. Pete squints at the sky, then looks at me with that little half-smile. "I've had a nice time," he says. "It's been nice to get to know you."

"It has," I say, and immediately want to make a joke to soften it. But I let it sit.

"So," Pete says after a moment, "how do you feel about meeting for a proper drink? Not now. Another day. Somewhere with chairs that aren't attached to the floor."

The words ping around my skull. I manage not to squeal. "Yes," I say, too quickly. "Yes, that would be…good. Very good. Medium good with strong potential to be excellent."

He laughs. “Great.”

We start walking again, and that’s when he clears his throat, the kind of clearing that signals a gear change. He looks straight ahead when he speaks.

“Before we make any plans,” he says, “I should say something. I prefer to be upfront.”

My stomach does a cautious little fold. “Okay.”

“I’m married,” he says. “I have a husband.” He waves the ring on his finger that I had missed all day, hiding in plain sight.

“Oh,” is all I can say at first. Like a gut punch.

“We’re in a polyamorous relationship,” he adds.

For a second, the words bounce off my brain like hail. Married lands first. Polyamorous lands second, a half-step behind, dragging a suitcase.

Somewhere in the distance, a seagull laughs.

I try to keep my face neutral, regretting my choice not to continue with my quarterly Botox injections last year.

“Right,” I say, channelling calm schoolteacher. “Okay. Right.”

He glances at me. “Maybe I should have told you before we started walking—"

“No! You didn’t need to!”

I feel like I’m shouting. Am I shouting?

I’m doing a very controlled internal panic. On the outside, I’m composed. On the inside, there’s a small choir singing ‘oh no’ in four-part harmony.

Pete winces a smile. “It wouldn’t be fair to not mention it before we go any further.”

“No, I appreciate the… mentioning now,” I say. “Pre-date mentioning.” I inhale. “So. Polyamorous.”

“Yeah,” he says. “James — my husband — and I have been together five years. We opened our relationship a couple of years in. We date other people. We’re not looking for a third or anything like that. We each have — and can have — separate relationships. James has a boyfriend.”

James. Husband. Boyfriend. So many questions.

I nod and remember to breathe. “So when you say ‘date’… you mean actual dates. Not hookups. Feelings. Intimacy. Moonlit dinners.”

“Yes.”

“And not a threesome thing”

He laughs. “No, nor a foursome thing.”

"And James knows about… all of this?"

"Yes," he says gently. "That's kind of the core feature. Communication. Honesty."

"Right, right, of course," I say, cheeks heating. "Sorry. I'm new to the glossary."

"It's okay," he says. "Ask anything."

I chew my lip. "So… how does it work? Like… do you have specific days when you get all polyamorous, or is it just 'as and when'?'

"Well, polyamory is allowed any day of the week," he says with a smile. "Even on Sunday."

"The lord's day, too. Controversial," I say, buying time while my insides reorganise themselves. "And do you…" I lower my voice,"…ever get jealous?"

"Sometimes," he says, nodding. "We both do. And that's perfectly reasonable and normal. But jealousy is just a sign that we need to talk. It's not necessarily a bad thing. It's just… information."

"And what are you… looking for?" I ask. "With me. With anyone."

"I don't know yet," he says. "I try not to plan my future with someone I've known for an hour. I just know I like being around you. You make me laugh. I felt something in Tesco. And walking with you now feels…easy and fun."

God help me, I melt a little at you make me laugh. Half of me is beaming, the other half is holding up a caution sign.

Daniel flashes through my mind: rules, conditions, the way love was a door you had to earn the key to. The idea of more than two people in an emotional equation makes my legs go wobbly. I'm still learning how to put myself first in a duo.

I couch it in humour. "So, if we went for a drink, I wouldn't be auditioning for the role of Live-In Boyfriend #2 who must love dogs and alternate Sundays?"

"No," he says. "You'd be meeting me. One person. If it grew, at some point, you'd meet James. His boyfriend, he's not a secret. People I meet aren't a secret. He's… part of my life. But I'm not looking to move someone into our house. I'm not… hunting a unicorn."

"Good," I say before my mouth can stop me. "I'm much more of a depressed Shetland pony."

He laughs so hard he has to pause, hand on the rail. The sound untangles something in me.

"Look," he says when we start walking again, "I get that this might be a no. I won't be offended. It's not everyone's cup of tea. Most guys are immediately put off by it. I just didn't want to pretend to be something I'm not. It wastes everybody's time."

We walk in silence for a minute.

Here's what's true: I like him. I haven't liked someone like this in a long time. Here's what's also true: the word marriedpokes a bruise I didn't know I still had. Part of me wants the simple rom-com, the monogamy montage, the "it's just us now" final shot.

But another part knows that simple isn't real life.

I try to hold all the truths at once without judging them. It's like juggling custard, but I try.

"I'm… surprised," I say finally. "And I'm also grateful you told me. I can't promise I understand it yet. But I want to understand you. You seem…just lovely really."

He exhales, shoulders dropping. "Thank you."

"And I do appreciate the honesty and the openness," I add. "I've dated men who hid far less."

And married them too, I think to myself.

Daniel's addiction to gambling only came out later in our relationship, when he got himself stuck in a financial hole, which was impossible to get out of without a significant other finding out. At the time, I did everything I could to help him out of this, and it nearly ruined us.

"Look," I say, finding myself again, "if we do go for a drink, you'll have to explain the rules like I'm taking a language class."

"I can do that," he says. "I'm very patient. And there's a quiz at the end."

"I'm not very good at quizzes," I admit. "Although I once won the '90s girlband quiz during a bottomless brunch at Blame Gloria."

He bumps his shoulder against mine, light and warm. "That's quite an accomplishment. You'll be fine."

Our circuit ends, and we're back outside the M Shed.

"So," Pete says, stopping, turning to face me fully. His face is open, a little nervous, the kind of nervous that means the answer matters. "Do you want to see me again?"

Chapter 9

TOM

Craig's front door opens almost instantly, like he's been waiting on the other side with a stopwatch and a wooden spoon. He fills the doorway, broad-shouldered, neat beard, his hair cropped close.

In his day job, he's DCI Craig Hollis with Avon and Somerset Constabulary, where he's worked for the best part of twenty years.

"Look who it is," he says, greeting me with a hug that smells part garlic, part laundry detergent. "Bristol's most eligible avocado consultant."

"I think I've heard the word aovocado more times in the last forty-eight hours than my whole life," I say, waving a bottle of red. "And I'm not mad about it."

We move into the kitchen, and I'm continually amazed by how exemplary this place is, even in the midst of a three-course meal being cooked. It's all thriving plants and gleaming copper pans, driven by the immense OCD of both its owners. Even the chaotic pinboard of postcards and gig tickets is orderly and precise.

Craig returns to the stove like a man in control, stirring a pan with one hand and flicking the oven light on with the other.

Craig's husband of ten years, Phil, appears from the hallway, buttoning a shirt with the kind of care you only give to buttons when you're hoping someone will unbutton them later. He's shorter and slimmer than Craig, with hair artfully tussled and a scruffier beard.

"There he is, our emotional support guest has arrived," Phil says, kissing my cheek. "You look well. Slimmer? Are we allowed to say that these days?"

"Probably not, but I'll take it," I say. "It's a new diet. Anxiety and panic-based."

"Oh, well, that's the best kind. Anxiety is huge this season."

"Let me take that," Craig says, relieving me of the wine and giving it a quick approving nod. He's in a navy sweater rolled to the elbows, forearms tanned from some recent weekend in the garden.

Phil reaches for his wallet on the counter, glancing at the pinboard. "Okay, I'm heading out. Don't wait up, kids."

"Text me when you get there," Craig says without looking. Then he does look, softening. "Have a good time."

"I will," Phil says, kissing him. It's unshowy, domestic, and entirely lovely. He kisses my cheek again on the way out. "If he burns the rice, don't let him gaslight you."

The door clicks shut behind him. Craig lifts a shoulder. "Hot date. Nice guy. Teaches pottery to children, if you can believe that exists."

"Children still exist?" I say. "I assumed we phased them out in favour of dogs with Instagram accounts."

He smirks. "You okay with him going out? I only remembered he'd planned it when you texted you were on your way."

"It's your house," I say. "Besides, he looked disgustingly happy. I'll allow it."

Craig returns to the hob with a pleased grunt. "Good. We aim for disgustingly happy around here."

I hop up onto one of their kitchen stools. "Smells amazing. What's on the menu?"

"Coconut rice, sticky aubergine, limey slaw. And something green to prove I care about your health."

"Please don't," I say. "I've had enough green for one lifetime."

He pours us both a glass of wine. "So," he says, "tell Uncle Craig about Tesco Mary."

So, then I start replaying all the main details: running into him again by the harbourside, our long walk together, the ease, the laughter, the natural chemistry.

As the story continues, Craig listens intently, his grin growing wider with each revelation. When I get to the part about Pete's offer of a drink, he claps his hands in delight.

"And then," I hesitate, inadvertently creating a dramatic pause. "Turns out he's married."

Craig's eyebrows lift. "Oh."

"And polyamourous."

The eyebrows lift higher. "Oh."

"Oh, indeed," I echo. "So, I did that thing where I tried to be all cool and adult about it, but ended up saying something about the Lord's day. I think I compared myself to a depressed Setland pont at one point."

"On brand," he says.

"As ever." I pick at the label on the wine bottle for support. "I don't know. It was just such a lovely romantic moment, by the harbour, the sun was shining. And then: Married. Open. Husband. Boyfriend." I rub my eyes as if that would help me process the words. "But, he was so lovely about it. Just honest and upfront. Unashamed. Can someone be genuine and married and ask me out for a drink all at once?"

Craig waves his wooden spoon around like a magical wand. "I mean, hello!"

I snigger. "Yes, obviously you and Phil are both wonderful and sensational." I sigh. "I think we need to talk through this open relationship thing again. We've not discussed it for at least a year."

Craig plates up with the theatrical flourish I've come to expect, almost like he's conducting an orchestra. "Right, food's ready," he says. "Let's sit and chat."

We eat at the little round table by the window. Craig forks rice into his mouth, nodding at my plate. "You will complement the aubergine. I don't make the rules."

"It's very aubergine," I concede, and he accepts this as the highest praise.

"Right," he says, settling back. "Polyamory. You know how it works for us."

"I know some of it," I say. "I know Phil texts when he goes out and you colour-code your calendars like a gay air traffic control tower."

"That's one way of looking at it," he says. "It's not complicated, but it's, let's say, layered. Like Lasagne. Or trauma."

"Don't ruin my relationship with lasagne," I say. "It means too much to me."

He kicks my shin lightly. "So, for us, it's all the boring things that are the most important: communication, consent, kindness. We'll always talk about what's working and what's not because it prevents any game-playing of late-night catastrophising."

"Ok, so there's a set of rules?" I ask.

"I like to talk in terms of boundaries rather than rules. It makes it feel less like a punishment. Think of them more like seatbelts."

"Seatbelts, right." I pause to take this all in. "And how about jealousy?"

"Oh, absolutely still exists," he says. "I'm still a human with emotions. Sometimes Phil goes out on a new date with a guy who looks younger and hotter than me, and I sit at home debating whether to call the bar they're at with a bomb threat."

"Rational."

"I have my moments," Craig frowns. "But jealousy isn't a crime, it's a valid feeling."

"Yes, Pete said something similar."

"Good," he nods. "It's just honesty. A sign to talk again. Why are you spiralling? What do you need? etc."

"So, I get that you're both okay with each other having emotional connections with others, but are you genuinely happy for him, in the same way you would if a friend did?"

"Oh yes, we call it 'compersion' in the trade."

"Which is…?"

Craig takes a sip of his wine. "It's that ridiculous feeling of joy when someone you love finds a meaningful connection with someone else. It's hard work, I won't lie. Kind of like a muscle you need to build. But when you get there, it's wonderful. Like watching your best friend discover their new favourite song."

I try to picture it: the man I love beside me, him beside his husband, us both living in a world where love isn't a finite resource that needs to be rationed.

"I mean, you make it sound so normal and healthy," I admit. "But I still don't get why you would want to be in this kind of relationship?"

Craig pushes his fork into his rice, thinking for a moment before answering. "Look, it wasn't because being monogamous was so awful, or we were desperate to shag half of Bristol. Our love for each other hasn't changed. We just kept coming back to the same notion that there was more to love than the box we were keeping it in. We wanted to allow ourselves the freedom to admit when we connected with someone else, without it feeling like a betrayal.

"But it wasn't from day one, right?" I ask.

"No, true. We had been together for at least three years before we even dared to talk about it."

I scrunch my forehead. "I don't know if I can get my head around it. Hooking up with randoms, maybe. But polyamorous?"

"And that's far enough. It's not like these are the only options. There are plenty of variations, different people view it in different ways, but, if it's a route anyone wants to consider, it's all about finding something that works for both of you"

Craig takes another sip of his wine and continues: "An open sexual relationship never quite fit for us. Sex without emotion. It's easy to get, but felt too flat, too clinical. We didn't want an endless string of random hookups with people we'd never see again. We wanted the possibility of real connections, even love, alongside what we already had."

"Some of us can't even find love with one man, let alone two."

"Are you calling me greedy?" Craig says, showing a fork of rice in his mouth.

I laugh. "Never. You're worthy of all the love you can get your hands on."

Craig nods. "Exactly. You can have as many friends as you like, as many best friends as you like, that you love dearly: no one will bat an eyelid. But having multiple romantic partners is always frowned upon. This just challenges that. There's always room for more love."

"It sounds so romantic when you put it like that," I say, maybe with a hint of sarcasm.

He aims his fork at me. "Look, I know it's different for you, being the single person and all. But one thing to remember, regardless: be clear about what you can and can't offer. Don't promise total boyfriend energy if you can only do every other Tuesday with no commitment. Don't pretend you're okay with casual if you imprint like a duckling.

"Which I do," I admit.

"Which you do," Craig confirms.

I chew, considering. "What if I don't know what I can offer until I try? What if I get it wrong?"

"You will," he says, cheerfully brutal. "We all do. But you'll understand why you got it wrong, and maybe it won't be for you. It's not a test with one right answer. It's something you learn by trying it."

Something in my chest loosens.

"It's not just sex for us," Craig adds, softer. "People assume it is. There's sex, sure, but there's also care. The point is joy, intimacy. A guy Phil's been dating helped me build a bookcase last month. We took him to Ikea, Tom."

"Wow, that's love." I laugh. "Is it weird if I say I'm jealous of how healthy you sound?"

"No, not weird," he says. "But don't be fooled. We've had the dramatic cry-on-the-floor nights. But we talk them through. We do it at our own pace. If someone is struggling, we slow down."

I nod.

Craig leans in. "I don't know, maybe this could be a good thing for you. Yes, it's not your traditional Disney princess romance, but it's fair to say you've spent years with Daniel equating love with control. Maybe a relationship where consent, honesty and communication are sacred."

There's a pause. And instead of thinking of Daniel as I often do when thinking of relationships, Guy pops into my brain.

Craig watches me, and because he's Craig, he doesn't push. He just slides the water jug closer, as if hydration were a metaphor.

"I used to walk that route with Guy," I say eventually, picking a piece of lime from the edge of my plate. "The harbourside , I mean."

Craig nods.

"We were… close. It meant a lot to me. I'd like whatever comes next to feel that same…connection."

Craig's mouth forms a small, understanding smile. "You deserve a genuine connection."

I change the subject. "Anyway, Daniel is still texting."

His expression snaps, and his forearms tense. "Again."

"He's been… insistent. Said we need to meet. Which… I may have agreed to—"

"What?!"

"He suggested later in the week, but I can't bring myself to say yes." I drink, as if wine is a courage remedy. "It's just, his name is always in my head, even now."

Craig's mouth is a line. "And he knows that. That's why he does it. Don't give him a corridor back into your life."

"I know," I say, smaller than I want to sound. "It's just hard to ignore the past when it keeps showing up in the present."

He reaches across the table and squeezes my wrist. "You're not who you were then. And you've got us. And… maybe Tesco Mary."

I smile helplessly. "Pete."

"Pete," he repeats. "I say just keep going with him. Go slow. Ask questions. See what happens."

We clear the plates, and he refuses my offer of help with the washing up on the grounds that I am a guest and therefore must sit on the stool and offer unhelpful critique.

At some point, the wine hits the bladder like a small freight train. "Need the bathroom."

"You know where it is," he says, flicking suds.

I step into their tidy little bathroom and lean on the sink. My face looks older than I feel. I think about Pete's laugh, and the way I felt when he said my name. I think about Craig and Phil and the way Craig's voice softened when he said compersion. The word sits on my tongue like a foreign language, strange but good.

Could I really do this? My instinct to Disney-princess everything is strong. Yes, I want orchestras and relentless stomach butterflies.

But I also want honesty and a kind of love that doesn't require me to change myself to be accepted.

When I return, Craig is at the table, my phone in his hand. He looks up immediately, eyebrows halfway to an apology.

"Sorry, just looking," he says, setting the phone down face-down and sliding it an inch toward me. "Thinking of getting a new one like yours."

"Thought you just got a new one," I say, casually.

"I did, but I'm not getting on with it."

We migrate to the sofa with bowls of something that Craig swears is pudding and I swear is just sugar and cream. We talk about small things: the dog that lives three doors down and looks like a retired judge, a TV show we both hate-watched, my cat Buster's new habit of sleeping on my head "for warmth" like he's a balaclava.

Then Craig steers us gently back. "You know," he says, "I worry about you thinking you have to perform the perfect response to all this. You don't have to decide what you are tonight."

"You make it sound easy," I say.

"It isn't easy," he replies, honest as ever. "It's work. But so is monogamy. At least with this one, we get better stories."

We talk until it's late. When I finally put my shoes back on, the city feels like it's a calmer place. At the door, Craig hugs me again, brief and hard, and we say our goodbyes.

On the walk back to Clifton, I get a message on my phone. The immediate pang in my stomach comes from the expectation that it's Daniel.

But, no, it's Pete. A simple line that warms me inside:

Hope you got home okay. So, what day works best for that drink?

I type, delete, type again, and then simply reply: Thursday?

Before I set off again, I look up at the night. It isn't a Disney sky: no fireworks, no orchestras. Just a city. And maybe that's all I need.

Open.

I test the word in my head. It doesn't need to be a door permanently flung wide. It could be like a window slightly ajar, letting in a cool breeze.

I can work with that.

My phone buzzes again.

I look at the message.

Not again.

I can't respond to these, not tonight.

Evelyn: *I lie in bed thinking about how the knife sliced through him.*

Chapter 10

TOM

As I arrive at the restaurant, I check my watch: fifteen minutes early as per normal. My brain still thinks punctuality equals attractiveness, which has never served me well.

A friendly waiter walks me to our table, but I'm too nervous to formulate enough words to generate any small talk, so I just smile at him as he walks away.

I feel like I'm entering a job interview for a role I'm underqualified for after getting ChatGPT to write my CV. While I wait, I switch from adjusting the cutlery to rearranging the salt and pepper shakers into different formations, like I'm planning some condiment-based military parade.

I try to sit still, my left foot anxiety-drumming on the table leg.

Then Pete walks in, like he's stepped out of a lifestyle blog. Casual but deliberate. Navy shirt, rolled sleeves, dark jeans. Stubble trimmed just enough to look accidental. He smiles when he sees me and — God help me — it's the kind of smile that makes me forget words exist.

I feel immediately underdressed in my Marks & Spencer shirt, which I ironed twice and still managed to crease on the walk over.

"Tom!" he says, striding over. "We meet again. And not surrounded by judgmental seagulls this time. Progress."

"Yes, and I'm sat down, so less chance of me tripping over a bollard," I say.

He laughs, loud enough to make heads turn, and I feel ridiculously pleased with myself.

We order burgers and chips, because let's not pretend either of us are salad people, and settle in.

By the time the food arrives, Pete is already mid-story about a guy he hooked up with once who asked for his Netflix password before they'd even kissed.

"You should've seen his face when I said I only had Now TV," Pete says, grinning. "Like I'd just told him Santa died."

I'm laughing so hard I nearly snort beer up my nose. This is Pete's thing: he's so relentlessly chipper it's impossible not to get swept along.

I take a sip of beer. "I once hooked up with a guy whose mum came home early. He panicked, shoved me in the kitchen cupboard, and I had to sit there for forty minutes while she cooked a casserole. Hugely uncomfortable, but I got a stonking slow cooker recipe I still use to this day."

Pete laughs so loudly that the couple at the next table glances over.

And this is the general tone of the conversation for the next hour: hookup stories, dating disasters, the kind of anecdotes that would make our mothers faint but which feel like currency here, between us. Every time Pete laughs, I feel like I've won a small prize, like my terrible romantic track record has finally found its true purpose: making him grin at me across a sticky table.

But eventually, a natural pause comes in the conversation. And I feel it's my time to ask.

"So, James?"

Here we go. The big one.

"Have you been dying to ask all night?"

"Maybe," I admit.

"You go for it. I'm an open book."

"Um, ok," I try to sound as chill as possible. "So, what's he like?"

"Well," he explains, chipper but not flippant. "We've been married three years, together for nearly six. He's brilliant. A better cook than me, better taste in music, absolutely useless at parallel parking."

"Right," I say carefully. "And he's… okay with you being here?"

"Oh yeah," Pete says brightly. "We're open about everything, without going into the lurid details. But we will talk openly about who we're seeing and how we feel."

"So, it's not all about sex?"

"I mean, sex and physical intimacy are really important, yeah. But we're not interested in one-night stands.

"So, you want a deep connection?"

"Of course," he says. "Our own connection is already deep. We don't want to replace what we have, more like…expand the cast list."

He says it so cheerfully, I almost forget to panic. Almost.

"So, James is also seeing people?"

"He has a boyfriend," Pete says with the same tone you'd use to say "he has a dog." "Sam. They've been together about two years. Lovely guy. Bit obsessed with Lady Gaga, but you can't have everything."

I raise an eyebrow. "So, you've got a husband, and he's got a boyfriend. Very modern. I feel like I need a flowchart."

Pete chuckles. "It's not as complicated as it sounds."

"Speak for yourself. I once got confused by the relationships on Love Island."

"It's much simpler than Love Island, I promise."

"And how do you feel about Sam?" I ask carefully.

Pete hesitates. "He makes James happy. That's what matters."

Which is technically an answer, but it feels a little hollow. I file it under red flags to obsess over at 2am.

I take a sip of my beer to buy some time. "And, this works? I mean, what about jealousy, drama, chaos?"

"Oh, don't get me wrong, there's plenty of chaos," Pete says cheerfully.

We laugh, but I watch him closely. When he talks about James, his expression softens. But Sam? Nothing. Indifference. Like he's describing a house plant.

He leans in. "Seriously, though, it's not about being greedy. There are things that James gets from Sam that he doesn't get from me, and vice versa. And it's about saying that's okay."

I'm, of course, desperate to know what these "things" are, but instead, I nod like we're casually discussing the weather.

"For us, that's about connection with more than one person. Doesn't mean James and I aren't committed. He's my anchor, my person. But we don't want to lock each other in a box either."

I nod, trying to absorb it all. My inner voice is screaming: *I struggle to manage one man, let alone a polycule.*

Pete must sense the heaviness, because he grins. "Okay, new topic. Tell me about your dad. You mentioned he passed away last time."

It knocks me sideways. I wasn't expecting that.

"There's not much to tell," I say, stabbing at my chips. "He died about a year ago. Heart attack. Classic mid-seventies cliché."

Pete's expression softens. "I'm sorry. That must've been hard."

"Hard and weird," I admit, "because I grieve, but I don't. I miss the idea of him more than the man. Miss what we never had. Which sounds pathetic, doesn't it?"

"No," Pete says firmly. "It sounds human."

Something in my chest cracks a little. I've talked about this before, with Craig, with a therapist, but Pete's response hits differently. Simple, no judgement.

"I think," he continues, "we spend so much time trying to fit our lives into other people's expectations — parents, partners, whoever — that we forget we're allowed to want something else."

I nod, relieved.

"So now," Pete says, lifting his beer, "I live by one rule: build the life you want, not the one other people think you should have. If that means polyamory, fine. If that means Netflix alone with your cat, also fine."

"Buster would hate that," I mutter.

Chapter 11

PETE

Pulling up outside Tom's place, they spill out of the taxi, still laughing. Pete can't stop looking at Tom's face when he laughs, his head tipped back, eyes creasing, the sound he makes warming his chest.

Tom fumbles with his keys like he's never encountered a lock before.

"Third time's a charm," Tom says, trying to open the door for the fourth time.

"Here," Pete murmurs, gently taking the keys from him. "Trust a professional." He shakes his head as if to recalibrate the alcohol level in him.

Soon, the door clicks, and Tom shoots him a look like he's just solved world peace.

The house is simple but beautiful inside. It has that quiet pride, three storeys of clean lines and quiet wealth, but still with that feeling of home.

One he's not felt for a long while.

A tabby cat pads into the hallway with the sort of disdain only cats and certain maître d's can pull off.

"Buster," Tom announces. "This is Pete. Be kind."

The cat gives Pete a long, unimpressed blink and leaves the room as if filing a complaint.

"He'll come back when he decides I'm worthy," Pete says.

"You and every man I've ever dated," Tom mutters, then flushes. "Tea? Wine? Water? A ceremonial handshake?"

Pete grins. "Wine. And I'll forgo the handshake if you promise never to say 'ceremonial handshake' again."

Tom returns with two glasses of red, sets them down, then hovers close enough for Pete to notice the flecks of grey at his temples.

Their first kiss makes time stand still. Tom tastes faintly of beer and the mint of the last mojito they had before leaving the restaurant. The kissing continues as Tom pulls him out of the room.

By the time they reach the stairs, they're laughing and bumping into the bannister like teenagers.

In the bedroom, under the soft glow of the lamp, the laughter softens, and their clothes fall to the floor. Not gracefully. Pete struggles to unbutton his shirt, leaving Pete to pull it off over his head like he's popping a cork. But soon, they're on the bed, aided by the alcohol and adrenaline coursing through them, their sex is passionate and natural.

Afterwards, they lie tangled in the heat, a sheet more decorative than functional. Tom breathes hard beneath Pete's palm, his arms wrapped around him, as they stare at the ceiling.

"That was…" Tom's voice falters. "Really nice."

"Nice?" Pete teases. "That's British understatement. File it next to 'it's a bit chilly' and 'my nan's funeral was fine.'"

Tom laughs, tips his face toward Pete, and kisses him softly. The room drifts into that delicate quiet where you either reach for your phone or you spontaneously confess something.

Tom chooses confession as they talk about Tom's ex-husband.

"He was… controlling," Tom says carefully, like handling glass. "I thought it was love…but I was being managed. Stripped apart bit by bit.

"He had a gambling habit too," he continues. "It was getting progressively worse. Which was making *him* progressively worse. It had put a big dent in our finances by the time I found out what was happening. I bailed him out too many times. I should have gone earlier, but he had this hold over me."

"No, I understand, I do," Pete admits. And he really does. "That must be hard to move on from."

"Yeah, definitely. I'm naturally the type of person who sees the good in people and trusts them. I don't want to get my defences up, but sometimes I can. Sometimes I hold back. I overthink. Question every little thing. Assume the worst. Think the most negative things about myself. It's not a trait I'm proud of, but…" Tom loses his words.

"It's something he's instilled in you?" Pete suggests.

After a pause, Tom can only nod.

"Was he ever violent?" Pete asks before he can stop himself, voice soft but blunt.

Tom's pause says enough. He stares at the ceiling, then shakes his head faintly. "I don't want to spoil tonight talking about my ex," he says.

"Okay," Pete says, meaning it. "Another time."

Tom exhales, presses his forehead to Pete's. "Another time."

Soon Tom drifts, arm heavy across Pete's waist, his breath evening into sleep. Pete lies awake, watching the streetlight's sweep across the ceiling.

This should only feel good. This night with Tom was everything he hoped it could be: how Tom laughed at his jokes, the electricity when they touched hands across the table, the tingling sensation of Tom's lips on his stomach.

And now, lying beside him, the warmth of Tom's body radiates in the summer night.

But dread slips into the room anyway, as punctual as ever.

Because Pete lied.

Too many times tonight.

Of course, James knew about our date.

Lie.

Yes, we're both happy to explore new connections.

Lie

James is a brilliant, loving man.

Lie. Lie. Lie

Pete had painted a picture of honesty, reassuring Tom that polyamory meant care, respect and openness. And Tom believed him. Because Tom, with those kind eyes, believes in people.

Pete had taken his trust and immediately stained it with lies.

The truth: James didn't know about tonight.

He wouldn't understand.

No doubt, his response would be aggressive, volatile.

But lying here with Tom, Pete knew this was something he had to explore.

Tom was caring, loving, honest: he knew that much already. And this was a relationship he wanted to progress more than anything. To take him to the next stage in his life.

James would not be happy.

And an unhappy James was more than just a complication.

As he'd witnessed before, this could be a matter of life or death.

Chapter 12

DANIEL

Daniel lies on his back, arms pinned at his sides, the wood cold through the shirt. The darkness is total, along with the feeling of dust and the sour scent of furniture polish. He thinks of coffins. Not metaphorically, literally. The narrowness around him, enclosed.

Above him, there is a rhythmic thud, once, twice, again, again, in a jagged tempo that refuses to calm. The vibration travels through the floorboards into his shoulder blades.

He tells himself to focus on counting, like the pulse in his ears. But the repetitive noise breaks his concentration.

His phone is in his pocket, and he can feel its physical weight and the weight of its messages.

His messages to Tom, plural now, sit unanswered above the read ones from a few days ago. A neat column of grey single ticks reaching into silence.

Can we talk?

I need to see you.

I'm nearby. Please, Tom.

It's like he's been blocked.

Above him, that thudding noise continues. He presses his head back, as if the wood could absorb it. It doesn't.

He closes his eyes.

Tries to think of something that will make him sleep, but he's hard, solid.

The need is not dignified; it never is.

He unzips his jeans slowly, slides a hand in and works at the feeling with the same angry efficiency he applies to everything else he wants to expel.

When he climaxes, it's like a black-out — brief, blank, a reset. He just lies there, the warmth on his hand, over his T-shirt.

The thudding sound that was aching his brain has also stopped. Silence settles like snowfall.

The release has only calmed his mind so much. His thoughts return to Tom not replying. He thinks about how Tom always needed help making decisions, how he so easily drifted unless someone anchored him. It wasn't cruel to be that anchor.

No, it was care. It was always about care.

He thinks about money, the money he owes, and the texts from the people who are calling in his debts. The pulse in his ear returns again like a ticking clock.

Tom will see sense.

Eventually.

He just needs the right kind of pressure to be applied. He's soft like that. That's not an insult, though. Soft is malleable. Soft can be shaped into something fit for purpose.

Giving it time, the house around him shifts into that late quiet where sleep is no longer a choice.

Eventually, when his shoulders begin to ache and his fingers tingle from being too still for too long, he rolls onto one side. He waits again, counting — twenty, thirty, fifty — not wanting to move too soon.

He turns over onto his front and uses his clammy palm against the wood floor as support to pull himself forward. The silence of the room stays intact as he slides out from under the bed in one controlled motion. Once his legs are out, he manoeuvres into a crouching position, staying low for a couple of heartbeats, until sure the only sound is the low, steady breathing ahead.

He stands, Tom's bed in front of him.

Tom lies turned slightly toward the window, mouth parted. There is another shape beyond him, a second weight in the bed. A man — unknown, uninvited, unannounced. The stranger's hand is draped over Tom's waist, proprietary in sleep.

Heat floods Daniel so quickly that he feels dizzy. His breath shortens, roughens.

Tom's throat, Tom's cheek, Tom's chest rising. He remembers the map of that body as if it were his own.

His right hand is still lightly sticky, his drying semen not yet crisp. He wipes it slowly across Tom's bedsheets, careful not to wake the sleeping duo.

He has been patient. He has been kind. He has been ignored.

He will not be ignored.

He needs Tom.

The other man's hand flexes in sleep, tightens fractionally at Tom's waist. Daniel's fingers curl into his palm until the nails hurt.

He remains there in the dark, standing, watching them.

Listening to the heartbeat, he can't mute.

Feeling rage climb, settle, and climb again.

Chapter 13

TOM

Following the success of our first get-together, I've ended up on a three-week bender of dates with Pete. Not a bender in the "ten pints and a dodgy kebab" kind (though, to be fair, one did involve a bunch of cocktails and a 2am dance off in the King'd Tuppence).

No, I mean, like an actual proper run of successful dates.

It's weird. I keep seeing the same man on purpose. Multiple times. In a row. Without being ghosted. Honestly, if there were a Guinness World Record for me, this would be it.

Pete plans actual dates.

Not "come over, watch Netflix, accidentally on purpose have sex while ignoring the film" dates. Real ones. With activities. I didn't even know those still existed outside of straight people's Instagram feeds.

Our next date was a simple coffee at Boston Tea Party on Park Street. Halfway through, it hit me that I wasn't "half listening, half rehearsing" what to say next. I was just talking. Unheard of. Normally, dates for me are 80% internal monologue about whether I trimmed my ear hair and 20% pretending to like Craft beer.

A few days later, we took a walk around Brandon Hill. Classically romantic and picturesque. Except I was wheezing like an asthmatic pug after five minutes. Pete offered to give me a piggyback up to the top.

Date three, and I still wasn't ghosted, which was suspicious in itself. Pete took me bowling at The Lanes. Bowling! Considering my "bowling technique" is a health and safety risk, this was high stakes. I once managed to flip the ball backwards and nearly killed a pensioner. That said, Pete was equally as useless, and we embraced the gutter as a collective.

Soon, we'd eaten our way through most of Gloucester Road, one too many pizzas, even a catastrophic attempt at eating ramen in Old Market, where I basically wore the broth down my t-shirt.

And now, nearly a month has gone by, and I'm at the stage where I've stopped counting how many dates we've been on, having effectively moved into "seeing each other" territory.

And during all this: no Daniel. Not a text, not a "we have to meet", not even a ghost of him in my head. After weeks of obsessing, I realised that he hadn't popped into my mind for at least a few days. Like he'd stopped existing. Or maybe I had stopped existing to him. Either way, it was bliss.

It made me reflect on how different this all felt. Normally, dating is an exercise in humiliation. Don't even get me started on the hookups.

By comparison, Pete felt… safe. Not boring-safe. Fun-safe. Like being on a rollercoaster with a bar that actually clicks down properly, not one where you spend the whole ride convinced you're about to be flung into the car park.

And yes, we've had all the sex. A whole load. Excuse the pun. I'd love to say it was cinematic lovemaking, candles and a Marvin Gaye soundtrack. In reality, it was me tripping over my jeans, Pete elbowing me in the nose, and Buster the cat watching us from the corner with deep moral judgement.

Still pretty great, to be fair.

The only problem is the elephant in the room.

The elephant has a name: James.

I try not to think about him, but I do.

I try to humanise him. Imagine him as just a man: maybe he gets nervous ordering coffee. Maybe he snores. Maybe he cries at Pixar films like the rest of us. But every time I picture him, all I see is the shadow looming behind Pete's smile.

It's all too good to be true. Which means it probably is.

I've lived in Bristol long enough to know that happiness here is usually followed by rain. You're sipping cider by the harbour, and suddenly the heavens open, and you're drenched, mascara running, trying to convince yourself it's "romantic." That's what this feels like: sunshine I don't deserve, with a storm cloud waiting to dump on me.

Still, I can't stop basking. Three weeks of dates. Three weeks of laughter and sex and feeling like maybe, just maybe, I'm not broken beyond repair.

Tonight, we're lying on my bed. He's half-asleep, one arm slung over me like a seatbelt I don't want to unbuckle.

But then reality hits.

Another text from Evelyn.

I can't bring myself to open it.

But I know what it will say.

The blood. Always about the blood.

I swore I'd never talk to her again after that night. After everything. My guilt is like a splinter: you learn to live with it, but then it snags on something, and suddenly you're bleeding all over again.

I shove the notifications into a box in my brain marked *do not open unless apocalypse.*

But it reminds me to leave the past behind.

My shameful past.

And make this work.

Live in the moment.

The thought derails my brain immediately. Instead, I go into self-destruct mode.

"Pete," I say. My voice cracks, like it knows what's coming.

He stirs, kisses the back of my neck. "Mm?"

"It's been over a month. I think..." I swallow hard. "I think I should meet James."

Silence. Heavy, suffocating silence.

And that's how it ends: me blurting out the one thing I know could ruin everything.

Because that's who I am. Tom: professional self-saboteur, part-time optimist, full-time idiot.

Chapter 14

TOM

Craig's voice comes through my phone as I sit in the taxi.

"You sure about this?" he asks. "Feels quick. Meeting the husband already. I mean, I'm sure Pete is lovely, but it's only been a month…" He trails off, the unspoken words left hanging.

"Yes, I'm sure," I say, sounding far more confident than I feel. "I'm driving this. I want to meet him."

I can feel Craig raising an eyebrow. "Tom, mate, last time you 'drove' something was at the pub quiz when you insisted Celine Dion was Swedish."

"She's Eurovision Swedish!"

"Yes, which is different to *actual* Swedish."

Still, I double down. "This is different. I need to meet him, just know who he is. I can't really move ahead with Pete until I know who my competition is."

This time, I can feel Craig frowning. "Tom, this isn't Love Island. The fact that you're calling this a competition suggests you're not quite thinking about this in the right way."

"You know what I mean."

"I know you shouldn't think of James as your competition," he says. "You're seeing if Pete fits in your life. That's the only audition that matters."

I huff. "Easy for you to say. You've already got Phil. You've got your setup. Your anchor."

Craig snorts. "Listen, if James is as important to Pete as Phil is to me, then meeting him isn't about sizing him up. It's about finding out if you can happily sit in the same room."

"Without clawing each other's eyes out."

"Stop! If they have a healthy, supportive, open relationship, James will genuinely want to get to know you, welcome you, make you feel comfortable, because he knows it's important to Pete."

Yes, Craig, very sensible. But also, I am currently sweating through my shirt and mentally writing my will.

I sigh. "Okay. Yes, you're right."

"And if James is even half as charming as Pete claims, you'll be fine. You'll hate yourself for overthinking it."

I chew my lip. "So… no competition?"

"Think of it more like Pete being a participation trophy. One for both of you."

I laugh despite myself. "Fine. But if he turns out to be some devastatingly handsome lawyer with a six-pack, I reserve the right to panic."

"Mate, if he's a devastatingly handsome lawyer with a six-pack, you'll be too busy imagining throuple Pilates to panic."

"You know what I mean,"

Craig sighs. "Okay. Just… be yourself. James will most likely be lovely. He'll want to welcome you and support Pete. So, relax. Enjoy it."

Easy for him to say.

I'm less about relaxing and enjoying, more catastrophising and overthinking.

We say our goodbyes, and I hang up.

I ask ChatGPT for tips on how to look casual when meeting your new boyfriend's husband, and it gives some questionable advice, though it does suggest I consider my exit strategy beforehand.

Damn, one more thing to think about.

The taxi drives me out past the Downs to Pete and James's place. From the address, I can somewhat imagine where I am going, but my stomach, along with my brain, is spiralling as we approach our final destination.

The house looms over me like something from a Channel 5 period drama. A massive, gated property, all stone pillars and lights glowing. I almost expect Judy Dench to answer the door.

Instead, it's Pete.

"Tom!" His smile is as bright as ever, and relief hits me as we fold into a warm hug. He looks so normal, comfortable here, even against the backdrop of all this grandeur. For a moment, it's easy.

Then he steps aside, and there's James.

Handsome, of course, he is. Tall, dark hair swept back. Shirt buttoned just enough to look effortless. He looks like he could comfortably audition to be James Bond.

Immediately, the air shifts. His look is cold, suspicious. Like he's sizing me up for a job interview.

"Tom," Pete says, voice light, "this is James."

James's handshake is firm, too firm, and his smile doesn't reach his eyes. "Hello," he says.

Very formal.

Cold as ice.

Immediately, my heart sinks. My rational brain had agreed with Craig's opinion that James would be warm and welcoming to support his partner.

But this was anything but.

I audibly gulp.

"Pleasure to meet you," I then say.

I feel like I should bow.

James offers a hand to shake.

Shake his hand normally. Not too limp. Not too hard. God, why are you thinking about limpness right now?

We shake hands, eyes locked. It's uncomfortably intimate.

Behind them, another voice cuts in. "Ooh, so this is Tom."

A young handsome chap darts across the room. Thirties, messy hair, energy like a golden retriever that's discovered tequila and decided to start a podcast about it. He bounds over, grinning. "I'm Sam. I've heard so much. Welcome to the lion's den."

Comforting.

He gives me a warm hug.

I wasn't expecting Sam, James's boyfriend, to be here.

This already feels messier than I had predicted.

And this was all my idea.

Idiot.

Dinner smells incredible, something with garlic and rosemary, but the atmosphere could curdle milk.

"Dinner's nearly ready," Pete announces. "Just a few final touches."

"Well, smells delicious," I say.

James stands around in the kitchen and pours himself a red wine, without extending the offer further.

We sit around a table big enough to host the UN, with me opposite James.

Pete hands me a glass of white with a forced smile. It doesn't take long for me to pick up on Pete's manner. He's on edge, I can sense his nerves, fussing with cutlery, talking sporadically to fill the silences, but also withdrawn, like a schoolboy waiting for exam results.

Sam, meanwhile, has clearly appointed himself Master of Ceremonies.

"So, Tom," he says, leaning forward conspiratorially, "how long have you and Pete been, what's the word, romancing?"

I nearly choke on my wine. "Oh, we're—we've just been seeing each other. A little while."

Sam smirks. "Cute. And you met in Tesco, I hear. That's some Rom Com shit right there. I've always been more of a tap on Grindr kind of guy. Pete, too."

"Sam," Pete warns softly, but the damage is done. James's eyebrow arches, and my cheeks burn.

"You're right. You're more Recon, aren't you?" Sam says, giving Pete a wink.

There's a long silence, met with a frown from Pete as the quip falls flat. James sips his wine slowly, Sam not even flinching at the atmosphere.

I awkwardly smile to relieve the tension.

"Well, it's lovely to meet you, Tom," Sam says. "Hopefully, this one lasts a bit longer."

James coughs into his wine glass.

Pete pushes his food around on his plate.

This one?

What does that mean?

Sam leans forward, resting his chin on his hand like he's hosting a talk show.

"So, Tom, tell us everything. How old are you?"

I clear my throat. "Um, forty-two."

"Cute," Sam says, nodding like I've just passed a test. "Star sign?"

"Er… Libra?"

"Oooh, balance and harmony," Sam says. "That'll help with the chaos of this place. Any siblings?"

"No, just me."

"Wow, only child. Explains the main character energy."

Pete coughs into his wine.

"And how about your parents? Are they local?"

"They're um…both dead."

"Oh my God, tragic!" Sam gasps, almost delighted. "Like Disney tragic! You're like Bambi."

I'm not sure how to respond, unsure if I'm being comforted or mocked.

Sam waves a hand. "Okay, next: worst date you've ever been on?"

"Uh…" I glance at Pete, but he just looks apologetic. I want to shift the attention away from me, but the people-pleaser within is sucked into responding to every question. There's a pause as I try to find any kind of acceptable dating disaster story. "I once went for dinner with a guy who brought his mum. To the third date."

Sam's jaw drops. "No! Was she hot?"

"I—what?"

Pete groans. "Sam…"

Sam ignores him, leaning closer. "Okay, let's get to the good stuff. Body count?"

"Uhh…"

"Don't be shy. Round up if you must."

My face heats up so much that I feel my ears burn. "I don't… I've never… counted?"

Why am I answering these questions?

James sips his wine so slowly it feels like a judgment.

Sam grins. "I bet it's respectable. Pete's is pretty high."

"Sam." Pete's voice is sharper this time, but Sam just winks.

"Fine, fine, we'll leave the stats for later. But what about kinks? Vanilla, chocolate, or full-on Ben & Jerry's Half Baked?"

I almost choke on a carrot. "Ummm…"

"Okay, maybe we should move on to something more—" Pete tries to deflect.

Sam beams. "So, Rocky Road."

"Sam," Pete moans, but he's laughing despite himself now, face in his hands.

And that's when I realise: I'm the comic relief tonight. The bumbling sitcom neighbour who wanders into the wrong apartment with his trousers on backwards. I plaster on a grin and keep talking, because what else can I do? At least if I'm the clown, nobody notices how terrified I am.

As the night continues, I appreciate Sam's presence more. James offers little except an occasional frown, Pete is quiet and awkward, a side of him I've never seen.

Sam, on the other hand, is in his element, filling silences with outrageous stories, most of which I suspect are only half true.

But I can't help but hyperfocus on James. He just watches. Watches in the way a hawk watches a field mouse. Or the way my mother used to watch me when I said I'd done my homework but hadn't.

Meanwhile, I'm overthinking everything. Am I holding my fork weird? Did I laugh too long at Sam's story? Should I compliment James's shirt? Why do his cheekbones look like they could cut glass? Why do I suddenly feel like I've turned up at the Hunger Games dinner table unarmed?

Sam takes a long sip from his glass. "Do you know who would have loved this wine?" he asks, to no one specifically.

No one responds.

"Who?" I ask, compelled to fill the silence.

"Chris," Sam says, casually.

The air shifts immediately. Pete stares at his plate. James' jaw tightens.

"Who's… who's Chris?" I ask.

Sam grins. "Pete's ex."

"Oh," I say, brightly, like a man who has just trodden on a rake.

Chris.

The name hangs in the air like a bad smell. I try to keep my face neutral, but inside, my brain is running a full background check on this mystery man.

Chris. Who is Chris? How serious was Chris? Is Chris hotter than me? Probably. Chris sounds like the kind of guy who runs marathons for fun and saves kittens from burning buildings. Is he taller? Funnier? Can he eat soup without it dribbling down his chin?

Pete is still fascinated by his plate, and Jame's jaw, still tight enough to crack a walnut.

My spiral continues.

Why do they both look like someone's just mentioned Voldemort? Was Chris The One That Got Away? The Big Love? Am I sitting in Chris's chair right now? Eating off Chris's plates?

I take a sip of wine, mostly to keep my mouth busy so I don't accidentally blurt out "So how often do you still think about him?" like a man mid-emotional breakdown.

"Yeah, this is some great wine. We need to get some more of this," Sam says, taking another big slurp.

Towards the end of the meal, I excuse myself to go to the bathroom. I need a break.

The house is vast, corridors stretching out like arteries. The bathroom itself is pristine, all marble and chrome, the kind of place you're afraid to exhale in case you fog the mirrors. I stare at myself in the sink.

What am I doing here? Craig was so right: this is far too quick, far too messy.

And James… something about him sets my skin on edge. So cold and brooding. The way Pete shrinks in his presence is unexpected and concerning.

But then I think of Pete's laugh, the way he looked at me by the harbourside, the warmth I feel around him. That's real. Isn't it?

I splash water on my face, breathe, and steel myself to go back.

On the way down the hall, I hear voices. Muffled, but distinct.

James. Low, dangerous. "…this was a fucking stupid idea."

Pete. Softer, placating. "I wasn't—"

"You just want to humiliate me."

I stop, frozen in place. I back against the wall and listen.

"James, please, just give him a chance—"

There's a bang, like something being slammed up against the wall, followed by silence.

My stomach twists.

I freeze.

I should step in like Pete's knight in shining armour, but I don't. I'm just solid like a statue.

Useless.

After a moment of pausing, I walk back into the dining room, heart hammering. Sam looks up with a knowing smile. Pete follows a moment later, a smile pasted on like wallpaper, eyes down. James strolls in last, face red, yet untouched. Our eyes don't meet for the rest of the night.

We finish dinner, but my appetite is gone.

Later, Pete squeezes my hand. "Thanks for coming," he whispers.

I smile, tell him it was lovely, but inside, I'm knotted.

The name Chris is whirling through my mind more than it should.

But more importantly, Craig told me James would be welcoming. Supportive. Lovely.

And all I can think is: *Craig was wrong.*

Chapter 15

PETE

Pete stands at the doorway as Tom pulls on his coat. The night air is cool, cutting through the tension that has clung to the house like static since dinner.

"Well," Tom says, his hand on the zip, voice light but not light enough. "That was… weird."

Pete smiles, soft, disarming. "Weird good or weird bad?"

Tom hesitates. "Just… weird. James seemed upset."

"He wasn't upset," Pete says quickly, too quickly, before softening it with a shrug. "Just nervous. That's how he is. He's protective. But he was pleased to meet you."

Tom's expression says he doesn't quite buy it.

"I …thought I heard you arguing," Tom adds carefully.

Pete waves it away with a hand, casual, like shooing a fly. "Oh, no, just a little disagreement. Nothing serious." He flashes a grin.

"Right," Tom says, unconvinced, his eyes flicking to the Uber that appears in the driveway.

For a second, neither speaks; they just feel charged air amongst the silence. Pete leans in and kisses him on the cheek, his smile fixed despite the twisted tension in the pit of his stomach.

Tom nods and disappears into the night.

The door clicks shut. The smile slides from Pete's face.

The house exhales into silence.

In the garden, Sam's silhouette glows faintly, a vape lighting his face like a cigarette in a noir film. James is slumped on the sofa, long legs stretched out, an empty wine glass hanging loosely from one hand.

At first, Pete doesn't speak. He just slips quietly into the kitchen, moving plates and cutlery almost mechanically, scraping leftovers into the bin and stacking the dishwasher.

Meanwhile, his mind is replaying the events of the dinner frame by frame.

Tonight was never going to be easy.

James was never going to play gracious host. He'd known that before Tom even arrived, and still he'd pushed for it. Should he have warned Tom? Probably. But he didn't want to scare Tom off when things were going so well.

Tom needed to meet James, needed to see him as a person, not just a shadow behind Pete's life. He wants this to work so badly, he and Tom.

James would come around eventually. He always did.

This was their rhythm: conflict and calm, storm and still water. It was what they'd built together.

But still, Pete had hoped it would go better than this.

And Sam, Sam couldn't help himself. Always the little arsonist, tossing matches just to see what burns. Mentioning Chris like that, so casual, cruel, watching Pete stiffen, and James go cold.

Pete clenches the cloth in his hand. Chris's name was going to come out eventually; it had to. But not like this. He wanted to do it in his own way, his own time.

What must Tom think now? That Pete is still hung up on Chris? That this house is one big mausoleum for failed love stories?

Maybe that's better than him considering what really happened to Chris.

Pete finishes clearing the plates and takes a long breath before walking back to the living room.

James hasn't moved. He's staring at the blank television, jaw set, eyes glassy from wine and anger.

"Sam," Pete says, not looking at him, "why did you bring up Chris?"

Sam exhales a cloud of vapour that curls lazily into the night air before dissipating. "Because it's true," he says with a shrug, leaning on the doorframe. "He would have loved that wine."

"You know what that does to James," Pete snaps, his voice low, careful not to ignite James further.

Sam smirks. "James can handle it. Can't you, babe?"

James doesn't answer.

Pete steps closer, crouching beside the sofa. "James," he says softly, "thank you for tonight. You knew this was going to be hard. But it was important."

James turns his head slowly, the look in his eyes enough to still Pete's breath.

"Important for who?" James asks, his voice deceptively calm.

"For us," Pete says.

James laughs—short, sharp, joyless—and sits forward suddenly. "For us. Right."

Pete swallows, tries to steady his tone. "This is what we decided, right? What would be good for us."

Pete takes a step closer, lowers his voice. "I'm trying to make this work, James. I'm trying to build something good here." He places his hand on James's shoulder. Soft, intimate.

Then James shoves him.

Pete stumbles, catches himself on the edge of the sofa, but James is already stepping forward, crowding him.

"James—"

The kick takes him by surprise, catching him in the stomach, knocking the air out of him. He doubles over, the floor rushing up to meet him.

Somewhere above him, Sam chuckles, a low, amused sound, and walks away, the back door sliding shut behind him.

Pete lies there, cheek pressed to the rug, the taste of blood in his mouth.

This is what love looks like, he tells himself.

This is what it costs.

When the house finally falls silent, he pushes himself up slowly, painfully, and sits back on his heels.

Tomorrow, he'll message Tom.

Tomorrow, he'll smile, make a joke, keep the illusion alive.

Because Tom believes in him. And that belief — fragile, dangerous — is the one thing Pete can't afford to lose.

Chapter 16

TOM

The next day, I'm sprawled on Craig's sofa like a teenager who's just been told his favourite boyband has split up. Which, honestly, is not far off.

Craig's making tea in that slow, deliberate way of his, like he's in an M&S advert and I'm the tragic audience they're trying to seduce into buying Earl Grey. He pops his head round the kitchen door.

"So. Dinner?" he asks, in the same tone a sexual health adviser might say, "So. Your tests."

I groan into his throw pillow. "You know when you meet someone's parents for the first time, and you're trying to be charming, but then you accidentally bring up Brexit or Meghan Markle or something, and the whole thing just implodes?"

Craig raises an eyebrow. "Did you bring up Brexit?"

"No." I sit up. "Although I may as well have."

"Okay, so how was James?"

I sigh. "So, you know how you said he would be open and kind and lovely, because that's what you polyamorous types are all into?"

Craig nods, suspiciously, sensing my tone.

"He was the *exact* opposite of that."

Craig winces. "Yikes."

"Yikes," I repeat, flopping back again. "James just… looked at me. Like I'd spilt red wine on his cream carpet. Except he didn't say anything, which was somehow worse."

"Did he try to get to know you at all?"

"No! Not at all, not one question! Not even, what do you do? Where do you live? Small talk basics. Nothing!"

"Okay, that's weird," Craig admits.

"Yes, weird! That's what I said!" I almost scream at the validation. "And Pete was kind of odd, quiet, on edge. In a way I've never seen before."

I pause for breath, before continuing: "And then Sam was there—"

"Sam?"

"James's boyfriend."

"Of course."

"Who, I don't know if he was making fun of me or flirting with me or planning to murder me in my sleep?"

"Presumably not the latter."

"And now, I just feel confused," I sigh. "It was supposed to be a lovely night, where I get to know this side of Pete, and everything was supposed to fall into place. But it just felt like the opposite.

Craig sips his tea. "So, this doesn't sound like the healthiest polyamorous setup, if I'm honest."

"It's just…complicated," I say, staring at the ceiling. "Pete's always amazing. Just funny and normal and easy to be with. I trust him , I do."

Craig frowns. "But he's got this whole housemate-slash-husband situation with a guy who glares at you across the dinner table like you've just eaten his dog."

"Okay, James wasn't glaring," I protest. "He was just… quietly radiating disapproval."

Craig smirks. "Oh, well, that's fine then."

I grab my phone. "Look, I found him on LinkedIn." I hold up the screen.

Craig squints at the profile picture, James's beautifully coiffured hair waving back at him.

"He's a 'Wealth Management Strategist'," I say.

"Oh, they're the worst," Craig says.

"And then there was the Chris thing," I add.

"Wait, who?" Craig looks confused.

"Chris. The Ex."

"Who's Ex?" Craig clarifies.

"Good point. Pete's Ex."

"Oh."

"His name just… came up. Like Beetlejuice. And then the whole table went silent, and I wanted to crawl into the floor and die."

"Oh wow," Craig looks bemused. "There's a lot going on here. What do you know about Chris?"

"Literally nothing, which makes me think he must be a supermodel or an MI5 agent or some beautiful fitness influencer or something."

There's a moment of pause, where Craig processes what he can of this mess.

"I'm just saying," he says carefully, "this might not be a situation you want to entangle yourself in too deeply. You're still—"

"Recovering, I know," I say, waving a hand. "But I like Pete. And maybe if I build a friendship with James, it'll make things less weird."

Craig sighs. "I'm not sure this is a good idea. Just… be careful, okay?"

Later that evening, I meet Pete for a drink. We're in a little pub tucked away off Gloucester Road, all wood panelling and ironic gin menus. Pete smiles when he sees me, and suddenly my shoulders drop; I didn't realise how tense I'd been until that moment.

"How are you feeling after last night?" he asks as we sit down.

"Like I survived a Hunger Games trial run," I say.

He laughs, and I feel absurdly proud for making him laugh. "James can be… intense."

"Yeah, I noticed," I say. "He barely said a word, but it was like he was in my head with a megaphone."

"Look, I probably should have warned you—"

"You think?" I cut in with a laugh.

"I just didn't want to put you off coming."

"It wouldn't have," I lie.

Pete nods, tracing a circle on the table with his finger. "He struggles with me… exploring the emotional side of things outside the relationship."

I scrunch my face up. "But you're in an open relationship, though? Isn't this the whole point?"

Pete nods. "Yes, you're right. It's something we both want. But he just finds it more difficult than me."

"That's the bit I don't get," I say, leaning in. "He has a boyfriend! And you're meant to feel, what, guilty?"

Pete gives me a small smile. "It's different when it's on the other side. For him, anyway. He wasn't comfortable with it at first. Casual sex he can manage. Romance? That's harder for him."

"But then he ended up seeing Sam."

Pete nods. “Exactly. They have their thing. And I’m happy for him that he has that. And we agreed that I could have the same. But the reality is hard for him, I understand that.”

I don’t even want to suggest this, but I do. “So, should we even be carrying on like this, seeing each other? Should we just cool it for a bit?”

“God, no!” Pete says. “I really want to keep seeing you and getting to know you.” He squeezes my hand as he speaks. “It’ll just take a bit of time for James to adjust. It’s not like we’re going behind his back.”

I can feel my overthinking engine revving up, so I take a sip of my drink to shut it up. “Do you think he even likes me?”

“James doesn’t dislike you,” Pete says quickly. “He just… worries. About me. About us. About everything.”

I nod.

There’s a pause, and I decide to go for it. “Pete, can I ask about Chris?”

He stiffens. “What about him?”

“Sam mentioned him last night. And then it got… weird.”

“Weird?”

“Weird. You all just looked weird and uncomfortable.”

“Well, no one likes talking about exes in front of the new boyfriend. Especially when I hadn’t mentioned him before.”

There’s a temporary burst of joy in my chest as Pete uses the word “boyfriend”, before my brain brings me back into the conversation. “No, I get that.”

“I was angry with Sam for bringing it up. He just loves to stir up trouble.”

He stares into his glass for a long moment. “Anyway, that’s all over now. Chris and I… we were together for two years. And then he… left.”

“Left?”

Pete shrugs. “He went away. Moved. I don’t know, it was all very sudden…” He trails off, swallowing hard.

I want to ask more, but I can see it’s costing him to even say this much. So, I nod, trying to make my face look sympathetic and not like I’m mentally rewriting this as the opening scene of a Netflix documentary.

“Okay,” I say softly. “I get it.” I take a short breath and continue. “I had a close friend, not a boyfriend, Guy.”

Guy. Why am I bringing up Guy?

"A work colleague," I continue. "We were really close. But then one day, he just wasn't around anymore."

"What happened?" Pete asks.

I don't really want to go into this now.

"Long story, I'll tell you one day, but I suppose what I'm saying is I know what it's like when someone leaves your life quickly."

Pete smiles and places his hand on mine, and the air between us shifts in a good way.

"I really want to make this work with us," he says quietly. "James just needs a bit of time to come around."

I nod, heart doing that embarrassing swoopy thing. "I want this too."

"Then we'll take our time," Pete says, grinning. "You'll win him over."

"Oh, absolutely," I say, my grin turning smug. "I'm very charming when I want to be. Give me three dinners and a bottle of wine, and he'll be asking me to move in."

Pete laughs — a proper laugh this time — and I feel something uncoil in my chest.

"Careful," he says. "He might take you up on that."

"Perfect," I reply. "I've always wanted to live in a house with a man who stares at me like I've broken into his garden."

We're both laughing now, and for the first time since last night, it feels easy again.

Later, outside, I feel light somehow. The tension of the previous night hasn't gone completely — there are still questions I need answering — but enough that I can feel comfortable with Pete again.

Pete gives me a warm smile before heading off in the opposite direction. I watch him go for a moment longer than is probably socially acceptable, then start walking myself, hands shoved deep in my pockets.

I pull out my phone as I reach the corner.

One missed call.

Evelyn.

I hover my thumb over the screen.

She's calling me now. Shit.

I can't stop thinking about the blood, her last message said.

I shove the phone away and keep walking. The evening air has that perfect August balance: just warm enough not to need a jacket. The street is quiet, just the occasional car passing, headlights slicing across the pavement.

And then I see him.

Daniel.

He's standing on the opposite pavement, maybe twenty metres ahead. Head down, hands in his pockets, like he's just waiting for the lights to change.

He looks up, and for a second our eyes connect.

I freeze. A shiver cascades down my neck.

Then a bus moves in front of us, coming to a stop.

But when the bus has gone, so has he.

The pavement is empty.

Chapter 17

CRAIG

Standing in the kitchen, Craig watches the rain out the window, making a drama on the patio. It's that annoying Bristol drizzle that isn't bad enough to cancel plans, but just makes everyone feel damp and miserable. He's spent twenty years standing in rain like this, while cordons go up and statements get taken. Twenty years in Avon and Somerset police, and it's always the drizzle he hates the most, not the blood or the lies. It's that darn drizzle.

Phil wanders down the stairs, whistling something jaunty and unnecessarily jovial for a Wednesday evening.

"Big night?" Craig calls, not moving from the window. He can see Phil's reflection, jacket on, hair done with the extra ten per cent care.

Phil steps into the doorway, tilting his head. "Just a drink," in the tone of someone who knows exactly how loaded that sounds. "Possibly two. We live in uncertain times."

"With?"

"Just that guy from Scruff. The one with the cute dog and the insane Kylie twelve-inch vinyl collection," Phil says, half expecting Craig to bat an innuendo back over the offer of twelve inches. Craig declines the offer and just nods.

"Anyway, just a quick catch-up. Very chilled," Phil adds, smiling.

Chilled.

The word lands between them. It's become their coded way of saying something isn't serious yet or is no big deal. Not a risk to their relationship. No intense feelings yet. You won't notice.

Craig forces another nod and a weak smile. He knows the rules because he wrote most of them. The boundaries, the check-ins, the honesty. He can give an exceptional talk on ethical non-monogamy: handouts, PowerPoint slides, the lot. He's lost count of how many times he's delivered that speech to friends about how they make it work.

"Phone, keys, dignity," Phil says, patting himself down. "All present."

"For now," Craig mutters.

"You want me to leave you the car?" Phil asks. "Or is this a pyjamas-by-nine kind of evening?"

"Every night is a pyjamas-by-nine-kind of evening."

It's intended to sound light-hearted, but there is an edge to the truth of it.

"Won't be late," Phil says, and the kiss on Craig's cheek is light, quick, careful, like a signature on a form. "If he's boring, I'll be home in time for tea and Celebs Go Dating."

Craig faintly smiles as he watches Phil close the door behind him.

The front door clicks. The house exhales. The rain gets bored and thins to mist. In the quiet, the fridge hums and the detective in Craig starts running timelines he doesn't want to run.

Another night, another date for Phil.

He picks up the tea towel, folds it, and unfolds it.

He thinks about the speech he gives: communication, boundaries, honesty. The trinity that keeps a polyamorous life standing upright. He wonders when he last asked Phil a question that didn't come preloaded with the answer he wanted. He wonders when Phil stopped giving details, and Craig pretended not to notice.

Phil has been distant lately, the way a landscape looks different after you trim a hedge. You can't say what has changed; you just feel more exposed.

His phone buzzes on the counter. Tom: You in? Can I call?

Craig sends back a thumbs-up emoji.

Tom calls immediately, like he's been perched on the edge of the bed waiting for permission. Craig answers on speaker.

"Evening, trouble."

Tom laughs, high and tired. "I'm not trouble. I'm delightful."

"You're both." Craig lowers his voice out of habit when he's soothing witnesses and friends. "So, what you up to tonight?"

"Well," Tom starts like he's about to drop some bad news. "I'm going to stay over at Pete's tonight."

"Like a sleepover?" Craig winces.

"Like an adult sleepover."

"Will James be there? And the boyfriend?"

"Yes, I think so."

"So, like an orgy?"

"No! No, not like an orgy. All very much a separate bedroom kind of situation."

Craig shakes his head. "Okay, is this wise?"

"It'll be fine. We'll hang out. I can get to know James a bit more, win him over with my wit and charm."

"In one night?"

"I know what I'm doing," Tom insists.

"I know you do." Craig looks at his own reflection in the darkened window: a man who is supposed to be unfazed by blood and secrets. "I'm not trying to parent you. It's just… fast."

"Fast isn't bad," Tom says. He laughs softly. "Craig, I'm forty-two. I've been slow for a very long time. Slow can feel lonely."

Craig looks back out the window. He wants to tell Tom to slow down. He wants to say a lot of things that will sound like interference. Because they're interference.

"Okay," he says at last. "If you're staying, text me the address."

"Why?"

"Just in case, you're drugged and child trafficked."

"This feels unlikely>"

"Well, because I'm a detective, then, and I worry. It's my love language."

Tom snorts. "Your love language is spreadsheets and suspicion."

"Both saved my life," Craig replies. "Humour me."

"Fine." Tom rattles off the postcode, and Craig writes it in his phone.

"Don't drink too much," he says. "Don't… don't try to win anyone over. Be exactly as lovely as you are and then leave enough of yourself for yourself."

"You think I'm lovely?"

"I think you're a nightmare," Craig says, soft as a smile, "and lovely."

"Okay," Tom says. "I'll call you in the morning."

"Do. Or I'll file a missing-persons report, and I'll make sure they'll use an awful picture of you on local news."

Tom laughs for real this time. "You would."

"I would." He swallows. "Night, mate."

"Night."

They hang up. Craig stands in the quiet of the kitchen. He stares ot his phone then flips it face down. He wants to be supportive, be trusting, be proud of Tom for going after something new. And he genuinely wants Tom to be happy and complete.

But there's another part, the part that has stood at too many doors in the drizzle because someone ignored their gut feeling. A colder, more practical part.

A part that would do whatever was needed to protect Tom.

His mind, traitor that it is, circles back to Daniel.

He knows the version of the story Tom tells himself: Craig, the loyal friend, the patient ear, the gentle nudge that helped him, supported him to leave his abusive ex.

It is true.

But, not the whole truth.

He told himself he did what he did because it was the best thing for Tom. He still tells himself that, because the alternative is admitting something uglier. There was a moment, a specific moment, when he stopped being a friend and started being an architect.

Last week, he'd crossed the line again. He slipped Tom's phone from the coffee table the moment he left the room, thumbed the screen open, and blocked Daniel's number without hesitation. A small domestic crime, committed with all the precision of a detective who knows how to make evidence vanish.

He told himself it was necessary. Daniel was a trigger, a wound that kept tearing open. Craig couldn't watch Tom bleed himself out one more time.

And yes, maybe that was part of it.

But it wasn't the whole story.

Daniel couldn't be allowed to get close again.

Not just for Tom's sake.

Because if Daniel ever spoke, if he ever spat the truth of what Craig had done into the light, Tom would never forgive him. He would see Craig not as a friend, but as the hand that tipped the first domino.

Craig sits with that thought longer than is comfortable, the weight of it heavy in his chest.

He doesn't regret it. Not yet.

And if it came to it again, he knows he'd wouldn't stop at blocking a number.

Chapter 18

TOM

I don't know why I agreed to stay over. Actually, that's a lie: I know exactly why.

Because when Pete asks me something, my brain doesn't do due diligence. I'm like one of those nodding dogs people stick in the back of their cars.

I'd told Craig earlier that I wanted this. That I was actively choosing to come back here. And at the time, I meant it. But walking up the drive now, away from my parked car, I have a growing urge to spin on my heels and drive myself back home.

Because I know what this is.

I know there are red flags here. Whole red bunting displays, doused in petrol and set ablaze, flapping in the breeze.

My rational brain is holding up a laminated sign saying: *danger, do not proceed.*

But my emotional brain? Oh, he's already inside the house, putting the kettle on, asking Pete how his day was, while stroking his hair.

Because Pete makes me feel wanted. Not tolerated, not managed. Wanted. Desired in a way that makes my chest ache.

And that's the bit I can't walk away from.

Seeing Daniel earlier, appearing out of the blue, like he was watching me, before he disappeared, was just another incentive to move ahead with this, to break away from the hold he has over me.

For years, I've convinced myself that feeling was for other people. That I'd missed my shot.

But with Pete… maybe I haven't.

And maybe that's worth ignoring a few flags for?

Inside the house, Pete greets me with that grin that should be prescribed on the NHS, and suddenly I'm a little less ready to bolt. The dining table is already set, candles lit, wine breathing in some fancy decanter.

"This looks nice," I say, trying not to sound like someone who has never seen placemats before.

He laughs, pours wine, and soon we're eating something involving lemon and garlic and a piece of fish that looks like it went to a very posh school. We talk, we laugh, we pretend this is just a normal date night in a normal house with no looming husband around.

And for a while, it works. I almost relax. Almost.

"So, where's the hubby?" I can't help asking.

"Oh, he's out for most of the evening. Date night with Sam."

"Date night," I repeat, trying to sound casual but probably sounding like a man who just accidentally FaceTimed his boss from the loo.

Pete grins at my expression. "Yeah, they do that most weeks. Go for dinner, a show, complain about the price of cocktails. Domestic bliss."

"Cool. Very modern. Very… Channel 4 documentary," I say, spearing a piece of lemony fish like it's offended me personally.

He laughs, the sound warm and low, and reaches for the wine bottle. "We aim for Channel 4. But most often we lean more into Channel 5."

"Ah, a bit filthier, and with more adverts."

"Exactly. But with a Jane McDonald soundtrack."

"Ah, yes," I nod. "So, we have the house to ourselves tonight?" I ask.

"Well, not all night. They'll be back at some point."

Hooray.

"And will they join us?"

"For a nightcap? Yeah, I'd imagine so." Pete looks at me, gauging my reaction to this news.

"And when you say 'nightcap'?"

"Relax. I mean a glass of wine, not an orgy."

I nearly choke. "Was that an option? Because I'm definitely underdressed."

"You'd be fine," he teases, topping up my glass. "You'd look great at an orgy."

"Well, that's very kind," I say, face reddening. "Although I get huge enough anxiety about whether to take my shoes off at other people's houses, so I'm not sure if a no-clothes environment plays to my strengths."

"Well, we're not exactly an orgy kind of household, so you can relax," he says softly, leaving his foot there, a warm line of pressure against my ankle.

I exhale, forcing a laugh. "Relaxing is not my default setting. I am an anxious man powered by coffee and worst-case scenarios."

"I've noticed," he says, eyes glinting, "you get this little furrow right here whenever you're overthinking."

Before I can respond, he leans forward and, with one finger, smooths the little crease between my brows.

"Better," he murmurs.

"I do not furrow," I say, furrowing. It feels nice to have him touch me.

"You do," he says, withdrawing his hand but not his gaze.

I pick up my wine. "I mean, yes, I was worrying about meeting James. And also about whether my cat is at home plotting my death for not feeding him on time."

Pete laughs, and this time he reaches over properly, covering my hand where it rests on the table. His thumb rubs absent circles over my skin as he says, "Tom, you are a grade A overthinker."

"I just—" I pause, staring at our hands. "I'm good at overthinking. Like, Olympic-level. Give me a situation, and I will catastrophise it until it looks like an episode of EastEnders."

"That must be exhausting."

"It is. But—" I swallow, looking up at him, "—it's also because I care. About getting things right. About not wasting time with the wrong people. When my dad died, it sort of… flipped a switch. Made me realise how much I'd been sitting on my hands, waiting for life to feel meaningful instead of doing something about it."

Pete's expression shifts, and he squeezes my hand firmly. "I get that."

"You do?"

He nods. "Yeah, I had a rough childhood. My dad was… well, not exactly father of the year. His contribution to my upbringing was mainly booze and shouting. Mum left early on, too. Stability has always been important to me. And a real connection. People who actually want to stick around."

The words hang between us, soft as the candlelight, and suddenly I'm very aware of how close we're sitting. His knee is still pressed to mine. His hand is still over mine.

"That's exactly it," I say, and my voice comes out quieter than I meant.

Pete doesn't say anything, just studies me for a beat, then smiles like he's made a decision. He slides his thumb across my knuckles one last time before withdrawing his hand and reaching for the wine.

"More?" he asks, but his voice has gone low, warm.

I nod, because speech is suddenly difficult.

Pete tops up my wine glass like he's on commission, and I watch the liquid swirl, pretending I'm the kind of person who knows how to appreciate the legs on a Pinot.

"So," he says, leaning forward on his elbows, like he's about to share a scandalous secret. "Are we going to talk about how we are both tragic clichés?"

I snort. "Define tragic cliché."

"You," he points at me with his fork, "the reclusive Bristol gay divorcee, who buys posh bread, has a cat with emotional issues."

I nod at his fair representation of me.

"And as for me, well, I'm…" he gestures vaguely at himself. "I'm a man who went no-contact with both parents since my twenties and spent the next decade trying to convince my therapist I don't have daddy issues. We're textbook."

It makes me laugh, but not just because it's funny, because it's so tragically true. "You make it sound like we're doomed."

"No," Pete says softly, shaking his head. "I think it means we're two people who actually get how much this matters."

Something shifts in me then. The wine doesn't feel so sharp on my tongue.

I pick at my food, trying to find the right words. "After my dad died, I… I thought I'd be devastated. And I was. But not in the way people expect. I didn't lose him because we never had a relationship in the first place. We mainly just talked about whether my car needed another MOT yet or not."

Pete nods as I continue. "I think the saddest thing was the realisation that we would never have a real connection."

I swirl my wine, watch it catch the candlelight. "Maybe I should have tried harder, maybe he should have, I don't know. But it's made me realise how much I value real connections and how rare they can be."

"Yes," Pete says softly. : Connections are worth exploring at the very least."

"They are," I nod. "And sometimes they work out… and sometimes they don't."

I take a breath. In the moment, t feels right to tell Pete more, so I do. "I told you about my friend, Guy, before," I say carefully.

Pete nods. "The one you used to work with?"

"Yes…it wasn't just a friendship. Not really. We had a…thing."

Pete doesn't look shocked, just quietly attentive. His gaze is soft but unwavering.

"He was married," I add, because it's all coming out now. "We started as just work colleagues, then lunch breaks turned into long walks and lots of talking. Then friends became something more." I pause, expecting some look of shock from Pete, but he remains calm , taking in my words.

"We started sleeping together," I continue. "It lasted months. I hated myself for it, but I couldn't stop. I used to say I would never be one of those people who cheated, but there I was… cheating."

"This was when you were with Daniel?"

I nod.

Pete tilts his head, his expression unreadable. "That must have been… complicated."

"That's one word for it," I say with a weak laugh. "It's not an excuse, but things were impossible between Daniel and me. Every day was a struggle, the mind games, the arguments. He had debts, big ones, from gambling, that weren't going away. And Guy was just a welcome relief from all that. Someone who made me smile."

My head hangs as the shame creeps in. "But I just felt like such a massive hypocrite. Cheating has always been a hard no. But then, there I was doing it in the worst possible way."

"So what happened?"

"Well, it ended suddenly," I admit. "But if I learnt anything, Guy made me realise that connections don't always follow the rules. And connections outside the rules can be special too—"

"If you rewrite the rules," Pete adds in.

I shrug. "Yeah, maybe."

Pete gives me a small, kind smile. "You don't have to justify yourself to me, you know."

"Yeah," I say, shrugging. "I just… The point is, although it didn't work out, I still believe connections are worth exploring. Even if they hurt. Even if they're complicated. Because sometimes, sometimes they can lead to something amazing."

Pete's grin softens into something warm, steady. "I think so too. When you find them, they're worth fighting for."

I place my hand over his. "Indeed."

"Thank you for telling me about Guy. And your Dad."

"That's okay. I'm glad you're getting to know me. I want to know you in the same way."

Pete smiles like he's been there, because maybe he has. "My dad…" He hesitates, twirling the stem of his glass. "He was just… absent. From about twelve, there was no more contact, no explanations. That was it."

I swallow hard. "I know my situation is different, but there's still a similar feeling, right? A hole where something should be."

He meets my eyes again. "Exactly. I think that's why we both take this seriously. We don't need casual or disposable. We want something real and genuine. Something that will last."

My chest heats in a soothing, warm way. "God, you make me sound like some hopeless romantic."

"You are a hopeless romantic," he teases, grinning. "But so am I. I think that's why this works."

And just like that, I'm smiling into my glass like an idiot, because he's right. This does work. Despite the awkward dinners, the James-shaped cloud hovering over everything, despite the red flags waving al over the shop, this is the first time in years I've felt understood.

"I'm really glad you asked me to stay tonight," I say finally.

Pete's grin softens into something warmer. "Me too."

For a long moment, we just sit there, grinning at each other like teenagers with a crush, and for once, I stop overthinking everything.

We end up on the sofa after dinner, the remains of dessert abandoned on the table because apparently, we are adults who can just leave dishes for Future Us to resent. Pete puts on some soft background music, and we curl up together, his arm slung across my shoulders like it lives there.

It's stupid how comfortable this feels. Like my entire body has been holding its breath all day, and finally lets go.

Chapter 19

TOM

We're on the sofa, plates from dinner still abandoned on the table, when the front door clicks open.

Great. *Company*.

Just what my anxiety ordered.

Sam's voice hits first, loud and cheerful, like someone's turned the volume up to eleven. "We're back!"

I sit up straight, instantly feeling like I've been caught doing something I shouldn't, even though the most shocking thing that has happened this evening is Pete showing me a video of a dog that can moonwalk.

James appears behind Sam, his expression unreadable, and my stomach jolts.

"Oh, hey! You're back early," Pete says, in that forced casual tone people use when they mean the exact opposite.

Sam drops into an armchair. "Well, date night was a success, Tom. A little Italian place, all candles and carbs. Nothing says romance like a bottomless bread basket."

"Sounds nice," I say politely.

Pete claps his hands together softly. "I'll grab more wine."

"Good idea," James says, his voice low. Then he follows Pete out of the room.

And now it's just Sam and me.

He grins, wide and wolfish.

"So," I say, sitting up a little straighter. "Do you, um… live here too?"

He smirks. "Not officially. More of a frequent flyer. I have my own place, but it's boring. And who wants to be boring when you can be here?"

I glance around at the house, which is admittedly gorgeous but currently feels like the setting of a psychological thriller. "Sure. And you do… what, exactly?"

"I run a CCTV installation business," he says. "Keeps me very busy. You'd be surprised how many people want to spy on their neighbours. Plus, you'd be amazed at the stuff you see when you're setting up cameras around other people's houses."

I smile weakly. I don't know whether to laugh or be slightly afraid. "Well, it's best to be safe. That said, I don't even have a Ring doorbell to my name."

"Oh, I've thrown up CCTV all over the place here. Because you never know," he says, with raised eyebrows.

I just nod.

Sam suddenly snorts with laughter for no reason. "So, I went to an installation job today for this guy, and his actual name was Wayne Kerr. And no, it wasn't a fake name. His driving licence confirmed it."

I laugh, shaking my head. "That's tragic."

"I mean, who in their right mind calls a baby Wayne in the first place. But with that surname too; were the parents drinking or just high on coke?"

I laugh despite myself. "I went to school with a girl called Fanny Tucker."

Sam cackles so hard he almost spills his wine. "No! That's not a real name!"

"Swear on my life," I say. "Her parents apparently didn't think it through until she hit Year Seven and everyone discovered euphemisms."

"Poor thing, that's just child abuse," Sam says, grinning.

"Isn't it?!"

"So, Pete's ex…" Sam leans forward, conspiratorial. And my heart jumps out of my chest.

Pete's ex.

"I still can't believe his name was Chris Christianson. Like, who does that to a baby? That's not a name, that's a witness protection identity."

I feel my face going red, but try to keep it cool. "Chris… Christianson? Wow…yeah… funny name."

"I mean, it's no Fanny Tucker, granted," Sam adds.

I nod and smile.

There's a momentary pause in conversation.

Don't ask about Chris.

Don't ask about Chris.

Don't ask about—

"So…Chris," I ask, as casually as I can. "What happened there then?"

Sam lies back on the sofa. "Well, I mean, he was lovely. A right doll. Blond hair, cheekbones, the works. Proper catalogue model energy." Sam grins wickedly. "And completely allergic to this house. Couldn't cope with James. Couldn't cope with Pete, in the end. One day, he just… poof. Gone."

"Gone?"

Sam shrugs. "Vanished. Not a text, not a note, nada. Pete was heartbroken for weeks, cried into his cereal. It was very sad. And also very boring. Don't recommend."

"And you never heard from him again?"

"Never, no. Just like that, he disappeared off the planet." There's a moment of silence, before Sam just waves his hands dismissing the mystery which is now playing out tenfold in my head. "But that was two years ago now, so Pete's moved on."

Sam stretches, clearly done with the topic of Chris like he's flicking ash off a cigarette, and grabs his wine. "Anyway. Enough ghost stories."

James walks back into the room, glass of red wine in hand. His handsome face is stern and unreadable.

"Right," Sam jumps up. "Need a wee. Back in a second," he says, scuttling out of the room.

No, no, no.

And then, just like that, I'm alone with James.

The silence is immediate and so heavy it's practically visible. I can hear the clock in the hallway, each tick feeling like someone is flicking my forehead. He sits opposite me, crosses his legs with calm precision, and just… stares.

My brain starts screaming at me to say something. Anything. "Nice… wine?" I manage, gesturing vaguely at his glass like an idiot.

"Yes," James says evenly. "We have a subscription."

A subscription. For wine. Of course they do. Probably artisan, ethically sourced, pressed between the thighs of French virgins.

"That's… efficient," I say, nodding like he's just told me he has solar panels.

"Mm."

I can feel sweat prickling the back of my neck. I glance around desperately for conversation topics like they're fire exits. "And… lovely house."

He inclines his head slightly, almost like I've complimented him personally. "Thank you. We've put a lot of work into it."

"Yes, you can tell," I babble. "It's very… symmetrical. Like if you filmed a murder mystery in here, the detective would definitely find a secret panel behind one of the bookcases."

He nods. "Well, Pete had a clear vision of how he wanted it when he moved in."

For a split second, I think I see his mouth twitch: not quite a smile, more like a private joke I'm not invited to.

"You and Pete seem… close," James says finally, voice smooth as glass.

My laugh comes out too loud. "Yeah, we, um, get on. Really well. I mean, quite well…"

He just looks at me until my words shrivel up and die.

"Pete's very good at making people feel seen," James says. "It's one of the things I always loved about him."

"Yeah," I say, my voice about an octave too high. "He's great."

Another silence stretches, thicker this time. My brain kicks into overdrive: compliment his shoes? Too weird. Ask about his job? Too personal. Pretend to choke and run out of the house? Not practical, though dramatic.

James leans forward just slightly, enough to make my stomach clench. "You should know this isn't… simple. Being with Pete means being part of this house. This life. It's not for everyone."

I try for a casual shrug and probably look like I'm having a small stroke. "Right. Yeah. Sure."

"It can be intense," he adds, almost kindly. "You'd be wise to think about whether you're prepared for that."The weight of his words hangs in the air.

Prepared. Like this is a storm I need to stockpile tins of beans for.

"Intense, in what way?" I ask before my brain can stop my mouth.

James smiles faintly, and it goes through me. "Living here isn't quiet. Multiple personalities. Lots of feelings. It can feel… consuming. All-encompassing. Not everyone's built for that."

I laugh nervously. "Oh, I'm very giving. Too giving, probably. Ask my ex. Actually, don't ask my ex."

James doesn't smile. His stillness is unnerving. "You'll find that the people who last here," he says, "are the ones who know what they're signing up for. Some think they do. At first. Then they discover what it really takes. Some get overwhelmed. Some leave."

I grip my wine glass tighter than is strictly safe. "Leave?"

James shrugs one shoulder, casual, like he's discussing bin day. "Sometimes quickly. Sometimes not quickly enough."

A prickle runs down my spine. My brain is screaming what does that mean but my mouth, traitor that it is, blurts out: "Like Chris?"

James's head turns sharply, his jaw tight. The silence that follows could freeze wine.

His eyes narrow just slightly.

"Chris is…in the past," he says finally, and his tone is soft, the kind of soft that makes my stomach drop.

Before adding a final blow.

"Where he belongs."

Before I can recover or dig myself in deeper, Sam's voice booms cheerfully from the hall, followed by Pete's laugh. James leans back again, face smoothing back into polite neutrality, as though the last thirty seconds didn't happen at all.

Pete re-enters, holding the wine like a peace offering, and my chest feels tight enough to snap.

Chapter 20

TOM

I'm perched on the edge of the guest bed like it's about to eject me, trying very hard to look like someone who stays in strange houses all the time and is totally fine with it.

Spoiler: I am not fine with it.

This is not the cosy romantic sleepover I'd envisioned on the drive over here. This is me in a house that feels like the setting of a middle-class murder mystery, packed with personality disorders.

Pete is so annoyingly calm. He's humming to himself as he plugs in his phone and lays his Apple Watch on its charging dock, like we're in some indie rom-com montage, not trapped in a gothic thriller.

"Why is your face all scrunchy?" he says, grinning as he tosses his jumper over a chair.

"It's not!" I lie, spectacularly. "This is just my face."

He sits beside me on the bed, takes my hand. The contact is grounding, annoying in the way only Pete can manage, like he's casually diffusing a bomb.

"I had a chat with James," I say.

"And how did that go?" he asks, cautiously.

"Well, he didn't kill me, so I'm taking that as a win."

"Oh, that well?"

"Yes, that well. He was intimidating to say the least."

"James can be a bit…intense sometimes. But that's how he can be with new people. Don't take it personally. He's just feeling you out."

"Feeling me out? Like a job interview?"

"Kind of. He'll be fine once he gets to know you and sees you're serious about this."

"And what do I do to get him to see that?"

"You don't need to do anything except just keep on being you."

"Well, I'm exceptionally good at being me."

"Perfect," Pete smiles.

"Where being me means making bad jokes when I'm nervous and accidentally trauma-dumping over dinner. Then replaying alternate versions of conversations in my head for the next ten to fifteen years."

Pete laughs and squeezes my hand, the tension in my chest loosening with his touch.

Maybe he's right. Maybe James is just being protective. Maybe I'm just overthinking, Craig tells me this all the time.

But still, the conversation with James, his voice smooth and deliberate, plays on a loop in my head.

You'd be wise to think about whether you're prepared for that.

Not exactly the bedtime story you want before staying over.

Pete moves to grab his T-shirt, and that's when I see it: a faint ring of blue and purple around his wrist, like a shadow that doesn't belong.

"Pete," I say quietly, catching his arm before I can stop myself. "What's this?"

He glances down like he's just remembered it's there. "Nothing. Banged it on a door."

"It doesn't look like a door bang."

"Because you're a door bang expert?" he teases, but his voice is a little too light.

"Pete."

He hesitates, then shrugs. "James and I had a…little disagreement earlier. Nothing major. It just got a bit heated, and he grabbed my wrist, that's all."

My stomach twists. "That's all?"

"Tom." Pete's voice is soft now, and he takes my hand this time. "It's fine. It was just a row. Forget it."

Forget it? How am I supposed to forget it when the image is burned into my brain?

"And does he do that often?"

"Do what?"

"Grab you? Hurt you?"

Pete shakes his hands in the air, pulling away from me. "No, I mean, not really, no."

His answer offers me no level of comfort.

"He can just be a bit passionate about things sometimes."

"I'm not sure if leaving bruises on your wrists can be classed as passion."

"Look, it's nothing; forget it," he says, trying to close this down.

But I'm not ready to end this conversation yet, so I take another approach.

"I used to say the same about my ex, Daniel, after an argument. 'It's fine, forget it.' But it wasn't fine."

Pete's expression shifts, first sad, then sympathetic. "I'm not Daniel."

"I know. *You're* not Daniel at all."

"Then trust me. Tonight is about you and me. We don't have to make this heavier than it already is."

I nod, but inside, my head is loud.

Because it is heavy.

I like Pete. No, I more than like him — he's the first person I've let myself want in years. But every new thing I learn about this house, this life, feels like a step into deeper water.

And I can't tell if Pete is pulling me closer to shore or further out to sea.

We climb into bed, and for a moment, things are simple again. He pulls me against him, kisses the top of my head like it's the most natural thing in the world. And I let myself melt into him, because it feels good to be wanted. To be chosen.

But in the dark, my eyes stay open.

I can still feel the ghost of James' stare.

I can still see the bruise on Pete's wrist.

And I can't shake the thought that I might already be in too deep. But I want to go deeper anyway.

Because if I don't find out what's really happening here, it'll eat me alive.

Pete's already yawning by the time we crawl into bed, like a cat who's had a particularly full day of being adorable. He rolls towards me, arm draped over my waist, and there's that flicker in his eyes – the unspoken so… are we going to…?

I kiss him softly but pull back, heart racing for reasons that have nothing to do with lust.

"I don't think I can, not here. Not with…" I gesture vaguely, as if James is lurking behind the wardrobe. "I just… can't relax knowing he's a few doors down. Can I get used to sleeping over for a bit first?"

Pete squeezes my hand. "Of course. I get it. We can take as much time as you need." I press my face into his shoulder, grateful for his understanding.

Soon, we're both lying in bed, sheet up to my chest, and before long, Pete's breath evens out into a soft, steady sleep.

Me? My brain has other plans.

It spins.

About James, about Sam, about that conversation earlier, where James basically auditioned to play the villain in my personal horror film.

And Chris. The ex. Who didn't get on with James. Who disappeared so suddenly.

Why does this leave such a bitter taste in my mouth?

Then Daniel pops into my mind, too. Still hovering around. Ever after all the years, still in my life.

And then Evelyn. Another name I want to remove from my life, but know I never can.

I lie in bed thinking about how the knife sliced through him.

How many messages like that can I take.

So many names buzzing around my brain. Sleep is not my friend this evening.

The wine doesn't help. I feel like my tongue is glued to the roof of my mouth. My head is starting to bang like the hangover is checking in early. Dehydration beckons, and eventually, thirst wins over paranoia. I slide out of bed, careful not to wake Pete, and pad barefoot into the hallway.

The house feels different at night. The quiet feels uneasy rather than calming. The lights are dim, with shadows stretching to every corner.

I find the kitchen, gulp a glass of water straight from the tap like a teenager avoiding parental judgment, and start back up the stairs and down the hall.

That's when I see it.

Halfway along the corridor, a door is ajar. Just a sliver of light spills into the hallway.

I hear noises.

Low, guttural.

Not just sex sounds.

Something rougher.

I should mind my own business. I should absolutely mind my own business. But I'm me, so I don't.

I peer in.

And I wish I hadn't.

James has Sam pinned against the wall, face pressed hard into the paintwork.

This isn't regular, romantic sex.

This is aggressive, relentless.

James's arm snakes up around Sam's throat, forcing his head back in a chokehold. Sam's face is flushed, straining, his gasps rasping through the air. James doesn't loosen his grip. His thrusts are sharp, punishing, each one punctuated by the wet slap of skin on skin.

Then, James breaks away from the wall and tosses Sam onto his back on the bed, like he's a ragdoll, and continues deep and hard inside him. James's hand wraps tight around Sam's throat, the other pinning him down by the chest. Sam claws at James's wrist, but James is stronger, his hips driving harder, faster.

As James's aggressive thrusts continue, he removes his hand from Sam's chest and slaps him hard across his face.

The sound is vicious, enough to make my stomach lurch.

Another slap, like the crack of a whip.

Then another.

James removes his hand from around Sam's throat, as the room fills with Sam's desperate gasps. But before he can catch his breath, James grabs a pillow, pressing it down over Sam's face as he thrusts, the sound of his breathing turning ragged, animalistic, almost a roar as he nears his climax.

I can't move. I just… watch.

James presses the pillow over Sam's face, while looking up to the ceiling, his moans sounding more like battle cries as he finishes with a ferocious, final thrust.

When he's done, he pulls the pillow away. Sam gasps desperately, sucking in air like he's been underwater.

But before he can catch his breath, in one last vicious act, James grabs him by his waist and physically shoves him off the bed entirely. Sam hits the floor with a grunt, a heap of limbs and sweat.

"Sleep somewhere else," James says, wiping sweat from his brow.

Sam doesn't move, just lies there, chest heaving, as James walks into the ensuite, door swinging shut behind him.

I stumble back from the doorway, my heart hammering so hard it feels like it's in my throat.

Back in Pete's room, I slide under the duvet as quietly as I can, staring at the ceiling for what feels like hours, pulse still racing.

James isn't just brooding.

Or complicated.

He's dangerous.

Chapter 21

JAMES

James grips the edges of the sink, breath ragged.

The porcelain is cool beneath his palms, the sensation making a meagre attempt to ground him. His reflection stares back from the mirror. His skin is slick with sweat, his pupils still wide.

He doesn't look ashamed.

He looks alive.

He turns on the tap, splashes cold water over his face, watching it stream down and drip onto the counter. The bathroom smells faintly of cedarwood and expensive soap, like every room in this house.

Sam pushed him tonight. Sam loves to push him. Tonight was like so many before: Sam running his mouth until James shuts it. He enjoyed the way Sam's body strained as James held him down. The way he gasped for breath from the chokehold.

The way the power tilted back in James' favour.

Control. He hates losing it.

The house felt unsettled tonight. All that laughter like everything was perfect. And that man, Tom, sitting on his sofa like he belonged there.

No idea what he's getting himself into, the fucking idiot.

It's a reminder of how fragile balance can be. One wrong piece on the board and the whole game tips.

James wipes his face with a hand towel and repositions it neatly on the rail. He has made mistakes before. He's trusted the wrong people. Let them get too close.

It has cost him.

It will not cost him again.

He won't be made a fool of. Not by Sam. Not by Pete. Not by anyone.

Lately, Pete has been testing the limits, letting new faces through the door, laughing too easily. To James, this only means that he's contemplating a world without him. It's a dangerous habit. Pete forgets who keeps the lights on, who gave him the life he now takes for granted.

James presses his hands against the counter and feels the veins in his forearms tighten. Pete needs reminding. Not with words. Words can be twisted and ignored.

But reminders that settle deep, that reset the balance.

When James steps back into the bedroom, Sam is still on the floor, pulling himself together, a bitter twist to his mouth. James doesn't raise his voice. He doesn't need to.

"Out," he says.

Sam hesitates for half a second, then smiles. "Of course, darling." He slowly picks up his clothes and slinks out without another word.

James strips back the duvet and lowers himself into the bed with a sigh. The room is silent now, just the hum of the house around him. His sanctuary.

He will keep it that way.

Whatever it takes.

Chapter 22

SAM

In the bathroom, Sam yanks his jeans back on, the zip catching for a second before sliding shut with a harsh rasp. His t-shirt is damp with sweat, still clinging to him, cold now.

He looks into the mirror, checking the red marks around his neck. He hopes they're gone by the morning. He's not really a turtleneck guy. He doesn't want to have to explain away bruises again over brunch.

James's bedroom light is off, door closed. Sam turns and pads down the hallway, bare feet silent against the polished wooden floor.

Downstairs, he pulls on his trainers by the door and glances back toward the stairs.

No movement. Good.

Sam's skin hums with restless electricity. He knows he won't sleep tonight. He never can, not after nights like this. His body is wired, his brain buzzing, like someone's turned all the dials up too high.

And then his eyes catch on Tom's coat, hanging on the back of the chair by the door.

Tom.

What do we really know about Tom?

Sam slips a hand into the coat pocket, fingers brushing against metal. Keys. He pulls them out, holds them in his palm, feels their weight.

Things are good between him and James. But Pete. Pete is reckless. Always has been. Throwing himself into someone new without a second thought, without a second's consideration about what it does to the rest of them.

He has a good life here. It's taken years to get the balance right. James can be…difficult, but Sam has learned how to give him what he needs to keep him steady.

Pete, for all his chaos, brings warmth into this house, softens the edges, makes it feel less like a fortress.

Tom could ruin that.

Not necessarily because he wants to, but because that's what strangers do. They bring chaos in their pockets and leave mess in their wake.

Yes, Tom comes with his own benefits, but are they worth risking the status quo?

If he's going to protect what they've built, he needs to know who Tom really is. Not the version Pete gushes about, that stupid Tesco story.

The real Tom.

He shrugs on his jacket and slips out into the night. On the street outside, Sam presses the key until a car parked alongside the house beeps. Door open, Sam slides behind the wheel of Tom's car. The Sat Nav pings awake, Tom's home address saved in its memory. Sam smirks. People are so careless.

The roads are quiet, the

The roads are quiet, slick with rain, as the streetlights glint off the tarmac. Sam drums his fingers against the steering wheel as he drives, every bump and turn making his mind work faster.

Before his life in this house, Sam had only ever known chaos and instability. As a young boy, he went from group homes to temporary placements to foster parents who treated him like a guest they couldn't wait to leave. Occasionally, he got comfortable and somewhere felt like home. But soon enough, he was moved on.

Another bag packed, another move.

Stability is built with your own hands and must be guarded like treasure.

This house is the closest thing he's ever had to a permanent address. And Tom? Tom is a risk. Sam isn't about to watch it all go up in flames because Pete has a weakness for sad men with nice smiles.

He pulls up outside Tom's place, kills the engine, and just sits there for a moment. The house is dark, quiet, the kind of quiet that makes your ears ring.

Sam slips the key into the lock and turns it, slow and careful. The door opens with a faint creak that makes his skin prickle.

Inside, the house smells faintly of laundry powder and cat litter. It's tidy, almost too tidy, like Tom lives here alone and hasn't had anyone around to make a mess.

Sam walks inside, closes the door behind him, and listens.

Nothing.

Good.

He moves quickly, methodical, pulling the small case from his bag. Cameras. Tiny, wireless, easy to hide. He sets to work, moving through the house like a shadow, placing them in corners, above doorways, tucked onto bookshelves.

It's not about spying, not really.

It's about understanding.

About seeing the truth of someone when they think no one's watching. People are always honest when they think they're alone.

Halfway through, he hears something.

A noise, soft and low, from the kitchen, maybe?

Sam freezes, hand slipping into his pocket, fingers closing around the knife he always carries. Just in case.

He takes a slow, quiet step forward. Another noise, closer now. A shuffle.

Sam pushes the kitchen door open with the tip of the knife, muscles tensed—

And there's a cat, sitting on the counter, blinking at him like he's the one being rude.

"Jesus Christ," Sam breathes, lowering the knife. "You nearly gave me a heart attack, you little bastard."

The cat yawns, hops down, and wanders out like it owns the place.

Sam exhales, shaky, and gets back to work.

By the time he's finished, the cameras are live, transmitting. He can watch from anywhere now. Keep an eye on things. Keep control.

On his way out, he stops by the door and looks back over the living room, the sofa, the neatly stacked books on the coffee table. It all feels so personal, like stepping through someone's head.

Tom doesn't know it yet, but Sam is inside his life now.

Watching.

Chapter 23

TOM

The next morning, after a quick shower, I throw back on last night's T-shirt and sit on the edge of the guest bed. Pete heads downstairs to pop the kettle on.

"Take your time," he says, on the way out the door.

In my head, this has been interpreted as: "take five minutes to have a mild breakdown before breakfast."

And I do.

My mind is whirling with too many thoughts.

Pete's bruised wrist.

The talk of James's temper.

The vicious sex I witnessed between him and Sam.

And Chris. The ex who vanished.

I rub my temples, last night's wine catching up with me.

Chris Christianson.

The name rattles around in my head like loose change. Sam had dropped it in so casually last night, like it was a punchline, but I can't stop thinking about it.

People don't just vanish.

I open Facebook, because of course I do. There are about ten Chris Christiansons, which feels excessive for a country this size. I scroll through them one by one: men holding fish, men holding babies, men holding beers. None of them looks like they used to date Pete.

And then I find him.

He's smiling in every photo, all white teeth and blonde hair, and, oh God, there's Pete, arm slung around him in one of them.

They look happy, genuinely happy: the kind of happy that makes my stomach twist. I don't know why it hurts. Pete's allowed a past, of course, but seeing it is like pressing on a bruise I didn't know I had.

Then I see the tag. Emma Christianson. Sister. I click.

Her timeline is a mixture of dog memes and increasingly desperate posts:

My brother has been missing for two years. He was last seen around the Bristol area. Please share. If anyone knows anything. Please contact me.

My brain short-circuits as I read this.

Missing.

Not just "moved to Spain and didn't leave a forwarding address," but missing-missing.

My phone vibrates, making me jump so hard I almost drop it. Craig.

"Morning," I whisper, glancing at the door like James might materialise there any second.

"You sound like you're hiding under a bed," Craig says.

"I might as well be," I say. "Craig, I think James is abusive. And controlling. And Chris, Chris Christianson, is missing."

There's a pause. "What? Who?"

"Pete's ex. Blonde. Cheekbones. Sam mentioned him again last night, got his full name. And I found his sister on Facebook. She's been posting for two years about him disappearing."

Craig sighs, the long-suffering kind. "Tom, you have a gift for choosing the most dramatic men possible."

"I'm serious," I whisper-shout. "I saw James and Sam last night. Together. Like having sex together—"

"So, it was an orgy?"

"No! No, I wasn't involved, I was just spying on them."

"You're not coming across great in this conversation."

"No, it wasn't like that," I say, exasperated. Although I realise it was exactly like that. "The point is, it wasn't… gentle. It was like, rough."

"Rough? Okay, who doesn't like a bit of rough play?" Craig admits.

"No, like *rough*-rough. Like 'I'm going to choke you until you pass out' rough."

Craig sighs. "I miss nights like that."

"Craig, listen to me: there's this whole tension with Pete that feels like…like—"

"Like what?"

"Like if I leave him here long enough, Pete's going to turn into one of those missing person posters, too."

Another pause. Then Craig says, more soberly, "Okay. That doesn't sound great."

"Doesn't sound great? Craig, I'm basically living in the set of a true-crime podcast."

"All right, calm down. You need to take a step back. If James really is controlling, this could end badly. I think you should keep your distance."

"I can't just—"

"You can," Craig interrupts, voice hardening like the detective he is. "You need to think clearly.

"Can you look into him?" I ask.

"Look into him?"

"Like police-look-into-him? His background. Does he have a violent history?"

"I can't just look into anyone for no reason."

"Please," I plead.

Craig sighs. "I'll see what I can do. But you need to keep your head down. And don't get any more involved. Have a few days away from Pete. It doesn't sound like anything good will come of this."

"And here's me thinking polyamorous relationships were the new healthy norm."

"Well, compared to this, mine positively is."

When I hang up, my hands are shaking.

I head downstairs, trying to look normal, which probably just makes me look like a guilty man in a BBC crime drama. James is in the hallway, speaking to Pete.

"I've left the spare key where the cleaner can find it, under the plant pot by the back door", he says, like Pete's too dense to have figured that out himself.

"Right," Pete murmurs.

James grabs his jacket and leaves, the door clicking shut behind him.

The house feels instantly lighter, like someone's opened a window. Sam is nowhere to be seen.

Pete pokes his head around the kitchen door, smiling. "Coffee?"

"Yes, please," I say, too brightly. So that's what I do: sit down, drink coffee, and play normal while I figure out whether my boyfriend is married to a monster.

Chapter 24

CRAIG

Craig stares at his phone. He doesn't go home after the call from Tom.

He tells himself he should, that he's done enough for one night, but he stays right where he is.

The call plays back in his mind: Tom whispering like a fugitive, the fear in his voice, the mention of Chris Christianson. The name means nothing to Craig, but the way Tom said it sets his teeth on edge.

He played it down on the phone. He had to.

But this situation is bad. Too many unknowns. Too many moving parts. And Tom, as always, is running headfirst into trouble with his heart leading the way.

Yes, a bad situation, a messy one.

Messy for Tom.

And for Craig.

He shouldn't be doing this. He explains it away as the detective in him, so impulsively doing his job.

But this isn't the same.

He's back here. Again.

In the garden, tucked behind a bush.

Looking through the window.

From here, he has a clear view of the kitchen. Pete is at the counter with his hands wrapped around a mug. James is packing something into his bag. Even from this distance, Craig can see it. The way Pete stiffens, how he lowers his head slightly, voice too quiet to catch.

Craig stays watching longer than he means to, breath misting faintly in front of him. His pulse slows into a strange, heavy rhythm.

Who are you?

Craig needs to know.

He pulls back as Tom enters the kitchen. There are some shared glances before James turns and leaves the house.

It's only then that the room softens. Pete offers Tom a cup of coffee. There are smiles, a hug, a gentle kiss. They look… domestic. Comfortable. Like they belong together.

Craig leans closer.

He tells himself it's for Tom's safety, that he's gathering intel for himself, that this is all completely acceptable.

But the truth prickles under his skin.

What he's really investigating for.

His phone buzzes once in his pocket. He doesn't answer.

Minutes stretch. He doesn't leave when Tom does. Doesn't leave when the lights in the kitchen go out. He circles the house slowly instead, checking each window, each room he can glimpse into.

Finally, when the house is empty and silent, Craig backs away, heart hammering.

It should feel wrong.

But it doesn't.

Chapter 25

TOM

I drive away from the house feeling like my brain has been put through a washing machine, tumble-dried on high, then folded badly.

Twenty-four hours ago, I was nervously convincing myself that meeting James would be fine, that this would be a wholesome, grown-up step.

But above everything, all I can think about is Chris.

Chris Christianson. God, what a name. I can still see his sister Emma's Facebook page, the posts pleading for information, the hashtags, the grainy pictures of them as kids.

Two years of searching.

Two years of silence.

He was in a relationship with Pete, who was married to James, who I know is both possessive and abusive. And who, as Sam was very honest about, didn't exactly click with him. There is no universe where they don't know more than they're saying.

I shake my head as I pull up outside my house. Buster needs feeding, and frankly, I need the normalcy of a grumpy cat and my own sofa to lie on.

When I get home, Buster greets me with the kind of enthusiasm usually reserved for tax inspectors: a disdainful look, a slow tail flick, and then he stalks off to sit with his back to me.

I fill his bowl, half expecting him to call the RSPCA.

He sniffs at it, looks at me, essentially does the cat equivalent of rolling his eyes with his stare and starts to eat.

My phone buzzes on the counter.

Evelyn.

Not again. I can't keep ignoring this.

I can't stop thinking about the blood.

Not now, I can't deal with that right now.

I stare at it until it stops. She leaves a voicemail. I don't listen.

I just need caffeine, so I grab my keys and leave the house.

Clifton is thriving with that overly enthusiastic Saturday morning spirit. When you're on the verge of an existential crisis, this feels personally offensive. I grab a latte from my local Spicer & Cole and perch on a bench outside, trying to look like someone with their life together.

I flick back into Facebook to Chris's sister Emma. I scroll through her feed again. Post after post about Chris.

Missing. Vanished. Help.

I look at her friends. After a quick scroll, I find Pete. Does this mean they actually know each other? Or just Facebook friends?

What did Pete say to her about his disappearance?

I start to type a message to Emma, just a few words, nothing heavy. But I stop and delete it.

Stupid. Too much. Not yet.

I take a sip of my coffee and look over my shoulder out the window.

And as I turn back, that's when I see him.

Or rather, I *think* I see him.

Dark hair. Familiar walk. A flash of a jacket, I swear I've seen before.

Daniel.

My stomach plummets. My hands start shaking so badly that I nearly drop my coffee. He just walked past the window, I swear.

I turn to look again, and he's gone. Just… gone. Like smoke.

That's the second time I've seen him in as many days.

My breath goes short. My chest tightens like a fist is closing around it. I grip the edge of the table, counting in fours like every therapist I've ever had told me to, but my brain is screaming too loud to hear anything.

Inhale, two, three, four.

Exhale, two, three, four.

People are looking at me now. A woman with a pram gives me the kind of pitying look usually reserved for stray dogs in charity adverts.

Eventually, it passes. My heart slows. My breathing evens out. But I feel hollowed out, like I've been scooped from the inside.

Daniel was here again. That's not a coincidence. Why is he hovering around here?

What does he want from me?

Again, another thing I don't want to think about today

Pete. James. Sam, Chris. Evelyn. Daniel.

They start to blur, like names on a memorial.

Too many names. Too many people grasping at my life.

There's only one I should be focusing on.

Pete.

Just Pete.

Heading home, I try to distract myself with chores. Laundry, hoovering, the ceremonial clearing out of the fridge (goodbye, three-week-old hummus). Anything to fill the hours until I see Pete again tonight.

By evening, my nerves have been wound so tight they hum. I shower, change into something casual-but-not-too-casual (the eternal gay dilemma), and drive over to Pete's.

The house is dark when I pull up.

I knock.

Nothing.

I try Pete's phone. Rings. Rings. Straight to voicemail.

I walk around to the back. Not in a creepy way, just a concerned boyfriend checking for signs of life. But the place is empty.

I get back in the car and start to drive home, stomach knotted.

It's halfway down the hill that I see it.

A car. Behind me.

Nothing unusual. It's a public road, but the headlights sit too neatly in my rear-view mirror.

I turn left. It turns left.

I turn right. It turns right.

Paranoia, I tell myself. It must be.

I need to turn left, but turn right instead, just to see. It turns right.

My palms go slick on the steering wheel.

I pick up speed, heart hammering. I take the long way round the Downs, weaving through side streets, doubling back, the whole paranoid-thriller-movie routine.

As I pull up to my house, the car just drives straight past. Too dark to see the driver, but I can make out the car following me is a grey BMW 1 Series.

Or maybe it was never following me at all.

I sit in the car outside my house for a long moment, forehead against the wheel, breathing hard. With everything going on, today is becoming all too much. I want to call Craig, tell him what just happened, but my phone rings first.

Pete.

I answer so fast I almost drop the phone. "Pete? Where are you? Are you okay?"

His voice is low, strained. "Tom, I… we shouldn't see each other anymore."

"What?" The word comes out sharp.

"It's James," he says. "He's not coping with this. With… us. It's getting bad."

"Then leave," I say, too quickly. "Pete, you don't have to stay there if—"

"Tom." His voice cuts through mine. Quiet, but final. "Please. Just… don't come round again."

The line clicks dead.

I sit frozen, phone still against my ear like the call is somehow still happening, like I can will him back onto the line if I just hold still enough.

Then I'm moving.

I don't think. I just drive.

By the time I reach their house, the sky has gone from grey to black. I park across the road and wait.

The house is still dark.

Minutes stretch.

Finally, headlights sweep across the driveway, and Pete's car pulls in. Relief floods me so hard I almost cry. He gets out slowly, head bowed. Even from here, I can see the bruises.

Big, ugly marks across his cheek, down his jaw.

I'm out of the car before I've even thought it through.

"Pete!"

He freezes, like a child caught doing something wrong.

"What happened?" I demand, crossing the road. "Who did this to you?"

He looks past me, anywhere but at me. "Go home, Tom."

"No," I snap. "You can't just show up looking like that and tell me nothing. Did James do this? Pete, tell me!"

He flinches at the name but doesn't answer.

"Pete!"

Finally, he meets my eyes. And what I see there scares me more than the bruises.

Fear.

"Please," he says, voice breaking. "Just go."

I open my mouth to argue, but he's already turning, retreating into the house. The door shuts with a finality that makes my stomach turn.

I stand there, frozen on the doorstep, heart thundering so loud it drowns out the night.

Whatever is happening in that house, something is dangerously wrong.

Chapter 26

PETE

In the house, Pete closes the door and stands there for a moment. With his head pressed against the wood of the door, his breath comes in short, shallow bursts. The house is quiet, still, a silence that emphasises his guilt as it floods in.

He can almost picture Tom still on the doorstep, wide-eyed, heart cracked open.

He needed to do that, though. As this is where Tom is now: past the line. Emotionally entwined. Connected to Pete.

This is what Pete wanted from the start. He knew Tom could be an important person in his life. So much empathy, understanding, a natural instinct to protect.

But now they're past the point where Pete can keep pretending this is all casual and easy. Tom cares too much, feels too much, and that is dangerous.

Because James is getting worse.

Tonight's blows still ring in Pete's head: the sharp crack of knuckles against cheekbone, one after the next, like punctuation marks. James doesn't just shout anymore; he hits harder.

Deliberate. Controlled.

Pete touches his face and winces at the swelling that's already blooming under his skin.

He never expected it to escalate like this. Despite everything, he always thought he had a certain degree of control over James. A feeling of understanding. Compromise.

But the dial of power has shifted rapidly in recent weeks.

So has the degree of violence.

He's been here before. Different man, same pattern. He fought then, too. And survived it. That's what he does. But tonight, he feels the edges fraying, how much closer the walls are pressing in.

Pete wonders if he has the strength to get through this again.

The house feels hostile now. Every room is wired with tension, every floorboard ready to creak at the wrong time. Pete moves through it quietly, checking locks, double-checking. James is out for the evening, but that doesn't mean safety. It only means time.

He showers quickly, water scalding, scrubbing until his skin is raw. When he steps into the spare bedroom and closes the door, he pulls the chair up under the handle and makes sure it's wedged tightly.

Then he lifts the pillow.

The knife is still there, cool against his fingers, reassuring and terrifying all at once.

Pete slides into bed, muscles aching, every sound in the house amplified: the tick of the clock, the hum of the pipes, the faintest shift of wind outside. He stares at the ceiling, listening, waiting.

Because he knows something is coming.

And he isn't sure how much longer he can hold everything together before it finally breaks.

Chapter 27

TOM

I sit in my car, engine off, but the dash lights still glowing faintly, a tiny galaxy of red and green light. My hands are locked on the steering wheel, knuckles white. I've lost track of time, but I've been here long enough for my chest to ache and my eyes to sting.

Pete's door is still closed ahead of me. Shut like a coffin lid.

My throat is tight. Every time I replay the look on his face, I want to headbutt the dashboard until the airbag bursts. The bruises, the fear, the way he wouldn't meet my eyes, I keep seeing it.

I want to help him. God, I want to drag him out of that house and never let him go back. But how? How do you save someone who won't — or can't — leave?

It's Daniel all over again.

I press my forehead to the steering wheel. The smell of leather and cheap car freshener fills my nose. Memories spool out in a fast-forward blur. Daniel's hand on my arm, tightening. Daniel's voice when it got dark and low. Me, shrinking. Craig, steady and relentless, holding up a mirror to my life until I couldn't ignore it anymore. Craig, driving me to his and Phil's place that night. Craig, telling me I wasn't crazy, that what was happening was not love.

He helped me escape. Helped me see the light. Helped me build something like a life again.

And now here I am, watching someone else drown and not knowing how to throw a rope without getting dragged under myself.

I stare at the front of Pete's house. The blinds are drawn. The windows are dark. That house feels like a fortress, a trap. It's eating him alive.

I think about calling Craig. I think about barging back up the drive. I think about sitting here all night until Pete comes out. All the options feel like failures.

And then my mind slides, unbidden, to Guy.

God, Guy.

It's been a year, and still his name lands like a fist to the chest.

I always hated the word "affair." Affair sounds like something trivial, like a fling you can sweep off a table when company arrives. What Guy and I had wasn't cheap or sordid. It was close, intimate, carved out of the loneliness I'd been drowning in.

He was married, yes. I know what that makes me in the eyes of the world.

But he was also kind. Funny. We used to sit in his car at night, hands tangled on the gear stick, talking about books, music, anything but the lives we were sneaking away from.

For the first time, I felt like someone actually saw me, not just the version of me I tried to sell on apps or at bars.

It was wrong.

And it was everything I needed.

The guilt was a constant hum, but some nights I thought this was worth it. This is worth all the risk, all the shame. Because connections like this are so rare.

And then, just like that, he was gone.

I don't even like to say the word.

Dead.

Just like that, he was dead.

As if the syllable could flatten the way he laughed, the smell of his jacket, the way he would reach across the table and tuck a piece of hair behind my ear. It was sudden. Heartbreaking. Torn away before I could even say goodbye properly.

I grip the steering wheel even tighter. I don't ever want that feeling again. I can't watch someone slip through my fingers and be left helpless as another door closes in my face.

But with Pete, it's starting to feel inevitable.

He's sliding deeper into something he can't name and won't escape from. And me? I'm already caught, already invested, already stupid enough to think I can save him.

I know I can't stay here all night, so I start my car and look into the rear-view mirror.

I blink, heart thudding.

A car is parked down the street behind me. Grey. Compact. Familiar.

The grey BMW.

Is this the same one that followed me?

I catch a glimpse of the driver's silhouette, but the streetlight is behind them, making a halo of shadow. My pulse spikes.

No. This is paranoia. This is me spiralling.

I put the car in gear and pull off the kerb. The BMW pulls off, too.

I take a left I don't need to take. The BMW takes it too.

Another turn. Another. The same headlights in the mirror.

My palms go slick. My chest feels tight. My therapist's voice pipes up in my head, calm and clinical: count your breaths, Tom. Four in, four out. Ground yourself.

But it's hard to ground yourself when you're sure you're being hunted.

I speed up, my heart hammering. The BMW stays back, still tailing me. I cut down a side street and loop back around. At the next roundabout, I circle it fully before carrying straight on. The BMW matches my route.

Okay. Not paranoia.

I drive faster, weaving through Clifton's narrow roads, past the Georgian terraces, past the coffee shops now shuttered and dark.

Another turn. Another.

Finally, at the bottom of a long hill, I slam on the brakes. The BMW is forced to stop behind me.

In a move driven by adrenaline, unlike anything I would normally do, I dive out of my car and approach the car behind.

For a long second, nothing happens.

Then the driver's door opens.

A woman steps out.

Streetlight catches her face.

And I know her.

It takes me a moment to place why. She's a little older than the photos, hair tied back, eyes sharper, but it's her.

Emma.

Chris's sister.

Chapter 28

TOM

For a beat, we just stare at each other, two strangers on a half-lit street with car engines ticking as they cool.

"You've been following me," I say. It comes out sharper than I mean.

"Yes," she admits instantly, like ripping off a plaster. "I'm sorry. Well… not sorry exactly. More like embarrassed I got caught." Her hands go up halfway, defensive, but her mouth quirks in something almost like a smile. "Once, I followed a man for three hours across London because I thought he'd stolen my brother's bike. Turned out it was his bike, and I'd basically stalked a stranger into a Pret. He bought me a coffee. Anyway, point is, my Miss Marple skills are ropey."

My pulse is still thudding, but there's something tired and brittle in her voice, like she's been running on fumes, that makes me hesitate.

"Why?" I ask, softer this time.

Emma exhales hard, like she's been holding her breath all day. "Because I'm looking for my brother. Chris."

I swallow. I almost say, *I know,* but it feels wrong to say it out loud.

She steps closer, tucking a loose strand of hair behind her ear. Up close, she's well-dressed but frayed at the edges: creased blouse, mascara smudged just slightly under one eye. Like she's been crying and then putting herself back together with duct tape and credit cards. A city girl gone feral.

"I'm sorry if I scared you," she says. "I just… I had to see for myself. Who you are. If you're another one of James's friends."

"I wouldn't call myself a friend of James," I say dryly, and something flickers in her expression: relief, maybe?

"Or Pete? You know Pete? I've seen you at his place."

I nod. "Yes, I know Pete. So, you've been following me a while?"

She sighs. "Look, I'm just trying to find my brother, Chris. He's disappeared." She clumsily fiddles with her phone before showing me his picture on her screen.

Chris's handsome face smiles back at me, like he doesn't have a care in the world.

"Do you recognise him?"

I shake my head. "No, sorry, I don't know him."

Emma's face sinks.

"But I know *of* him, Pete has mentioned him."

Her eyes come to life. "What did he say? Did he say where he went? I need to know he's alright." Her voice edges toward desperation.

"Sorry, no," I reply, trying to stay calm. "I don't know anything, just that he disappeared.

She falters.

"What do you think happened?"

Her voice cracks slightly as she speaks. "Before he vanished, I'd been getting some strange messages from him, saying he was sorry and had to leave. Then I never properly heard from him again. I'll get a message from him randomly saying he's safe, and then months will go by with nothing. When I call him, it always just goes straight to voicemail. Pete told me he had no idea where he'd gone. He was devastated. But then I found out about James being in the picture. I didn't know about him before. And then they were living together in this house."

Her shoulders drop just slightly. "All I want is to find him. To know he's safe."

I hesitate, then gesture toward my car. "Look, this isn't the best place to talk. Let's go back to mine. Have coffee. We can talk this through properly."

She looks at me, surprised, then nods. "Yes, that would be nice."

As we get back into our cars, my heart is hammering again, but this time not from fear—this time from the feeling that I've just stepped further into something I won't be able to step back out of.

Buster is waiting at the door when we get back, glaring like I've ruined his life.

"Don't worry," I say, stepping over him. "He's harmless. Just a touch judgmental."

Emma crouches by him, offering Buster her hand like she's greeting royalty. "He's gorgeous," she says softly.

"He's a tyrant," I reply, heading to the kitchen. "Tea? Coffee? Wine?"

"Coffee. No, Wine. No, coffee. Do you do an espresso martini?" she says erratically. "No coffee. I need a clear head."

Fair. I put the kettle on. She perches on the edge of the sofa, hands folded tightly in her lap. Up close, she's even more of a contradiction: expensive coat, tired eyes, a jittery energy under her stillness.

"I'm sorry," she says after a moment. "For following you. When I saw you with Pete, I just had to know who you were. Whether you were someone I could trust."

"You can," I say, maybe too quickly.

She gives me a wary, questioning look.

"I'm not exactly James's biggest fan," I add. "And I care about Pete. I don't know what's going on in that house either."

Her shoulders relax a fraction. "Chris adored Pete," she says quietly. "They were good together. It wasn't perfect. Chris could be intense, always falling too hard, too fast, but he loved Pete. And Pete loved him. I don't think he would've just walked away."

The idea of Pete and Chris being in love lands hard in my chest, but this isn't the time to entertain these thoughts, so I just nod.

"And what was he like?" I ask.

She glances around as if the houses might be listening. "We grew up in Chelsea. He was successful, a business consultant and travelled a lot. Meanwhile, I was getting banned from casinos in Brighton for counting cards badly."

I blink a few times, not knowing how to respond.

"Anyway," she continues, "Chris was always the golden boy; I was the family liability. When he met Pete, he was happy. The happiest I'd ever seen him, actually. And then…"

She hesitates.

"And then he just vanished."

Emma's fingers tighten on her mug. "But that's not Chris, though. He wouldn't do that to me. Something happened."

She glances at me, searching my face. "But I know he's alive. I know it."

"How?" I ask.

She hesitates, then leans forward, lowering her voice. "At first, I had a few messages from him saying he was leaving, and it was safer not to be in contact with him. He still messages me occasionally, but he won't tell me where he is or what happened, just to stop looking for him. The police said he made a large withdrawal of money just before he disappeared; perhaps he went abroad."

A shiver runs down my spine. "And the police haven't been helpful?"

"No, they think he ran off on his own accord."

"Why?" I ask

"It's a long story, but two years ago, his firm got embroiled in a financial investigation, a big one, government-level." She lowers her voice. "Chris wasn't some criminal mastermind, but he was directly involved. Or adjacent. Or complicit. I'm not sure, but the blame was landing firmly on him. I'm sure he was the scapegoat."

My stomach tightens.

"He didn't tell me everything," Emma says, "but he told me enough. He was going to lose everything: his job, his career, his reputation, his money. He was facing some serious charges. He said he needed time to figure things out. Then… he vanished."

Her voice cracks, but she continues.

"At first, he sent messages saying he was safe, but needed to stay hidden. Then the messages became less frequent; sometimes months would pass before I got one. They were always vague, always different numbers." She takes a shaky breath. "The police thought he'd just run away. Happens all the time to people like him, rich, facing public humiliation. They just leave the country and start afresh somewhere else."

"And you think that's not true?"

"No," she says firmly. "Chris wasn't perfect, but he wasn't a coward. You don't disappear off the face of the Earth because of a tax investigation. There's something else."

She leans closer, eyes dark and shining.

"I think he found something out about James. And Pete knows more than he's letting on."

I swallow. Hard. "Like what?"

"I don't know, something bad. And I think he went into hiding. Pete… he as good as told me to stop digging. Told me I'd get myself hurt. But how can I stop? He's my brother."

"And what did the police say?" I ask.

There's a pause of silence, and then she shakes her head, almost laughing bitterly. "The police were useless. Too much evidence that he left voluntarily. No foul play. Case closed. They think I'm obsessed. Which, okay, fair, but they also believed me when I said I was just sleepwalking when I was found breaking into my neighbour's garage in my twenties. Long story. Point is: they don't exactly scream thorough to me."

"Okay," I say quickly, because I can hear the edge of hysteria in her voice and I know exactly how that feels.

"So maybe he got involved in something and then had to escape from it?"

She shakes her head. "No, no. I've been through this in my head. I talk to Pete sometimes, when he will listen. He always alludes to it being about James, not explicitly. But I can see the fear in his eyes. He knows something."

I nod. I've seen that look of fear.

"But the point is: I know Chris is out there. He's hiding. And he's scared."

She sits back, staring into her coffee. "All I want is to find him. Even if it means following strangers in my car. Even if it means looking crazy. Honestly, looking crazy is my strong suit. I've had exes call me 'chaotic neutral with a driving licence.'"

Emma's words are erratic, but I still swallow hard as they sit heavy in the air. Suddenly, the missing man isn't a neat story or a Facebook post: he's a ghost sending warnings from the shadows.

"I know enough to know James isn't a good person. Pete needs to escape from him, and I want to be able to help him do that."

"Maybe if he's not with James, he'll be more open about where Chris went?"

"Then we work together," I say, surprising myself.

Emma blinks at me, then nods slowly. "Okay."

Buster jumps up onto the sofa arm, tail flicking like a metronome of disapproval. But I feel something lock into place inside me.

Whatever is happening in that house, whatever secrets James and Pete are keeping, I'm not walking away now.

Chapter 29

EMMA

Emma slides behind the wheel and lets the door thud shut, like a stamp on paperwork. She looks at her reflection in the mirror and picks out a clump of mascara from her eyelash.

Well, that had gone better than anticipated.

Tom seemed just lovely.

Sweet Tom. Soft voice, careful eyes.

She pulls away, Clifton's terraces yawning like tidy teeth, and lets the evening unravel. She runs back through the conversation: Tom's tentative questions, his earnest nodding. He wants to help. Of course he does. He's a rescuer. She can see it in his eyes. One of those men who believes in better versions of people.

Emma can see the way Tom's eyes glint as he speaks of Pete. He loves him. He thinks he can save him.

A perfect alignment of interests.

Venn diagram heaven.

She signals left, the indicator ticking impatiently. The road curves toward the expensive part of town, where cars sleep in garages larger than her flat. Everything here just feels expensive, and it drags her back to childhood like a hook under the ribs.

She was raised on privilege, a childhood both gold-plated and chaotic, in a Chelsea townhouse big enough to hear echoes down the hallway. There were the holidays in Provence, winters in Verbier, summers on whichever yacht her family were borrowing that year. Life was all tailors, tutors and tantrums that were rewarded with presents. In place of God, extravagance was her parents' religion. A life Emma took for granted at a young age.

But with this life came expectations.

Chris fit the mould beautifully.

Emma… did not.

Her phone vibrates; she ignores it.

Chris liked it up here, the city glittering below like a jewellery box. He'd stand with his hands in his pockets like some postcard of success: classic Eton boy turned corporate success, money pouring through his life like water through fingers. He was always the calm one, the sensible one.

She was… not.

Her parents were all about optics. Saying the right thing at the right time to the right people. As children, this meant one thing: stay silent.

Chris learned to fold himself into the spaces. Emma wouldn't fold for anyone.

She checks the date on her phone out of compulsive habit.

Nineteen days left.

So little time.

Streetlights flicker across the windscreen like a film reel. She thinks of Tom again, his careful way with words. He'd looked… frightened. That pleased her more than it should; fear means he'll move fast. Men like Tom only need one push, and then they push themselves. He'll go back to the house. He'll listen for cracks in the walls. He'll get what she needs.

Her phone vibrates again. This time, she reads the message:

Any progress?

She types back, one eye on the road, the other on her device.

Working on it.

Time is short. Only 19 days until this all comes to a head.

Yes, she wants her brother home safe.

But she also wants her freedom.

Sweet Tom is a step on that staircase.

Empathetic. Pliable.

Useful.

She presses harder on the accelerator, humming some soft, shapeless melody from childhood.

James is the door.

Pete is the lock.

Tom is the key.

And Emma?

Emma is the hand that turns it.

Chapter 30

SAM

Sam watches the feed in real time, hand on his chin, like he's tuning in to a late-night soap he definitely isn't supposed to be watching.

And there she is.

Emma Christianson. Eyeliner like war paint, posture like a lit fuse. The camera in the hallway, a perfectly placed buttonhead lens, placed behind the coat rack, captures her leaving, Tom closing the door behind her.

He leans closer, amused. "Well, well," he murmurs to himself. "Look who crawled out of the comments section of life."

He recognises her immediately. Chris's sister. He's seen her before, always a shade too frantic. Like grief mixed with a shot of espresso. She's been hunting for the truth for two years.

Tom wanders back to the living room, falling back into the sofa, a man deep in thought. Such clean emotion, Tom. Bless him. He'll break his own heart tying neat bows around other people's mess.

The living room camera, tucked into the spine of a fake plant, gives him a nice, soft-focus view of the sofa. Sam watches him and, despite himself, feels a tug of something that might be fondness.

Irritating.

Still, Emma + Tom = … interesting.

He toggles wide: exterior cam, front door; hallway; living room; kitchen; study; upstairs landing; bedroom, obviously. Enough coverage to know the shape of a day, not enough to be noticed.

Tom's cosy home sends a warm ache through his chest, and he hates that. He's always been somewhat sensitive to the idea of home. An idea he craved for years, a feeling he tries to smother these days.

The last place he called home was over twenty-five years ago, and even then, the word was being oversold. Those final months with his family are blurred memories these days: the slammed doors, dinner thrown across the room, low voices switching to yelling and back with practised ease. He remembers the biscuit tin, out of reach, no doubt empty, but worth a stretch on tiptoes when another mealtime was forgotten.

Care was the same, just a different frequency. Too bright, too grey. Some homes were fine, in the way a hospital corridor is fine. Others not so much. He soon learnt that words like 'comfort', 'warmth' and 'security' were borrowed, temporary.

Now, watching Tom's home, like some tranquil haven, presses on old bruises he wants to forget.

He files that feeling away in a stuffed box in his head marked "Later" and shuts the lid.

Instead, Sam thinks about Pete's place in contrast: rooms designed by consensus and money, immaculate surfaces reflecting nothing back. Tom's living room would survive a hysterical meltdown and still smell like Febreeze.

He takes a sip of coffee. It's cold, but the caffeine helps his focus. Scrolling back ten minutes, he freezes on Emma's expression mid-plea, Tom's brow folding in sympathy.

She's good.

Sam rewinds further, catches the moment they step through the door. Tom ushers her in, while Emma hesitates on the threshold as the house might bite. He pauses, zooms. Her eyes drag the room with a practised scan. She's done her share of doorway decisions. She's the kind who spots exits and alarms without thinking.

Useful. Annoying. Both.

He knows her reputation. Erratic, hungry for answers, good at blowing up bridges and then acting surprised she can't get back across. People like to call her crazy because it's easier than calling her right. He doesn't think she's right, not yet, but he respects a person who refuses to be bored by her own life.

And she's not Tom's only visitor.

There's another man he needs to keep his eye on this week.

A man entering the house by the back door like he owned the place, but never when Tom was there.

This needs further investigation.

Back to the living room. Emma's crying now, quick, angry tears she keeps trying to blink back into her head. Emma wipes her face and says something. The word please is in it; he can tell by the mouth shape. Tom nods again.

He's going to help her.

Of course he is.

He flips back to the live feed. Tom has not moved from the sofa.

He will absolutely agree to something generous and foolish because he's the kind whose heart has never met a boundary it didn't want to climb over and hug.

He closes one eye and imagines the strings crisscrossing the city: Tom to Pete, Pete to James, James to Sam and Emma threading through all of it like a needle.

The tapestry is ugly at some angles and stunning at others. Either way, it's going to be expensive.

Yes. Emma and Tom connecting is interesting. It changes shapes. It opens doors.

And there's someone who will definitely want to know about this.

Chapter 31

TOM

Craig's door opens before I've even knocked, like he's been standing there with a stopwatch and a lecture prepared.

"Get in," he says, scanning the street behind me like I've turned up with a press pack and a marching band.

Inside smells like coffee and laundry. It's as comforting, domestic and excessively competent as I've come to expect from this house. Phil appears in the hallway, tying his laces, all flushed cheeks and power-cardigan, like a man who could host a Radio 4 show on a Tuesday afternoon.

"Hey, Tom," he says, smiling. "I'm heading out. You two behave. Craig, don't interrogate him for sport."

Craig kisses him like a man who absolutely will interrogate me for sport. "Back by ten?"

"Or eleven," Phil calls, already halfway out.

The door shuts. Craig folds his arms. "Right. Sit. Talk."

I flop onto their sofa. "So," I say, "yesterday was… a lot."

He gives me a neutral detective face. It's the look he wears when suspects are about to confess to parking on double yellows. "Start at 'a lot' and proceed chronologically."

"Pete told me not to come back." The words come out too fast. "He had bruises, Craig. Real ones. Dark. Cheekbone, jaw. He wouldn't say, but—"

"From James?" Craig says, as if reading from a script.

"Yes. Probably. And then," I inhale through my teeth. "I got followed by a car. Again. I thought I may have been imagining it the first time. I'm self-aware enough to know both are possible."

He doesn't even flinch. "What car? Registration?"

"Registration? No idea. I was busy panicking. Grey BMW. Could also have been a toaster."

Craig sighs in a way that suggests I've let down the entire constabulary.

I continue. "But that doesn't matter, because I confronted the driver."

One of his eyebrows tries to make a break for it. "You what?"

"Yes, like slammed on the brakes and forced them to stop—"

"Very unlike you."

"Yes, very, I was high on adrenaline. But, I'm glad I did."

"Who was it?"

"It was Emma, Chris's sister."

Craig blinks, processing. "Chris? The ex?"

"Yes, the mysteriously vanished ex, who disappeared two years ago. She says he was with Pete for a while, but wasn't getting along with James."

Craig huffs. "So, why was she following you?"

"She's desperate to find her brother. Thinks he's gone into hiding. Thinks James knows more than he's saying. Thinks I can help."

"Help how?"

"Help by getting through to Pete."

"And you think you can?"

I muster a shrug. "Maybe. But I think Pete needs more help than she does."

Craig nods. "I agree. So, what's she like?"

"Emma? She's… interesting."

"Define 'interesting.'"

"Like someone who keeps emergency mascara in the glove compartment and also believes she could hot-wire a helicopter."

He pinches the bridge of his nose. "Great." He grabs a notepad from the side and flips it open. "Look, I've been doing a little digging myself. This stays within the room," he says sternly. "Here's what I've found."

I sit up.

"James Whitlow," Craig begins, and the surname feels expensive. "Forty-five. Property, private equity, some tech businesses, too. A few shell companies. A very good accountant. The sort of chap who appears on charity boards in photos where everyone is wearing navy."

"Of course he does," I mutter.

Craig continues. "He's been looked at before. Various allegations, but nothing stuck. Assault twice: one from a former employee, one from a former partner. In both cases, he was initially charged, and then they were dropped after witnesses went quiet. Money has a way of muffling noise."

My stomach drops like a lift. "Jesus."

"Intimidation complaints around a planning dispute. Again: charged but withdrawn."

"So, violent, connected, and rich," I say. "Great. My favourite flavour of villain."

Craig gives me the Don't-Be-Flippant-With-Crime glare. "I'm serious, Tom. This man doesn't need to break the law to get what he wants. People do it for him."

I feel the fizz of panic bubble under my ribs. "What do I do?"

"Stay away."

I make the kind of face small children make when told broccoli counts as a treat.

Craig points at me. "No, I mean it. I know that look. It's the look you get before you adopt a problematic cactus. You are not equipped to take on a man whose lawyers have lawyers."

"I know," I say, lying so hard the sofa should eject me. "I will. I'll stay away."

"Tom." He gives me stern detective face.

"Okay, okay." I hold up palms. "I will. But I can't just leave Pete."

Craig's voice softens. "I know. But you can't save someone who doesn't want saving."

"There was a time when I would say I didn't need saving."

Craig frowns. "This is different."

"Is it?" I ask.

"Of course. I'd known you years before you met Daniel. There was a very clear benchmark of what your normal, if slightly erratic, overthinking and melodramatic behaviour was—"

"—Melodramatic?"

"—So, I could tell how you changed, became a shell of yourself."

I pause. This was true.

"And you've known Pete for like twenty minutes, and you're, what, trying to swoop in like Batman and save the day?"

"But I feel like I've known him forever. He knows so much about me. My life, Dad. I told him about Guy."

"Oh," Craig says.

"Everything, about how I was seeing Guy behind Daniel's back. The truth." I stop for a moment before continuing. "Well, nearly everything. I didn't talk about what happened when Daniel found out."

Craig just nods.

"Or how he found out," I add.

"No, I suppose that's not important."

"No, but it is to me. Even now, I'd love to know how he found out."

"Maybe solve one problem at a time, hey?"

"Yeah," I agree. "And now Pete's my main priority. You should have seen the bruises on his face. I can't just leave him in that house."

Craig leans back in his chair. "I get it," he says. "You want to help Pete. But you're not equipped to fix this. None of us are, not in the way he needs."

That hits like a slap, though not an entirely unfair one. I open my mouth to argue, but he keeps going.

"If Pete's in a violent relationship, he needs professional help. Proper safeguarding. People who do this day in, day out."

I sigh. "So what? Helplines? Leaflets? It feels so… impersonal."

Craig shakes his head. "It isn't. Refuge runs a twenty-four-hour line. Completely confidential. They'll talk him through safety planning, even housing if he needs it. He doesn't have to commit to anything, just… talk. And there's Galop: they specialise in LGBTQ+ domestic abuse. There are local services that can give him counselling, legal advice, the whole lot. If Pete ever feels ready, I can make a referral. But it has to come from him."

It's valid advice, but it feels useless, like giving someone an umbrella in a hurricane.

Craig's tone softens. "His GP could help too. If he talks to his doctor, it goes on his record and builds a picture. If things escalate, that picture matters."

He says it like it's all practical and simple. But the weight behind it is anything but.

I laugh nervously, trying to cut through the heaviness. "You're telling me to stop playing the knight in shining armour, aren't you?"

"I'm saying, leave it to the professionals."

I nod, pretending to be calm when my insides feel like a washing machine on spin cycle. The suggestion of *leave it to the professionals* feels optional, but I don't share this opinion with Craig.

"Okay, but one last minor thing…" I hesitate, because I know I'm pushing my luck. "Can you look into Chris?"

Craig scrunches his face, but I continue. "Emma said the police think he left of his own accord, but… I don't know. She's convinced there's more to the story."

Craig stares at me for a long moment, then nods once. "I'll see what I can do off the books. And if I find anything, you let me decide what's actionable. Promise."

I nod, which we both understand is not legally binding.

He takes his notebook and scribbles a few lines. "And if James contacts you, or if you see him near your house—"

"I call you," I recite. "Or 999 if he's wearing gloves."

Craig doesn't laugh. "I'm not playing, Tom."

"I know. Sorry." I take a breath. "Thank you."

"And in the meantime, just step away from all this for a bit."

I nod. Although inside, I know this is a promise I may very well not keep.

Leaving Craig's place, outside, the air is cold and sensible. I sit in the driver's seat and stare at my phone. It's only when I see my own reflection in the black screen, looking pale and older than yesterday, that I realise my hands are shaking.

The phone vibrates like it's had enough of my introspection.

Evelyn.

Fuck.

I stare. For a second, I consider letting it go to voicemail and pretending I was in a tunnel or fleeing a bear.

I can't stop thinking about the blood.

I can't do this now.

I lie in bed thinking about how the knife sliced through him.

But I know I can't put this off.

I answer. "Evelyn?"

Chapter 32

TOM

"Tom?" Her voice comes through cracked and breathless, like she's jogged here through static. "It's me. I—I didn't wake you, did I?"

"No, it's like seven thirty," I say, already hating the brittle brightness in my voice. "Hi, Evelyn."

There's a tremor of relief on the line that makes me feel worse, which I didn't think was possible. "Good. Good. I've been trying you."

"I saw," I say, and immediately wish I hadn't, because it sounds accusatory. I add, "Sorry. Yeah, I saw your messages."

I can't stop thinking about the blood.

"Things have been…busy."

She doesn't respond to the apology so much as swallow it. "I...I just needed to speak to you again, about it all. I just can't get it out of my mind."

I lie in bed thinking about how the knife sliced through him.

I close my eyes. My throat goes dry in that quick, efficient way it has when life decides to be a horror film. "Right."

The part of me that likes to fix things rifles through a mental first-aid kit: platitudes, distractions, tea. Another part, bigger and more cowardly, just wants to hang up and climb into a cupboard. Talking to Evelyn is like putting my face too close to a wind machine: everything flaps, and nothing feels like it's in the right place.

"Where are you?" I ask because that feels like a solid, practical question. "Are you at home?"

"Yes," she says, quickly. "Yes. Sorry. I didn't mean to — I just… I was thinking about him, and then I was thinking about you, and then—" She inhales sharply. "You knew him. You knew him in a way I could hear when we spoke at the… at the thing." She can't say funeral. I can't, either. "You're easy to talk to," she says. "I know he liked that about you."

My tongue is a useless animal. "He was easy to like."

Silence. A brittle, balancing silence. Then a jagged laugh. "Yes. God, yes. That smile." She clears her throat. "I keep going back there. I know it's stupid. I know. I think if I walk the route again, something will…." She swallows. "I keep picturing him on the ground. I know I shouldn't, but my brain is a bully."

Before I can respond, I close my eyes to ground myself. I can hear Evelyn breathing. It feels like a responsibility.

"Evelyn," I say softly, "you don't have to walk it again."

"I do," she says, and there's flint under the fatigue. "I have to keep him alive in some way. He was my husband. Guy was my husband."

Her words ping around the room, ricocheting off my ribs.

Guy, Evelyn's husband.

Guy, my lover, my heart and soul. The man I loved.

Guy, the man who was mugged and stabbed to death one night a year ago.

The world tilts, and memories of Guy come flooding back, overwhelming my heart: holding my hand under a cafe table, 2am texts with a stupid meme that would make me grin, the way he whispered my name.

But then I think about how I processed grief for a man I wasn't supposed to love, the way I had to swallow it whole and pretend it tasted like nothing.

"I keep thinking about the blood," she says, her texts coming to life. "It was on the pavement. The police washed it away, but you can't wash away the shape. Not really. I still see it."

My heart beats against the back of my sternum. I open my mouth to speak. No useful words are formed.

"I know we haven't talked in a while," she says quickly, as if reading my mind. "I'm sorry. You were… kind, after. And then I went quiet. And then you did. And I understand. It's… a lot."

"It is," I say, because I'm incapable of lying convincingly for longer than four seconds. "I'm sorry too."

"You were his friend," she says. The word *friend* hits me like a sharp prod in the stomach. "One of the good ones, one of the few who stuck around. People get tired of grief, I get it. They want you to have an end date for it, so they can get back to normality."

I stare ahead into the distance.

His friend.

One of the good ones.

If only she knew the truth about what we were.

"People are rubbish," I say, and it makes her exhale a small laugh.

"I keep thinking about what he went through, how it felt. I keep thinking about the knife. Slicing into his skin." Another pause. Then she says, almost dreamily, "The doctors said he didn't suffer long. That it was quick, and I cling to that. But I still think about the pain. How much it hurt. How alone he must have felt." Her voice splinters. "I keep thinking: was he frightened? Did he call out? Did anyone—" She stops. "I'm sorry. This is… I'm doing it again."

"It's okay," I say, because what else can you say? No, it's not okay, it's awful, and it will always be awful. Hitting Evelyn with a truth bomb is not on my agenda today.

"I phoned because I was scared," she says suddenly, the words tumbling. "I woke up, and it felt like a wave was over my head again, and I thought: I'll drown if I don't hear a voice that knew him." A breath, ragged. "And you did. You do."

My guilt sits up and stretches, smug as a cat. She doesn't know. She will never know, if I can help it. To her, I'm the kind friend from work, the listener, the man who will say kindly things about a husband I met on lunch breaks. She has no idea that every memory she brings up has two sets of fingerprints on it: hers and mine.

"And the police have given up. They'll never catch who did this now. And I'll never know. I just… I just lie in bed thinking about how I want to stab them back, slice them up, hurt them in the same way."

I pinch the bridge of my nose until stars pop. "I'm so sorry," I say, and the uselessness of the phrase makes me want to set something on fire.

"I know," she whispers. "I…I don't want to keep you," she adds quickly, because Evelyn always does: apologises for existing while phoning to prove she still does. "I just…Thank you for answering."

"Of course," I say, even though answering feels like my tongue is covered in ulcers.

"Can we… could we meet?" she asks. "Not right now. Sometime. Coffee. I'd like to talk about him with someone who knew him. Remember our best memories of him."

Best memories. Jesus. I guarantee Evelyn would not want to hear mine. The truest memories that I will never forget.

For a second, I consider the clean sever: a polite no, or maybe a slow fade into voicemail. But then I think about Guy, and despite everything we did, I knew he loved her very much. I hear myself say, "Yeah. We can do that."

"Thank you." I feel the relief in her voice, pouring down the line like warm water.

We do the clumsy dance of goodbyes, and then I hang up.

I lower the phone into my lap and stare at the blank screen until my reflection comes into focus. I look older, worn down, like someone who has been living under a fluorescent light.

Talking to Evelyn is like dragging a net through a sea I'm not supposed to swim in anymore. Everything I pull up is sharp.

Guilt climbs into my lap and makes itself comfortable, but before I can properly acknowledge it, my phone buzzes on the passenger seat.

A text from a number I don't recognise.

I pick it up. It reads:

Why are you ignoring me? Why did you block my number? Daniel

Of course it's him.

Because who else would send something that passive-aggressive, wrapped in fake vulnerability? Classic Daniel. Pretend to be wounded, make me feel like the villain. Even when he got us into thousands of pounds worth of debt from his gambling, it was still somehow my fault for driving him to it. He's like a magician who pulls guilt out of thin air.

I haven't blocked his number. What the fuck is he talking about?

I should ignore this. I should absolutely ignore this.

I'm not sure if it's the post-Evelyn adrenaline, my anxiety around Pete, or just my lifelong inability to make a single healthy decision under pressure, but I stab at the screen, hit "call back," and press the phone to my ear.

My hand shakes so badly I nearly drop the phone again.

Then, a click.

A breath.

And Daniel's voice, cool and sharp, slides through the line like a knife.

"Tom."

Chapter 33

DANIEL

Daniel answers on the second ring.

"Tom." His voice is smooth and practised, the kind of tone he uses in court, calibrated to sound reasonable, in control.

On the other end, Tom's voice spikes. "Why are you following me?"

Daniel smiles faintly, rifling through a stack of papers on Tom's desk, a mix of bank statements and receipts. Tedious, but sometimes the banal hides the important.

"I'm not following you," he says, pitching it light, almost hurt. "Honestly, Tom. That paranoia of yours again. I just wanted to talk. Clear the air."

"I've seen you. Twice. Don't lie to me."

"I'm not lying." His fingers slide open a drawer. Pens. Cables. A spare set of keys. He pockets them without hesitation. "You've blocked my number. What choice do I have? I've been trying to reach you, to be nice. You can't fault me for that."

"Being nice?" Tom's laugh is sharp, bitter. "You call showing up in the street, stalking me, 'being nice'? Stop texting me. Stop following me. Just…stop."

The line quivers with Tom's anger. For a moment, Daniel lets the silence stretch, savouring it, because anger is still attention. It means Tom still feels something.

"Tom," he says softly, coaxing now. "You're being aggressive. Why? I don't understand. I've always been here for you. Always. I never stopped caring."

He sits down on the desk chair in Tom's office.

"And I never will."

There's a sharp inhale on the other end. Then Tom's voice, final and shaking: "Stay away from me."

The line goes dead.

Daniel lowers the phone slowly, staring at the dark screen. The rejection hits sharply, but he doesn't flinch. He's used to this dance. Push, pull, block, unblock. Love, fury, silence. He knows Tom better than Tom knows himself. This outrage is a doorway later.

He'll take another approach. He has time.

At the desk, he pulls Tom's laptop towards him, flips it open, and types with practised ease. Passwords are never difficult; Tom's used the same one for years.

He scrolls fast and deliberate. Not here for browsing, not here to wallow in nostalgia. He's looking for something specific. Something he needs before it's too late.

His fingers drum against the keys. He's a lawyer, after all. He knows exactly what he can get away with.

And exactly what he's willing to risk.

Because Tom may think he's finished with him.

But Daniel knows better.

There's far too much at stake.

Chapter 34

TOM

Two days.

That's how long it's been since Pete told me to leave him alone, his voice quiet and broken, like the words weighed ten tonnes just to lift out of his mouth. Two days since the bruises on his face burned themselves into my brain.

Two days of silence.

And here I am, sitting in my car outside his house like some sort of amateur stalker.

Irony isn't dead; it's alive and well, laughing at me from the passenger seat. Just yesterday, I told Daniel to stop stalking me, stop circling my life like a vulture, and now look at me. Parked like a creep, checking my mirrors every five seconds, rehearsing imaginary conversations.

All very Baby Reindeer.

The truth? I didn't call ahead because I thought he'd say no. Better to ambush. Terrible strategy for healthy relationships, great for emotionally fraught stand-offs.

As I wait, Daniel's face barges into my thoughts like it always does. That phone call, his voice, the way he denied everything, like he hadn't been following me, like I was making it up.

That I'd blocked him.

I hadn't. I know I hadn't. Regardless, I check. I scroll through my phone, thumbs clumsy with nerves.

And there it is: Daniel. Blocked.

My stomach drops.

I didn't block him. Did I? Maybe I did during some breakdown haze, but no, I would remember. Wouldn't I?

No, no, someone must have done it.

But who? And how? Paranoia twitches in my brain like a faulty light switch.

I shove the phone back down, my chest buzzing with frustration. I want Daniel out of my life. Out of my head. Instead, he's like mould: grows back every time I think I've scrubbed him clean.

And then Evelyn.

That phone call still sits in my gut like a lead weight. Her voice cracking, her words tangled, talking about the blood, the pain Guy must have gone through.

She doesn't know.

She can't know.

To her, I was just his friend. Someone to cling to in grief. She has no idea that Guy and I were… more.

But then, I know someone told Daniel about Guy and me. The revelation that sparked our eventual breakup. In the back of my mind, I always considered that it was Evelyn. That she always knew, and this was her way of punishing me. She was the only one with a real motive.

But she's never given any indication that she knew the truth.

Guy. My Guy.

And now he's gone. Stabbed. Brutal. Quick. The kind of ending that doesn't make sense, not when you still feel the warmth of someone in your skin.

Evelyn can't move on. Neither can I. Different reasons, same result.

Guy and Dad. Two losses back-to-back like cruel dominos. I thought I'd never breathe properly again, never love again. I was wrong. Because here I am, camping outside Pete's house like some lost dog, desperate for scraps of hope.

Saving Pete feels like a step towards redemption. Or maybe it's distraction. Probably both

Headlights flash in my wing mirror, and my chest tightens. Pete's car pulls up into his drive. He gets out and slowly moves towards his front door, shoulders hunched.

I climb out of the car before I can second-guess myself. "Pete," I call.

He freezes, keys in hand, then turns. The bruises have dulled to yellow and green now, faint shadows instead of raw wounds, but I see them anyway. My anger flares at James.

"Tom," he says, guarded. "What are you doing here?"

"I had to see you," I say. "To know you were alright. To talk."

For a second, I assume he'll tell me to leave again. But there's a flicker in his eyes: exhaustion maybe? Eventually, he nods once and walks to the door. I follow, my pulse hammering.

He unlocks it and punches a code into the alarm panel. 2020.

Of course. The year the world shut down. The year everyone was locked inside, gasping for air.

How appropriate.

And while I want to blame James for this nugget of irony, I know it's the same code Pete uses when he puts on his Apple Watch.

The door clicks open. We step inside.

Pete drops his keys on the counter and rubs a hand across his face. He looks older tonight, lines carved deep around his eyes. For a long moment, silence fills the space between us, thick as smoke.

He looks at me. "I can't do this anymore."

My hand immediately reaches for his. "Do what?"

"This." He gestures around the house. The word covers everything: James, us, the bruises, the lies. "The pretending, the covering up. Hoping it will one day get better, when it never does."

I step closer, cautious. "Pete… talk to me. Tell me what's been happening."

His mouth twists. He shakes his head. "You already know. You've seen enough."

"Please," I say, gently. "Just… tell me."

I stand there, not sure what to do with my arms.

He finally lifts his head, and what I see in his eyes makes my stomach twist. Not just exhaustion. Not just pain. Something deeper. Resignation.

When he speaks, his voice is quiet, stripped bare. "It didn't start with fists."

The words catch me off guard. I don't breathe. I don't even blink.

Chapter 35

TOM

"That's the thing people don't realise. It wasn't obvious, not at first," Pete starts. "With James, it was gradual. A few comments, a few little rules. What to wear, who to see. When I should be home. It felt protective."

My chest aches. I want to reach out and hold him, but I wait.

"And I liked it. At first. It made me feel special. Loved. Like I was the most important thing in the world to him, and he just wanted me to be perfect.

"But, then, instead of lifting me up, it ground me down. Over and over again. One remark after the next. Putting me in my place. Knocking me down. Rewriting conversations we'd had.

"And then," Pete continues, "it was a shove. A grip too tight on my arm. A bruise I couldn't explain. But by then, he'd already done the groundwork. I believed I had nowhere else to go."

The silence between us buzzes, alive with everything unsaid.

Pete rubs at his jaw, where the bruise is fading. "It's not even the violence that breaks you. It's how he makes me believe I deserve it. If I'd just done things right, kept him calm, it wouldn't have happened. He's… he's very good at that. Making me feel like I'm the problem."

MY throat is dry, and I find it hard to swallow. The urge to scream and shout is unbearable. I want to fix this instantly, but I know I can't.

"There are good days," Pete continues. "Days when he's kind and charming and generous, and I feel like the luckiest man alive. And then the next day, he'll beat me to the floor so hard I can't even look in the mirror. That's the cruellest part, really, being built up to be torn down when you least expect it."

My hands curl into fists at my sides.

"It's been years of walking on glass," Pete whispers. "Of calculating every word, every expression. One wrong move means shouting, silence, or worse. That's what my life is."

I finally sit down next to him, not touching him yet. Just close enough for him to know I'm here.

He exhales shakily, then glances at me. "You want to know why James lets me… see other people?"

I nod.

Pete gives a humourless laugh. "Because it's not about him letting me do anything. He wants me to think I'm free. He dangles the carrot to see what I'll do with it, knowing he can whip it away at any time. That's what he gets off on: the power. The leash around my neck."

The word makes my stomach lurch.

"So, it's about control," I whisper.

Pete nods. "He tells me he's not jealous, that he wants this for both of us. He wants me to explore other relationships, like he has with Sam. It always sounds so enlightened and modern. But it's not freedom, it's just another test. The second I feel anything, he yanks."

I don't know what to say. My head is full of static.

"That's what happened with Chris," Pete says finally, voice breaking.

The room holds its breath.

Pete's jaw clenches, eyes glassy. "Chris wanted more. He wanted me to leave, to build something real. James saw that. Hated it. That's when the leash snapped."

My thoughts barely keep pace with my heartbeat. "Pete…"

"I swore I'd never let it happen again," he says. "Never. But then you came along."

His eyes meet mine, and it's like being pinned in place. "And I told myself it was different. That you wouldn't be a threat, because it was casual. Just a connection. Just… a chance to breathe sometimes, away from him."

I can't move. I can barely breathe.

"But you knew the risk," I manage.

"Of course I did. But Tom—" His voice fractures. "Do you know what it's like to go years without being touched kindly? Without someone seeing you as anything other than property?"

Tears slip down his cheeks. "I knew I shouldn't. I knew I was repeating the same mistake. But I was so fucking lonely. And you, you made me feel like maybe I wasn't gone already. Like maybe I was still me."

I can't hold back anymore. I reach for his hand. He grips mine tight, desperate, like a man clinging to a rope in a storm.

"So, James let me happen," I say slowly, "because he knew at some point, he would tear me away from you."

Pete nods, swallowing hard. "That's what he does."

"So, why now?"

"It's when he realises I care too, that's when it turns. That's when it gets dangerous. I thought maybe, if I kept it small and low-key, James wouldn't notice. Or maybe he wouldn't care. But James always notices. And James always cares."

He pulls his hand away from mine and presses his palms flat to his thighs, grounding himself.

I want to scream. I want to storm upstairs and smash every single hidden camera I know is in this house, rip the place apart until James has nothing left to hide behind. I want to take Pete and drive as far as the roads will let us go.

Instead, I sit here. Holding his truth like it's glass, fragile and sharp at the same time.

"I don't care how messy it gets," I whisper. "I'm not walking away from you."

Pete shakes his head, tears streaking down his face. "That's what Chris said."

And in that moment, the air between us isn't just heavy, it's suffocating.

"Did you two ever talk about leaving, going away together?" I ask.

"We talked about it, but… it was never going to happen. The risk was too high."

For a while, neither of us speaks. I listen to the sound of his breathing, uneven, shaky. My own heart is thundering, threatening to drown everything else out.

"Pete, what did happen to Chris?"

Pete presses his fists against his eyes, like he's trying to squeeze the truth out.

He shakes his head. "I don't know. One day, he was here, and the next day, he texted to say he couldn't be a part of this anymore. He was moving away. There was something going on with his job; the police were involved. Talk of him being charged. I'm not too sure of the details, but I never heard from him again."

I think of Chris, his name like a ghost. Or a warning. Chris, who wanted Pete to leave, then vanished into thin air. Chris, whom Pete once held, just like I am now.

"Do you think it was James's doing?"

I picture James, looming and controlling, pulling invisible strings. Pete's words echo in my head: the leash.

"In one way or another, yes," he says.

I hate myself for asking the next question, but I need to. "Why me? Why did you let yourself fall into it again, after everything?"

"Because you made me feel alive again. Because you smiled at me like I wasn't broken. Because for one stupid second, I believed it could be different this time."

His shoulders shake. He lets out a sound that's halfway between a laugh and a sob.

All I want is to take it all away. To fix it. To save him. But I know Craig's words are true: this isn't something I can fix with hugs and declarations. This is bigger, messier. Still, right now, it feels like the only thing I can offer is to hold him together while he falls apart.

Silence stretches. His breathing shudders. Mine feels tight, thin.

Pete's body tenses when he glances at the clock. He shakes his head. "You can't stay. James will be back soon."

My stomach drops. "So what? I'm just supposed to vanish?"

He moves quickly, already heading towards the study. "No, Tom, listen to me. You have to go. And I need to delete the CCTV of you being here."

I freeze in the doorway. "What do you mean, delete the CCTV?"

Pete speaks with urgency. "James has cameras all over the house. Sam set them up for him. He'll review them sometimes. If he sees you here—" He doesn't finish the sentence as he sprints into the study. I follow behind him.

He opens the MacBook on the desk, which automatically opens when it connects to his Apple Watch. He double-clicks on an icon on his desktop, SecureTech, which pings open.

Pete doesn't look at me. He clicks quickly, deleting files with the efficiency of someone who's done it before. So quick, I'm not sure what I've just witnessed. "Best to be safe. He'll never know."

The screen blinks back to the feed, empty now of evidence. Pete stands, finally looking at me.

"I'll call you in a couple of days, when things quiet down," he says, and we share a warm hug.

His face is pale but determined. "You can't go out the front now. You'll be filmed again. Go through the back door, left around the house, and cut through the trees. You'll come out by the lane."

I open my mouth to argue, to tell him how insane this sounds, but his eyes stop me cold. He's deadly serious.

So, I do what I'm told. I slip out the back door, my breath catching as it shuts quietly behind me. The night air hits my face, sharp and damp. I keep low, moving left along the wall, the house glowing like a watchtower at my back. Through the trees, branches snapping underfoot, my heart pounding like I'm already guilty.

By the time I hit the lane, my chest is burning, and my hands are shaking. I glance back once, and swear I can feel James watching, even if the cameras no longer are.

Once in my car, I just sit in silence.

Despite everything we've just talked about, all I can think about is Guy.

How I thought he was my second chance, my lifeline after Dad died. How I clung to him like he was the only thing keeping me upright. And how he was ripped away in a single violent moment.

I can't do that again. I can't lose someone else I care about.

I think of Pete, broken and beautiful and terrified, and the thought hits me hard: I don't just want to save him because I can't stand seeing him hurt. I want to save him because I'm falling for him.

Because somewhere, somehow, despite everything, I still believe love might save me too.

Chapter 36

TOM

I pick the table by the natural light of the window because if I'm about to become an amateur detective, I'd like it to be bathed in a flattering glow.

Emma arrives like a weather front in expensive boots. She doesn't so much sit as orbit: coat half-off, sunglasses pushed into hair, phone, tote, keys, another phone, all of it landing across the table like she's laying out evidence in some café-based murder mystery.

"Flat white. Actually, no, make it an oat latte. No, scratch that, flat white. I can't drink oat, it makes me cry. Long story," she says to no one in particular, then to me, "How are you? Terrible question. Don't answer. Tell me everything. Actually, wait, have you seen the traffic on Whiteladies? Criminal. Speaking of criminal: James."

A waitress appears, takes my order and hers, and leaves looking faintly winded.

"I'm… good?" I try. "And by good, I mean brittle. Like a posh cracker."

"Perfect," she says. "We love brittle. Brittle keeps you sharp."

Emma's energy is like someone pressed fast-forward on her brain, and her body is playing catch-up. She's attentive in short sprints, but it's like her thoughts are playing hopscotch. That said, there is something oddly comforting about being with her. I'm a chronic overthinker, she's a chronic over-sharer. Between the two of us, we almost make one functional adult.

"Well, thanks for meeting me again," she starts.

"Oh, of course," I say. We hadn't swapped numbers after our first encounter, but she messaged me later on Facebook Messenger. I was surprised to hear from her so soon, but I felt it was important for us to keep talking.

Emma leans in, eyes bright with an intensity that could scorch paint. "It's nice that I didn't have to tail you around Clifton again before you agreed to it this time."

I nod. "Yeah, well, I spent 3 hours stalking Pete outside his house last night, so I'm in no position to judge."

"So, you saw Pete?"

"Well, yes—"

"Is he safe?" she cuts in immediately.

"Define safe," I say, and she deflates a millimetre. "He… talked. More than before. He told me about what it's like with James. The years of abuse. It sounds terrifying."

"I thought as much," Emma says, grabbing the menu in front of her.

"I need to speak with my friend, Craig. He's working today, I can't get hold of him, but he's in the Police—"

"Police?" Emma cuts in. "What kind of police?"

"Um, well, the…normal police," I respond.

Emma frowns. "How can he help?"

"He mentioned support systems that could help Pete—"

Emma scoffs. "That won't help! Not with someone like James around. Did Pete mention Chris?"

"Um, kind of. He said he doesn't know what happened to Chris, just he got a text, and then he disappeared."

Emma makes a face like she's chewed a lemon she found in a handbag. "That's what he says. And I like Pete, I really do, but that man could hide a cathedral under that smile. And trust me, I know smiles. I once dated a magician. He could smile while stealing your watch and your car keys. And my flat. But that's another story."

I blink a lot.

"Anyway," she continues. "I've always had the feeling he knows more than he lets on. Especially when James' name comes up."

The coffees arrive. Emma immediately sugar-bombs hers with three sachets. "Don't look at me like that. I once lived for six weeks on Haribo and full-fat Coke. Perfectly fine, hallucinations aside."

I nod, feeling the need to recalibrate the conversation. "So, you and Pete keep in touch?" I ask.

"Of course." She stirs, clinks, stirs again. "I check in every few weeks. I ask very nice, open-ended questions; he gives me very nice, closed answers. But there are moments… tiny slips. Fear, Tom. I see it in his eyes."

"Yeah," I say softly, thinking of bruises. "I've seen it. He told me all about it"

She studies me, radar pinging. "I think Pete knows exactly what happened to Chris. And if James were out of the picture, even temporarily, Pete would tell us what really happened."

"Us?" I repeat. It comes out like a high-pitched squeak.

She waves a hand. "Yes, you and me. Like Mulder and Scully, but with fewer aliens and more trauma. Look, in the weeks before Chris vanished, his messages got increasingly odd. Some of them seemed like nonsense. He'd talk about videos, videos in the house telling the truth or something."

A chill slides under my collar. I swallow. "Like cameras?"

"Maybe, I never really knew what he was talking about." She takes an unladylike slurp.

I breathe out slowly. "Pete showed me their CCTV."

Emma's eyes widen like I just admitted to owning a dragon. "He what?"

"There are cameras around the house," I explain. "Sam put them up. I don't know where exactly, but he said he had to delete them after I left yesterday, just in case James saw them."

Emma sits back, triumph sparking. "Then it exists. Proof exists."

"Proof. Of what?"

"Abuse. Coercion. Something worse." She looks around the cafe at the mums with prams and the professionals on their laptops. Moving in closer, she lowers her voice. "If there's footage of James hurting Pete, if we could get it, the police will have to take it seriously. It might not fix everything, but it would buy us some time. Enough for Pete to breathe and listen to us."

"Surely James would delete anything incriminating?"

"Maybe, but also why put it up in the first place? Clearly, he has some voyeuristic fetish for being filmed. Maybe he saves them to watch them back while he rubs baby oil over his misters."

This is not an image I was hoping for today, so I just nod.

While I'm not sure this is exactly the route I wanted to go down to help Pete, the tired, irrational, overly emotional side of me that feels he could double as Ethan Hunt to save the day is switched on.

Could I find some video evidence of James that could be used to convince Pete to leave?

“How would we get it?” I ask, hearing how treacherous my voice sounds and deciding not to fix it.

Emma’s smile is sharp. “Well. This is where we leverage your… excellent rapport.”

“I’m not sure I like where this is going,” I sigh.

Tom, listen. Pete trusts you. He invited you back, didn’t he?”

“Sort of. I may have… shown up,” I mumble. “I’m aware of the hypocrisy.”

She pats my hand. “We’ve all stalked someone for good reasons. You should see my search history.”

For a brief moment, we breathe. Two ridiculous people in a Bristol coffee shop, discussing how to ethically obtain illegal evidence.

“I can’t go through him,” I say. “If Pete’s terrified, he won’t risk it. And if James catches a whiff…”

“Then we don’t go through Pete,” Emma says. “We go around him. You said the footage is stored somewhere in the house?”

“Almost certainly,” I say. “There’s an office. Mac on the desk.”

Emma’s attention scatters to the window, then zips back. “Do you think you could get to it?”

“Do I think I can commit a crime with panache? No. Do I think I can bumble a crime with high anxiety and snacks? Possibly.”

“Snacks are crucial,” she deadpans. “I once tried breaking into my ex’s place with nothing but Pringles and optimism. It didn’t work.”

We sip. I overthink. My internal monologue starts a chorus of "*You cannot do this / You absolutely will do this*" on repeat as the caffeine fires up my brain.

“This is a really terrible idea,” I say, surprising myself with a sensible sentence.

“It is,” she says simply. “But I’ve been in this for two years. Two years of terrible ideas. And I’m prepared to try them over and over again until I find the truth.”

“You know,” I say, “you’re very weirdly inspirational.”

“Yes,” she says. “It’s my brand. My other brand is unpaid parking fines and men who ghost me. But inspirational sounds better.”

We go quiet long enough to notice the café’s playlist has slid into melancholy acoustic covers of songs that don’t deserve it.

This really is a terrible idea.

But in a world of regret and desperation, an idea I have to try.

Chapter 37

EMMA

"Tom," Emma says, softer again. "Thank you. I know you don't owe me any of this. I know you barely know me, and you should probably run away fast. But you're here. And I think you might be… good."

"I'm very medium," Tom says. "But I care about Pete. And I care about…" he glances around and lowers his voice, "not letting men like James write the ending."

"Then we're aligned."

We sort the bill. Emma insists on paying, then lets Tom pay anyway. At the door, she pauses, eyes flicking to every face in the café like she's memorising them for a quiz.

Emma gives his arm a quick squeeze, then launches herself into the street like a decorative missile. She walks away from the café like she's leaving a theatre after a standing ovation, with the faint whirl of triumph under her ribs.

She leaves Tom at the window, his fingers circulating the rim of his coffee cup, eyes lit with that peculiar mixture of terror and determination she has learned to recognise as valuable.

It's always the same: people who feel useful will do whatever it takes to keep feeling that way. Tom is prime.

She tells herself, aloud and to the thin, damp air of the street, that she's being pragmatic. That this isn't manipulation so much as persuasion on an urgent timetable.

But the truth is slipperier.

Emma has always been a connoisseur of leverage: a little honesty here, a well-placed omission there, a theatrical tear at precisely the right dramatic moment. She knows how to bend people toward the shape of her need and make it look like their idea.

Two coffees and a half-hour of breathless anecdotes are all it takes to have him humming with a dangerous goodwill. He wants to be the person who rescues.

She does not tell him everything.

She does not tell him about all the other people she has bent before. She will not whisper about the ways she learned to read the rooms of desperate people until she could lay her hands on the panic and pull it open like a suitcase.

That archive of small betrayals is private.

This is different, she tells herself. This is life or death.

She whips out her phone and fires off a message.

Think I have a way in.

She tells herself, again, that she would do anything to get what she needs.

If she has to weaponise kindness, to lace compassion with deception, she will. She will be the unreliable narrator of her own life if it keeps her life from falling apart.

Chapter 38

TOM

I shouldn't be here.

I know I shouldn't be here.

But here I am, parked halfway up a quiet suburban road like the world's most incompetent private investigator. If anyone looks out of their window right now, I look less like a man on a noble mission and more like a divorced uncle waiting to kidnap the family barbecue set.

My rational brain reminds me I need the voice of reason, and I try Craig's number once again. He is the human equivalent of a safety instruction leaflet after all. It rings once and goes through to voicemail.

Excellent. My one sensible friend is unavailable. Again.

Right. Without Craig to talk sense into me, I'm limited to two options:

Go home, have a bath, and admit I've already gone further than any sane person should.

Break into James and Pete's house.

I sigh and open the car door. Option two it is.

The street is unnervingly quiet. Daylight, but hushed, like the houses know something's about to happen and they don't want to get involved. James's hulking black SUV and Pete's smaller, neater Audi are both absent from the drive. Hopefully, they're off somewhere long enough for me to play junior burglar. I pray Sam isn't home either. He unsettles me in the way feral cats do: watchful and unpredictable, probably prone to scratching if cornered.

I cut through the side path, through overgrown bushes that make me feel like I'm in a low-budget spy film and appear by the back door, the route Pete told me wasn't covered by the cameras.

The back door waits. I crouch and peer behind the plant pot. There it is. The spare key, just as James had said it would be for the cleaner a few days ago. I shouldn't be pleased at how cliché this is, but honestly, if all crimes were this simple, the prisons would need more bunk beds.

I slide the key slowly into the lock as I feel my heartbeat hammering in my ears. The alarm pad flashes red at me.

I punch in the code.

2020. The same code I've seen Pete punch in before.

The pad beeps, then goes blank. Relief washes over me.

Step one: successful illegal entry.

Inside, the house is too quiet, and my breath is too loud. My shoes creak. Even my heartbeat sounds suspicious.

I move through the kitchen first, looking through a few drawers, the kind of kitchen drawers where you chuck unwanted mail and knick-knacks. Nothing incriminating. Shiny surfaces. A fruit bowl so polished the bananas look contractually obliged to stay bright yellow.

The dining room houses nothing but expensive chairs that probably cost more than my car. The living room, nothing but aggressively plumped cushions. No damning evidence.

Okay. The office.

It's tidy, of course, in that way that feels both sterile and threatening. A desk. Shelves. Files stacked neatly. And there it is: a sleek, closed MacBook, gleaming like the crown jewels.

I open it up. The login screen slides up, demanding a password like an offended maître d'. Of course it does, hardly a surprise.

But I had planned for this.

The bedroom is two doors down, and I step inside like I'm entering a boutique store I can't afford to shop in. Bed made. Wardrobe shut. On the bedside table, an Apple Watch sits on its charging stand.

Bingo.

Pete doesn't always wear it. He told me once that it annoyed him when it buzzed with every email, so he often leaves it at home.

I lift it carefully. It comes to life, bright screen glowing, and prompts for a passcode.

Again, it's a code I've seen Pete type in before.

2020.

The watch unlocks instantly. Relief makes me want to sit on the bed and cry. Instead, I strap it to my wrist, feel faintly ridiculous, and hurry back to the office.

I tap the Mac's spacebar. The login screen pops up again. I raise my wrist. The watch buzzes. And like magic, the Mac unlocks.

"Oh my god," I whisper. "I'm a genius hacker."

Thank you, Tim Cook.

No, I'm not. I'm a man in someone else's house, breaking several laws simultaneously, but still, the thrill is real.

The desktop is ordinary enough at first: bland wallpaper, neat folders. But then I see an icon labelled "SecureTech."

I click.

A program opens, displaying the cameras across the house. I vaguely remember Pete whizzing through this yesterday. I go to the video history, which contains rows of videos, labelled with dates and times.

My stomach drops. This is it. This is what Emma was talking about. The house is riddled with cameras.

I open one at random: two days ago, kitchen. The video plays in eerie silence. Pete is there, standing by the counter, shoulders tight. James is making a cup of coffee. A simple daily task. There's no audio, but the body language is clear.

I open another. The empty dining room, then Pete wanders in to set the table. I flip through a few more. Same story. Mundane life at the house. So many files, this could take forever.

And I don't have time.

What else is on this laptop?

I pull up a Finder window and search "Video". Reams of videos files pop up. I can see from the thumbnails that a lot are from the CCTV files. I click on one. A video pops up and starts playing. It's from the kitchen: James is screaming at Pete, his arms flying around in the air in anger. I click back to the file, select it and select Show in Enclosing Folder. A folder pops up full of video files, simply named "Saved Files." There must be 25 videos in here. I click on another. A video of James in the dining room; this time, he hurls a plate across the room at Pete, which nearly hits him.

These have been saved for a reason. I've got no time to look at them all, but this is evidence. Real evidence. Emma was right.

I need to save them.

In preparation for this, I had come armed with a small USB stick, which I whip out of my pocket like some criminal mastermind. I go to slot it, but after several attempts, I deflate.

There are no fucking USB ports in this stupid MacBook.

Fuck you, Tim Cook.

I panic-look around the desk, in a few drawers and to my delight, like a ray of sunshine, there's a Mac-compatible memory stick.

This will do nicely.

I slot it in and copy the folder of saved videos. The progress bar creeps across the screen with agonising slowness, like it's mocking me.

Every second feels like a countdown.

In the meantime, I flip back to the SecureTech UI and delete the most recent recordings, me rummaging around the kitchen and dining room. Gone.

I can slide out the back again without being noticed.

I truly am an actual lawless virtuoso.

And then—

A sound.

The faintest click. A door shutting?

My whole body locks up. The progress bar crawls. 47%. 52%.

Footsteps.

Definite footsteps coming up the stairs.

No. No no no.

64%

I glance at the watch on my wrist, the Mac glowing in front of me, the files still copying. Every instinct in me screams to run, but the transfer isn't done. If I pull it out now, the files might be useless.

76%

The footsteps grow closer.

I clamp a hand over my mouth, heart battering like it's trying to escape. Whoever's here, they're inside the house.

And I'm trapped.

Chapter 39

SAM

Sam comes back to the house like he owns half of it, which, in his head, he does. He's spent the last hour going for a run around the Downs and back, sweat running down his face and in his hair.

He hums to himself as he opens the door, because if you are going to be a houseguest with free rein, you might as well supply the soundtrack.

And with two cars not in the drive, this means he has the house to himself.

In the kitchen, Sam removes his headphones and peels off his sweat-drenched t-shirt, chucking it in the washing machine in a way that suggests he's been doing this for years.

Sam knows the domestic rhythm of this household well by now. His role changes here day to day: occasional lover, regular nuisance, highly competent events manager, and unofficial surveillance tech. He likes having a role in a place like this. Not that he would call it home in the way Pete and James do, but it is important to him.

Pausing, he remembers the darker places: hostel rooms with bedbugs, foster houses with peeling wallpaper. Places he tries hard to forget, but memories don't allow him that luxury.

A small, muffled sound snaps him out of his thoughts.

Sam tilts his head, listening.

Instinct — call it street-sense, call it having grown up in places where unexpected movement means you look over your shoulder twice — tells him to be careful.

Not anxious-careful, more practical-careful.

Check. Confirm. Prepare.

From the kitchen, he slides out a knife from the block, one of those long, dependable things with a black handle that makes everyone feel like Gordon Ramsey or Michael Myers, depending on your objective.

With the knife by his side, he moves around the house with the footed stealth of someone who has sneaked around places he shouldn't be far too many times.

He checks the usual places: dining room, living room, before moving to the office. Its door is almost closed.

Strange.

James leaves that door open. It's always been more of a show-office.

If the door's ajar, someone's been in there.

He pauses at the threshold.

Slowly bringing the knife up higher, he raises his hand to the door.

With a flip, he pushes the door wide open.

He looks in.

Empty.

He tightens his grip on the knife a fraction and steps forward, because the sensible thing to do is to check thoroughly.

Sam takes a slow step forward before something clamps over the back of his shoulder in lightning cold stillness.

He spins, reflex, and the blade is at a throat before his brain has time to narrate what's happening.

"Jesus, Sam!" James shouts, his eyes wide as the tip of the blade touches his skin

"Fuck!" Sam shouts back, whipping the knife away.

"Christ, what the fuck are you doing wandering around the house with a knife?"

"I heard a noise. I thought someone was in the house. Your car's not here."

James rubs his throat where the knife pressed against him. "I had the car in the garage for a service," he says. "I was just having a lie down."

"A nap? On a weekday? You must have had a busy night," Sam grins.

James doesn't acknowledge the comment.

"If I'd have known you were still in, I wouldn't have put the alarm on when I left for my run," Sam says.

"Just make sure you put it on when you leave. I'm heading out," he says, turning and heading down the corridor.

"Anywhere nice?"

"Post office."

And then he's gone.

With a final look in the office, Sam turns and heads to the bathroom. The sweat from his run is starting to dry into his skin, and he needs a shower.

In the bathroom, he places the knife on the side and turns the shower on, stripping off the rest of his clothes.

The bathroom hums with the sound of running water, but Sam's attention has already drifted. Steam ghosts up the mirror while his thumb flicks idly across his phone screen.

The CCTV feed from Tom's place flickers to life.

A familiar rush hits him, that small, private thrill of seeing without being seen. He loves the feeling of power it gives him. He scrolls through the angles: Tom's hallway, the kitchen, the living room.

And then the study.

There he is again.

The same man. Always the same man.

He moves like he belongs there, confident and practised. His hands are in the drawers, flipping through papers. The same laptop open on the desk, the same focused intensity.

Sam frowns. He's seen this man twice before. Once late at night, once early morning. Always in the office, always digging.

He's looking for something.

Sam leans closer to the screen, heart beating faster now.

Who the hell are you?

A friend? A nosey neighbour? An obsessed stalker? No, that's far too Eastenders for Tom's mundane life.

He has a key. That's the thing. He uses it like he owns the place.

But one thing is clear: he shouldn't be in there.

If this man's in Tom's life, that makes him part of Sam's, by proxy. And Sam does not like unknown variables.

The shower hisses behind him, forgotten. Steam curls around the room like smoke.

On-screen, he watches as the man closes the laptop, smoothing everything back into place, every movement neat enough to make a forensics team cry.

Then the man pauses. He doesn't leave. Instead, he turns and heads upstairs.

Sam flicks the feed. Bedroom cam.

The man appears in the main bedroom. Lingering, like he's waiting for something to start.

What are you looking for now?

The man goes to the basket at the end of the bed. He reaches in and pulls out something black. Presses it to his face. Holds. Breathes.

Sam raises an eyebrow. "Oh. Oh, okay."

Definitely underwear.

Sam brings the screen closer to his face as the man wanders over to the bed and opens the bedside table, pulling out a chunky white block, along with a small bottle.

It takes a moment for it to register. A Fleshlight. Lube.

This is about to get interesting.

Climbing onto the bed on his knees, pulling his trousers down to his ankles, he stacks a few pillows together and rests the Fleshlight on top. After fiddling with the lube bottle, it's only a few moments before he's inside the Fleshlight, slowly moving in and out while pressing the black underwear to his face.

Sam doesn't flinch. He should. Any normal person would. But he's somewhere between fascinated and wildly impressed by this sad car crash happening in front of him.

The man builds up speed, thrusting in and out of the Fleshlight, his face inhaling the underwear like he's auditioning to be a Dyson, until he crashes forward onto the pillows in a moment of climax.

Sam exhales through a low whistle. "Tom, Tom, Tom… what have you got yourself mixed up in?"

Pushing himself off, the stranger stuffs the toy back in the drawer with not even a rinse under the tap.

Then the man wipes himself down with the same underwear, tosses it back into the basket, and leaves. Businesslike.

Sam exhales slowly, sets the phone down on the counter, and grins at his reflection in the fogged-up mirror: half amusement, half something colder.

Whoever this man is, he's made himself very interesting.

By the time he's finished, this stranger won't be a stranger anymore.

Chapter 40

TOM

I don't breathe so much as sip the air in tiny, panicked teaspoons.

Back in the study, in the moments before Sam opens the door, I go into full-blown gay panic: the level reserved for when you accidentally like your ex's holiday photo from 2017

As the progress bar copying the videos hits 100%, I yank the memory stick out, close the MacBook, while my eyes dart around the room for a hiding spot.

Hide under the desk. Not with my dire lack of flexibility.

Pretend to be an IKEA coat rack. Ridiculous idea.

Fake medical emergency. Collapse, whisper "diabetes," hope for mercy.

All useless.

My body enters DEFCON Glitter status: gay panic so pure it could power a disco ball.

With seconds to formulate a plan, I do the only logical thing: I become one with the wall behind the door. There's a sliver behind its hinged side, ridiculous for a man of my height, but I flatten myself into it like I'm auditioning to be a poster.

The handle turns.

The door swings inward, stops a whisker from my nose. If I exhale, the game is up. I hold in all bodily functions, including the ones that make life worth living.

A figure leans into the room, weight shifting on polished floorboards. I can see the edge of a forearm, a knife blade catching the light.

A knife. Fantastic. Because what this moment was missing was cutlery-based jeopardy.

"Jesus, Sam!" James barks from behind the door.

"Fuck!" Sam's voice.

"Christ, what the fuck are you doing wandering around the house with a knife?"

"I heard a noise," Sam grinds back, breath quick. "I thought someone was in the house. Your car's not here."

"I had the car in for a service," James says, tone flat and irritated. "I was having a lie down."

A nap. Of course. The one time I break into a house, I stumble into a power-snooze-kitchen-slasher crossover.

Their voices shift away. I keep my cheek pressed to the cool wall and listen to footfalls. My legs have progressed to advanced levels of trembling. I silently negotiate with my calves. Please stop. I will hydrate better. I will buy magnesium. I will stop drinking coffee as a personality.

"I'm heading out," James says.

"Where?"

"Post office."

Post office. Somehow that sounds more ominous than "underground vault" or "secret lair." Only a true villain pops to the post office after a nap.

A few seconds later, pipes clank. A rush of water. Sam's shower spits to life, the sound thick as rain on a tin roof. He's in the bathroom. Knife presumably put down. Or maybe he showers with it. Who knows with him?

This is my sign to leave.

I ease the door a fraction wider and step out. I slide the memory stick deeper into my pocket until the rectangle digs like a talisman.

Twenty-five video files.

Twenty-five little bombs.

Now I have to get out of here.

I head straight to the back door. No cameras on the back path.

Outside, I breathe, re-plant the key under the pot with the kind of care reserved for ancient relics and scoot through the bushes.

On the pavement, my head is a radio changing stations every second. Go home. Watch the files. Call Craig. Go home. Follow James. Post office.

The memory stick digs again, reminding me I have twenty-five tiny reasons to leave.

But curiosity is my most toxic trait, after pastries.

I glance up the road and there he is: James, hands in his pockets, face calm, walking like he owns the street.

I follow at what I hope is a casual distance.

We drift onto the main road. James moves with purpose. I move with panic.

We cut through the side streets, past Victorian terraces with doors the colour of expensive moods, until the trees begin to thin and the Downs open up ahead. The grass is still damp from earlier rain, that silvery kind of damp that soaks into your shoes and your soul.

On the downs, it's all going on. A woman in a puffer jacket throws a ball for a golden retriever who clearly identifies as upper-middle-class, while a cyclist zips past with the sort of aggression only achievable through Lycra.

James strides on, unbothered. I follow a good fifty metres or so behind him.

We pass an elderly man walking a dog that looks like a footstool with eyes. The man nods politely. I nod back, trying to look casual, as if I'm not halfway through a light espionage mission disguised as cardio.

And still, we keep walking.

Definitely not towards a post office.

No, James is heading for the south side of the Downs. The part that overlooks the gorge.

My phone vibrates. Craig. Finally. I stare at his name and let it go to voicemail because obviously, the worst time to be sensible is the exact moment sense calls you.

The landscape opens out into wind, space and drama. The Clifton Suspension Bridge stretches ahead, all graceful arches and bad decisions. Below, the Avon Gorge glints dully.

James doesn't even pause to admire it, which somehow makes it worse. He walks right to the edge near St Vincent Rocks, where the ground slopes down in patches of scrub and limestone. It's quieter here. The joggers have thinned out, replaced by couples taking photos and teenagers pretending not to vape.

The wind picks up, sharp and metallic. It tugs at my coat, my nerves, my common sense.

James stops, checks his watch, then looks down the path leading to the viewpoint.

Someone's already there, waiting.

A face I recognise.

Phil.
Craig's husband, Phil.

Chapter 41

TOM

Phil.

For a second, my brain refuses the data, like a computer that's decided "no thank you" to the update.

Phil, cardiganed, kind-eyed, king of Bakewell tarts, standing at the railing by St Vincent Rocks as if he's meeting a man to talk about bin collections and not James Bloody Whitlow. He doesn't look shocked to see James. He looks… ready. Braced. Arms folded, jaw set, like someone who has rehearsed a speech on the drive over and intends to deliver every word without blinking.

How do they know each other?

Does Craig know? Of course, Craig knows. Craig knows everything. But also: surely not? If he knew, he would've said. Wouldn't he?

I duck behind a clump of gorse that is doing nothing for my outfit or dignity and pretend I am simply a shrub with trust issues. From here, I can see them in profile. James says something first, short and clipped. Phil shakes his head. James's shoulders go up. Phil steps closer. Whatever Phil says next makes James flinch like he's been tapped on the sternum.

I'm too far to hear, which of course means my mind obligingly supplies dialogue.

PHIL: "Stop hurting Pete."
JAMES: "Mind your own business."
PHIL: "This is my business."
JAMES: "I have exquisite cheekbones."

PHIL: "Irrelevant, but yes, you do."

It isn't that, obviously.

Phil doesn't gesticulate. He's very still, which is somehow worse. James's hands come out of his pockets and then go back in. A cyclist rattles by with the bell of an ice cream van, and both men ignore it, which tells you everything about the mood.

Then it happens: the shift. The argument curdles. Phil says something that makes James step back. His mouth is a hard line now. He looks over Phil's shoulder at the view as if reminding himself he could throw a person off a cliff with one arm (I don't think he would; I absolutely think he thinks he could). Then he turns on his heel and storms away along the path, down towards the trees.

My legs move before my ethics can vote. I follow, keeping enough distance to look like a coincidence if anyone ever asks.

Phil just turns and looks out to the view, oblivious to me.

My pocket buzzes. Craig.

Of course.

I nearly let it go to voicemail out of pure cowardice, then remember that this is my one sensible adult in a world of lunatics (me included), so I answer. "Hi."

I can't stalk and talk, so I make the sensible decision to pause behind a tree and pick up the phone.

"Where are you?" he says, with the "no hello" cop voice that makes you look for a seat belt even when you're on the sofa.

"Uh…I'm out," I say.

"Can you come by tonight?" he asks. "I've got updates. Would rather do this face-to-face."

"Updates?" My chest tightens. "On… which part of my terrible life?"

"Chris." He pauses. "And some things that might intersect with… other things." It's the vaguest I've ever heard him be. "Half seven?"

"Yeah. Yes. I'll be there." I hesitate.

This would be the moment to say, "By the way, your husband and James just had a surprise cliff-side summit meeting." But the words get stuck behind my teeth. The idea of hurling that into a phone call feels wrong, like defusing a bomb by text. "Thanks, Craig."

"Tom—" he begins, then changes tack. "Just… keep your head down for the rest of today, alright?"

“Absolutely,” I lie, while stalking a man through shrubbery. We hang up.

I pocket the phone and peek out from the tree. James is way off into the distance now from the path, too far to catch up without breaking into an unsubtle run. I make the decision to end my Jessica Fletcher cosplay and head back to my car.

It’s a long trek back. I didn’t realise how far we’d come, so I up the pace. I have a memory stick full of potentially incriminating videos that need to be reviewed, plus the knowledge that James and Phil are heated acquaintances to stew over.

I need to formulate a plan for how I’m going to tackle this with Craig.

Ultimately, I need wine.

Eventually, I reach my car, a few streets down from James and Pete’s place. As I fiddle with my keys, a recognisable voice comes from behind.

“Tom.”

My heart does a Broadway leap into my throat. I spin.

Daniel is standing two paces away, like he’s been conjured by the word “red flag.” He’s in a dark coat, hair too neat, that lawyerly cleanliness that looks like you could wipe a verdict off his cheek.

“Daniel, what are you doing here?” I fire back.

He ignores my question.

“How do you know Emma Christianson?” he asks.

The shock propels me into petulance. “How do you know Emma Christianson?”

A flicker of annoyance. He steps closer, lowering his voice like we’re co-conspirators. “Don’t be cute. She’s trouble.”

“No, you’re trouble,” I say, which is not the slam-dunk I think it is, but my hands are shaking, and my mouth is a different person with different goals. “Why are you following me?”

“I’m not,” he says with extreme confidence. “I was walking. I saw you. I wanted to talk.”

“I’ve told you not to follow me, Daniel.” I’m struggling to interact and unlock my car in the moment.

“We need to talk.”

“We have nothing to talk about.” The door unlocks, and I rip the door open and jump inside.

“You can’t trust Emma,” he says firmly, as I slam the door.

Getting the keys in the ignition is my next mental challenge I fail at, as Daniel shouts at me through the window.

"She's a liar!"

Keys in.

"And a fraud!"

The engine fires and I pull away too fast, tyres gritting on fallen leaves.

It's only when I'm a street clear, do I let the breath go.

Okay, what just happened?

Chapter 42

DANIEL

Daniel watches the taillights of Tom's car shrink into the distance and feels the pressure behind his eyes. It's not so much the walk-off that stings so much as the drama of it: Tom's moral grandstanding.

He stands on the pavement and lets the city breathe around him. A slow, precise anger fills him up, the kind that cools and hardens.

Tom's become stubborn and dismissive, now disrespectful of what they once had. He was trying to help, to warn him. And what does he get: a slammed door and the smell of burnt rubber.

How does he know Emma?

Emma Christianson had been a surprise he hadn't expected. His heart took a taxi to his mouth when she'd walked away from Tom's house, as Daniel had been watching from the shadow of the poplar.

But, as ever, he smelt an opportunity. He thought this would be his way back in. He thought this could be the connection he was looking for, the ignition to bring them back together.

Emma was trouble. She was a fraud, a liar.

Dangerous.

His time in her presence back then was enough to recognise that. And now she's here, sniffing around Tom.

What's her game? Is this about him? Daniel cannot think of a viable situation in which they would become friends.

But here we are.

He thought he could use Tom's relationship with Emma to get back inside, but that ship has sailed.

And now he's out of time.

No more time to reignite a relationship with Tom.

No more searching through Tom's house.

Daniel jumps into his car and speeds off home. When he reaches his street, something feels off immediately.

It's subtle. The usual quiet hum of the road is there, the orange glow of streetlights, the familiar outline of his building.

But his front door is ajar.

Just an inch.

Enough to notice.

His body reacts before his brain catches up. He stops. Listens. The air feels thick and stale.

He doesn't move straight in. Instead, he steps to one side, scans the windows. No lights on. No movement. His heartbeat thuds hard and steady, each beat a reminder of how much he has to lose.

He pushes the door open with two fingers.

Inside is quiet.

The hallway smells wrong. Sweet and rotten at the same time.

His shoes stick slightly to the floor as he steps inside.

"Fuck," he murmurs.

The living room is untouched. The kitchen is the same. No drawers pulled out. No obvious chaos. That almost makes it worse, the deliberateness of it. Whoever's been here wasn't searching. They already knew where everything was.

He moves toward the bedroom.

The door is open.

The smell hits him first, sharp enough to make his eyes water. Then the sight lands, heavy and irreversible.

There is a fox laid out on his bed.

Its body is twisted unnaturally, fur matted dark with blood. The tail — impossibly bright, almost theatrical — has been severed and placed carefully across the pillow, like a gift. The sheets are soaked through, red blooming outward in obscene patterns.

Daniel doesn't scream.

He doesn't move.

His gaze drifts past the bed to the wall beyond it.

Smeared there, in uneven, dripping letters, are two words.

DEADLINE

TONIGHT

Written in the fox's blood.

A sound escapes him, somewhere between a sob and a gasp, as something inside him finally fractures. His hand comes up to his mouth too late, his stomach lurching as the reality of it crashes in. This isn't a warning. It's not a reminder.

It's a promise.

He stumbles back, knocking into the doorframe, breath coming shallow and fast now. His phone vibrates again in his pocket, but he doesn't need to look. He already knows.

From the bedroom window, he sees them.

A car idling at the end of the street. Watching.

The brake lights flare red.

Then the car pulls away, taillights shrinking into the distance, as calm and unhurried as if they've just dropped off groceries.

Daniel sinks down onto the edge of the bed, careful not to touch the body, hands trembling now despite himself. The heat behind his eyes returns, sharper this time, no longer masquerading as irritation.

This is fear.

Pure and undeniable.

Tonight is no longer a deadline; it's a reckoning.

Tonight is his final chance to get what he needs.

And he will get it by any means.

Chapter 43

TOM

On the drive home, my heart keeps doing that anxious tap-dance it does when the universe has presented me with too much plot for one afternoon. By the time I'm home, my shirt is damp through from sweat, driven by the mix of adrenaline and excessive overthinking.

How did Daniel know that I was even speaking to Emma? I've only met her twice, shared a few messages on Facebook, nothing more. We met in the street when she was tailing me, then we went back to mine. Then went for that coffee. Not many opportunities to "accidentally" see us together.

I knew he was watching me. Seeing him around so often over the last few weeks was no longer a coincidence. After I told him to leave me alone the other day, there was a small part of me which thought that maybe I was just imagining it.

But now. No way.

Daniel is following me, watching me. God knows how often.

How does he even know about Emma?

He spat out allegations like a charge sheet. Liar. Fraud. Daniel is overconfident at the best of times, but spouting these claims with such conviction only adds to my confusion. What do these two have in common? They move in totally different circles. Emma is expensively feral, a hurricane in decent boots. Daniel is… Daniel. Polished, precise, the human equivalent of a cease-and-desist. The Venn diagram of those two should be two lonely circles drinking alone at opposite ends of a bar.

All that aside, what was Daniel playing at? Was he genuinely trying to warn me?

No, of course not. This is a game, a tactic he's using to get to me, get under my skin, control me.

Classic Daniel.

Whatever he thinks he knows or doesn't about Emma, he's just using this as an opportunity to get to me.

And I won't let him do that.

I lock the car, unlock the house, lock the house again because paranoia is cardio, and Buster materialises in the hallway like I owe him rent.

"Big day," I tell him.

He blinks the ancestral blink of a creature who has never once paid a bill and pads away to a sun patch.

In the kitchen, I put the kettle on out of deeply British instinct, then realise my hands are shaking. I sit at the table and let my brain melt for a full thirty seconds.

Daniel and Emma are one question.

Phil and James are the other.

How *do* they know each other?

I can't get the image out of my head. The two of them on the edge of the Downs, the suspension bridge floating behind like a postcard, and them… arguing. Not a friendly "what shall we have for tea" bicker; the rigid kind, the kind you overthink in bed for the next seven years.

Why are they meeting? Does Craig know? Surely, he'd have said something. But they share everything, open about everything, right? That's what Craig said. They have no secrets.

But Craig isn't stupid; he's a detective. He'd never let that go un-catalogued.

How do I even bring this up? Not one I can casually drop into dinner conversation between lasagne and moral panic.

And just as my brain is trying to process this, too, another nugget of drama pops into my head.

The memory stick. Still stuffed in my pocket, following my light spot of illegal tourism this morning.

What have I become where a casual breaking and entering isn't the most dramatic thing that has happened to me since breakfast?

I head to the study. My laptop sits on the desk like a lifeguard. I fish the memory stick from my pocket. It feels too light for the amount of hope I've invested in it.

After a frantic search for an adapter, I slot it in. The computer makes the cheerful "I recognise this" noise, which feels jarringly upbeat given the content. I open the drive. The filenames are not helpful: CAM-KITCHEN-DATE-TIME, CAM-DINING-DATE-TIME, CAM-BEDROOM-DATE-TIME. Cold, tidy. Of course, James's surveillance system would be clinically labelled.

I select all, drag them to my desktop, and the little progress bar appears. "About 6 minutes remaining." Great. Plenty of time to overthink myself into nervous collapse.

I pace. I open the fridge and stare at it like answers live behind the hummus. I close the fridge. I check the front window to make sure the street looks like a street.

And that there's no sign of Daniel outside.

My hands still shake.

I should message Emma to say I have something, but I don't know what it is yet. Better to look first. Better not to give the hurricane a reason to generate more hysteria.

Back on the screen, a collection of videos has been copied, with 3 minutes of copying time remaining.

I stare at the video files that have copied over so far, like it's a moral test I'm about to fail. A collection of tiny windows into someone else's life, into Pete's life. Every one of them is a trespass with timestamps.

I pause before playing the first file. This is a huge invasion of privacy, the digital equivalent of rifling through someone's underwear drawer. But this isn't idle voyeurism; this is evidence which could help rescue Pete.

Granted, it's that moral grey area, borderline deceitful/heroic, enough to make a priest sweat, but a choice I'm ready to take.

"Right," I say to nobody, and click the first video.

It's the kitchen, with a clear view of the island. No sound, which makes the video feel even more ominous. James strides into frame like a storm. Pete is by the sink, hands fidgeting with a tea towel. James is shouting, his mouth open, the lines in his face sharp. Pete is shaking his head, small, quick movements bred by fear. James slams his clenched fist on the counter. Pete's hands fly up to placate him. James leans in, crowding him. It's all mime, yet I can understand the intensity of the room.

Feeling sick, I scrub forward. Pete backs out of frame. James pursues him like gravity. My knee bounces so hard the table shivers. The video ends.

I click on another file.

Same room. Different day. Morning light. Another argument. James is screaming. Pete is across the kitchen. James grabs a plate from the rack and, without warning, hurls it across the room. It explodes against the wall, white shards spraying across the floor like confetti from a bad wedding. Pete flinches so hard he almost falls. It ends there.

My phone rings, and I jump like I've been tasered.

Pete.

I answer. "Hey."

"Tom," he says. He sounds small and careful. "Are you… free? Could we talk? Coffee?"

"Yes," I say so fast, I worry I've cracked a rib. "Yes, absolutely. Where?"

He suggests a café not far from the house. "Twenty minutes?"

I agree, and we hang up.

I should go. Sensible me says close the laptop and leave. But there are files copied, and one more won't kill me. Famous last words.

I click another.

Night. The room is low-lit, shadowy. James and Sam stumble into frame, and the energy is not dinner. It's charged and sharp. There's nothing wrong with sex in kitchens when everyone is up for it, but this… this looks like the opposite of tenderness. James grips the back of Sam's neck, hard, and pushes him against the counter. I wince because a face-plant like that has to hurt. James's hand closes around Sam's throat. He's saying something and thrusts with a fury that reads as punishment. My stomach knots. I scrub forward because I know how this will play out. I witnessed it myself when I watched them that night. It ends with Sam sliding to the floor, eyes screwed shut, and James walking out without looking back.

I close the window, breathing too fast.

I look at my watch. I'm going to be late for Pete.

But I can't help myself, I need to watch one more.

Front hall. James steps in, coat on, movements clipped. Pete follows, carrying a bag, speaking animatedly. James turns and says something sharp. Pete stops. James takes a step forward. Another. It's like watching the weather roll in. Pete lifts a hand, a fragile, desperate stop. James swats it away and launches. There's no wobble in the movement.

Then, a punch.

Another.

Pete's head snaps to the side, to the other side. He goes down to a knee. James hits him again.

My mouth fills with that hot, metallic taste you get before you cry or before you say something you can't take back. I slam the spacebar. The image freezes with Pete mid-fall, eyes shut, mouth open. I sit very still because if I move too quickly, I'll throw up.

There it is. Proof. No interpretation needed. No "maybe it was an accident" or "maybe we're reading this wrong."

A fist hitting a face can't be denied.

All the files have been copied over to my desktop now. Still, at least another twenty to watch.

I stand. I need to move. I pull the memory stick out of my laptop, put it in my pocket, and grab my keys, phone, and courage. I give Buster a panicked kiss on the head — he endures this with the stoicism of a soldier — and I head for the door.

How do I broach this with Pete?

Chapter 44

TOM

I park a street away and head towards the cafe where I agreed to meet Pete. It's a bright, wet day, the sun reflecting off every window, catching the reflection of my tired eyes.

As I walk, I receive a Facebook message from Emma.

How did you get on? Any news? x

Of course, she uses an x. People who weaponise affection via punctuation are dangerous. I consider replying, then stop myself.

Daniel's voice from earlier slinks back in:

She's a liar, Tom. Don't trust her.

I don't want to give Daniel space in my head, but he's already rented the loft conversion and installed skylights.

I slip the phone away. See Pete first, think later.

The bell of the door tinkles when I step into the cafe. The delightful scent of coffee and pastries hits me immediately, at odds with the twisting sensation in my gut. Inside, it's busy with patrons and two waitresses, who must only be sixteen, working busily. I see Pete sitting at a side table, hands wrapped around a mug. He looks tired, his shoulders bowed. I give a half-wave as our eyes meet, and I feel a comfortable warmth through my body.

"Hey," he says, standing. He reaches out his arms, and we enter into an extended hug, one that lasts longer than you would expect in polite company. I feel conscious of the couple at the next table staring, but I don't let go. It's a wonderful relief to feel him in my arms again.

We break apart and take a seat. "You look..." I search for the least loaded adjective. "Human."

He huffs a laugh. "You too."

We sit. My heart is a drumline. I don't know what to say first. I stole your house's memories feels like a bit of a conversation killer.

Pete nudges a second mug towards me.

"I ordered you a latte. One sugar. Don't @ me."

"That's exactly my order," I say, mock-surprise.

"Yes, I can order a coffee under extreme trauma." He smiles again, small and bright, then glances out the window. "I just wanted to see you. Yesterday was a quiet day at the house." A pause. "Well. Quiet-ish."

"Quiet-ish is good," I say. "Quiet-ish is underrated."

For a little while, we skate on safer ice. Work. Weather. We feel obliged to make fun of the woman nearby who keeps loudly mispronouncing "cha-cuterie". My shoulders loosen a fraction. It almost feels normal.

If you ignore the rogue hard drive-shaped guilt buzzing in my pocket like a wasp.

Pete traces a finger along the rim of his cup. "I missed you," he says simply.

And there it is. The sentence that kicks my chest from the inside. "I missed you, too."

We hold that thought between us for a moment. Then I clear my throat before I continue. "I, um… spoke to someone."

"Oh?" He's wary now, like I've produced a small bomb from my jacket.

"Emma," I say. "Chris's sister."

His mouth lifts, surprised. "Emma?"

"She was… following me," I admit. "In a not entirely subtle way. We ended up talking."

Pete blows out a breath and leans back. "She's determined, I'll give her that."

"She said she liked you," I say. "That you keep in touch. She seems… intense, but nice."

He smiles properly at that, then sobers. "She wants answers. And so she should." A shadow crosses his face. "I feel guilty. About… all of it."

Guilt. That word sits down at our table and orders itself a pastry.

"And is she trustworthy?" I ask.

"I mean, she comes across like an erratic hamster wheel on speed, but she's trustworthy," he confirms, and I feel a knot in me slacken an inch. Emma: one. Daniel: zero. It shouldn't be a scorecard, but my brain loves a league table.

We talk more about Emma, how she messages him regularly, how she flips between calm and frantic. More often frantic. Pete squeezes the bridge of his nose. "I just wish I had some information that would help her."

"What does she think you know?"

"She's convinced I know where Chris really is. She thinks I know where he ran off to, or we're still in contact. But I don't know anything."

A silence hangs between us. Pete sips his coffee, and I know we've reached the point where I need to unload my guilty conscience.

"Pete," I say, and my voice comes out thinner than intended. "I did something. And you're going to be… annoyed. But I need you to know why."

His eyes lift to mine, wary. "Okay…"

"I went to your house. When you were out." The words tumble now, trying to outrun each other. "I used the spare key behind the plant pot — don't hate me — and I got into the office and… I went through some of the CCTV files."

"You what?" he says, very softly.

"I know," I rush. "I know it's a massive invasion of privacy. I know. I hate myself. But I…Emma said there might be evidence, and I've been so worried, and when you told me about the cameras—"

He puts his hand up. "Tom."

I stop. The café becomes extremely loud, then extremely quiet, then normal again. Pete stares at the table for a moment, jaw working, then looks back at me. "How?" he asks.

"How…?"

"How did you get past the computer?"

The question is so practical, I blink. "Your Apple Watch," I say, embarrassed. "It was on the charger. I know the code. It's the same as your alarm."

He closes his eyes like he's praying for patience. "And how did you guess that?

"I memorised it when you typed it in the other day."

He shakes his head, in no way marvelled by my apparent criminal genius.

"Of course you did."

"I'm sorry," I say. The two least useful words. "I shouldn't have. But I thought if we had proof—"

"Stop." He says in a firm whisper. The charcuterie lady looks over for a second before returning to her coffee. "That was stupid, dangerous. What were you thinking?"

"But I've seen what's on some of them—"

"What did you see?" he asks.

"Him shouting at you. Hitting you. There was a folder with them all saved in there. I've got it all," I confess.

"What do you mean, you've got it all?"

"I copied them onto a memory stick."

"Tom, for fuck's sake! You had no right to do that," his voice was solid but low against the hum from the café.

"I'm sorry, I just saw the memory sticks there, and I grabbed one—"

"The sticks in the office? The silver ones." His gaze bores into me. "Did you move them?"

"I—" I fumble. "I used one, yes. I… didn't think—"

"James will notice," he says, almost a whisper. The colour drains slightly from his face. "He notices everything. Remembers everything." He swallows. "If he thinks anything's missing, there will be hell to pay. He'll check the CCTV—"

Guilt floods me hot. "I deleted the footage of me in the house. I'm so sorry. I didn't think it would matter for a day."

"It matters," he says, not unkindly, just urgently. The way someone says there's a fire.

"You can put it back," I blurt. "Right now." I pull out the memory stick from my pocket.

"Have you watched them?" he asks.

"A few," I admit. I feel suddenly like a kid confessing to peeking at Christmas presents and finding a crime scene instead. "Enough to know…"

"*I* saved those videos," he says. "Sometimes I thought, if I ever needed to… you know." He doesn't finish.

I put my hand over his. It's warm and tense. "You can."

He shakes his head, quick, like a horse twitching off flies. "It's not that simple."

"Because you're scared, I get that—"

"Because," he says, a little sharper, "there are things you don't know." He squeezes his eyes shut, then opens them, staring past me. "I've made mistakes, Tom." The words come out flat with self-disgust. "Things I've done. Things he could… use. Against me." He meets my eyes again. "I'm not proud. I'm not… innocent."

Something cold slides under my ribs. "Pete—"

"It was once," he says quickly, seeing my face, misreading the direction of my fear. "Years ago. I thought I was protecting him. It doesn't matter what now. He won't let me forget it." His voice frays. "I can't just walk. He'll bring me down, too."

I nod like I understand, because in a way, I do. Shame is a padlock, and fear is the key that keeps it locked.

"Okay," I say softly. "Okay." I squeeze his hand. "Then we do what we can, safely. We'll make a plan. But first—if the missing stick puts you at risk—take it." I slide the memory stick across the table. It looks ridiculous there beside the muffin crumbs. "Put it back before he notices."

Pete exhales, shaky with relief, and pockets it immediately."Thank you," he mutters, and I can't tell if he means for returning it or for not running away.

"I shouldn't have taken it," I say.

"No," he says, quietly honest. "You shouldn't." He scrubs a hand over his face. "But I know why you did."

He's calmer now, but wired, like a man who's walked away from the edge and only now registers how close he was. He glances at the door, then back to me. "I'll go straight home and put it back."

"Do you want me to come?" I ask.

He hesitates. "No. Better you're not seen." Then, gentler: "I know you want to fix this, Tom. I want to fix this, too."

I swallow the instinct to argue that "fix" is my middle name, along with "overthink." I nod.

There's a silence neither of us fills. I look at his cheeks, the faint fading of the bruises still there like storm clouds retreating.

"Emma messaged me," I say. "Just for an update, but I didn't reply."

Pete's eyes soften. "She means well."

"She said the same about you," I say. "That you're a good person caught in a bad thing."

He looks away. "Maybe."

"Definitely," I say, too quickly.

He smiles, sad but grateful, then glances at his watch. "I should go. James might be back this afternoon."

My chest tightens. "Right."

He stands, and I follow suit. Another hug, a little tighter this time. When we pull back his eyes shine for a second, like he's about to say something else, but he doesn't.

He leaves with a gentle urgency like he's carrying a priceless and fragile artefact under his jacket. I watch him go until the door shuts behind him, then slump down into my seat. My latte is cold. I drink it anyway.

The guilt eases… and then re-forms in a different way.

Because the stick I gave back is not the only copy.

The files are on my laptop.

I tell myself this is safety, insurance. If James does go looking, there's a version he can find and a version he can't.

That sounds like sense if you tilt your head and squint.

Chapter 45

TOM

Craig opens the door before I knock and scans the street behind me like I might be trailed by an entourage of poor decisions. Which, to be fair, I am, but they're all internal.

"Come in," he says, stepping aside. "Shoes off, please. We're not animals."

I toe off my trainers and kick them into the corner. The guilt about the CCTV sticks to me like kitchen steam. I won't tell him. I can't. If I say the words *I broke into James's house*, Craig will hear the rest (*and I'm about to do more stupid things*) as loudly as a fire alarm.

But that's only the mini-secret versus the fact that I saw James and Phil together earlier. I've still not planned how I'm going to bring that one up, but I know I'll have to.

I've never kept secrets from Craig before. It's impossible to do so. He's like the FBI, MI5 and Mystic Meg's long-lost son combined.

"How's Phil?" I ask, sounding casual in the way a man sounds casual while hiding a live grenade under a tea towel.

"Good," Craig says, stirring something ambitious on the hob. "He's out tonight. He's on a date with some guy from Bath who makes miniature copies of famous buildings out of cardboard and sells them on the internet for excessive amounts of cash."

"Oh, well, there's definitely an opening in that market," I say.

Craig nods.

"And by date you mean..?"

"Probably getting railed by him right about now, next to his guillotine."

“Oh, well, lucky Phil,” I applaud. “So, you’ll be expecting a miniature Houses of Parliament on the kitchen table by the morning?”

“Which I will sell on eBay at the earliest opportunity,” Craig explains.

“Of course. And no railing to be had for yourself?” I ask.

“No, I’m far too busy to even flick on Grindr, let alone organise any form of railing.”

“So, everything’s… normal?” I test.

“Painfully so,” he says. “Wine?”

“Yes,” I say too quickly. Wine is honesty lube; I should say no. “A small one.”

He pours me a glass that would get you a VIP seat at the local AA meeting. I perch on a stool at the breakfast bar and watch him move around the kitchen with the tidy grace of a man who labels his spice jars.

Soon we’re sat down working our way through dinner, which is a tray of roasted vegetables, salmon with lemon, and a bowl of exceedingly fluffy couscous.

“Right,” he says, finally, when our plates look lived-in. “Chris.”

I grip my glass. “Go on.”

“I pulled what I could,” Craig says. “Spoke to a mate who owed me a favour.” He pulls his chair closer to the table, and I do the same. “So, Christopher Christianson. Thirty-two when he went missing. Born in London. Clean record, mostly. A few parking fines, nothing juicy. Up until just before he disappeared.”

My stomach tightens. “The corporate financial crime stuff?”

“So, he was part of a corporate advisory team that handled high-value acquisitions. About eighteen months before he disappeared, the firm he worked for was at the centre of an investigation. Serious Fraud Office stuff. There were… irregularities.” He taps the counter with two fingers. “False valuations and inflated asset reports. There was some shell-company trail that didn’t add up.”

I blink. “You mean he was committing fraud?”

Craig shakes his head. “Kind of. Someone in his department was laundering funds through a consultancy project Chris had signed off on. Whether he knew it or not… that’s murkier.” He pauses before lowering his voice. “But what is clear is that when internal auditors started sniffing around, Chris suddenly became a liability. If he cooperated, a lot of very wealthy people would go down. If he didn’t… well, he’d go down with them.”

“So he panicked.”

"And then bolted," Craig says. "He transferred whatever assets he had into cash, closed all his accounts. Then just disappeared before anyone could question him properly."

I grip the edge of the table. "So, he disappeared to avoid being arrested?"

Craig looks at me gently. "Or to avoid being used as a scapegoat."

"But Emma kept pushing," I say.

"She did," Craig says. He sips wine, watching me over the rim. "And she didn't help herself."

I brace. "Meaning?"

"From what I've found out, Emma Christianson is known for being…problematic," he says. "She's already got two years inside for fraud. Came out last year."

My mouth drops open. "Fraud?"

"Fraud."

"In a real prison?"

"Yes, a real prison."

I think of Daniel's warning — *She's a liar and a fraud* — and hate that, for once, he might not be entirely wrong.

"And that's not all," Craig continues. "A handful of previous for things that suggest she's more improvisational than truthful. Plus, she's recently been charged with arson."

"Arson?" I can't believe this.

"Yeah, and she's having her day in court over that soon. On top of that, let's just say she's known for being very… elastic with reality. And she antagonised the investigating team. Turned up unannounced. Made allegations she couldn't support. The quickest way to make the police stop listening is to lie flamboyantly."

"She told me she thinks Chris found something out about James," I say. "That he was scared."

Craig's mouth flattens. "Lots of people are scared of men like James."

"I know," I say, softer.

"I'm not dismissing your instincts, Tom. But Emma's version can't be our only map."

I nod and swallow more wine, which is a terrible strategy because it greases my tongue. "I, um… ran into Daniel. He knew Emma. Or at least, he knew of her."

Craig's eyebrows do a small theatre show. "And how would Daniel know Emma?"

"I don't know," I say. "He told me not to trust her. Called her a fraud. Literally."

His eyes narrow. "So, Daniel followed you again?"

"Yes," I admit. "Warned me off Emma, but then I ran."

"I hope you put him in his place."

"When he said Emma was trouble, I said, 'No, you're trouble.'"

"Jesus..." Craig puts his head in his hands.

"I can't do unexpected conflict, you know this." I push couscous around. "He's definitely being persistent."

"Stalkerish," Craig translates.

"But that said, he was right. About Emma, I mean."

Craig scoffs. "Maybe, but that doesn't excuse him from being a monster. You know he's just trying to manipulate you, use this to get to you."

"I know, I know." And I do.

Craig leans back, his voice edging from friend to officer. "Tom, listen to me properly for a second. You need to start keeping records of all this stuff. Every time he shows up, every message, every weird call: write it down. Keep screenshots. It builds a pattern."

"Yes, I will..."

"If he turns up again, call it in. You don't wait for things to escalate."

"Craig..."

"I'm serious. I could flag it quietly if you want. A harassment notice, an informal one, just a warning to back off. If he ignores that, it becomes official. You'd have grounds for a restraining order if it kept going."

"I'm not ready to be someone who files a restraining order just yet."

"Then start by being someone with a diary," Craig shoots back. "You've got history with him. That matters legally. He's already been violent with you once before."

I nod.

Daniel had been violent once.

A punch to the face one evening after a heated row, which fast-tracked the ending of our relationship.

I had never gone to the police about it. The guilt over the row that triggered it was too much.

The night Daniel found out about Guy.

Why am I thinking about this now?

Craig gives me a supportive smile, and we hug.

He means well, but the conversation has opened something heavier in me. It's the same look he gave me after Guy died, that quiet, anchored worry.

Back then, I remember sitting in this very flat, half-drunk, looking at a photo of me and Guy on my phone. Craig was the one who told me that grief isn't something you heal from, it's something that moves in.

He'd been right. Guy's death had hollowed me out, made space for other people's disasters to move in rent-free.

Maybe that's why I keep trying to fix everyone else: Pete, Emma, even Daniel in some fucked-up way. I'm still trying to save the version of me who couldn't save Guy.

And my dad, too, in a different timeline of helplessness. His heart, gone too early, leaving me with the belief that men I love tend to vanish.

"We need to think more seriously about Daniel," Craig says, pulling me back.

But I can't think about anything like that right now. Daniel is the least of my problems.

"Anyway, I saw Pete today—" I start.

"I thought I told you to stay away?"

"Yes, I know, but then he messaged, and I just wanted to check up on him."

"Look, I know you want to save him, because that's what you think you do. I know you have feelings for him. But you need to stay out of this. This is a messy situation. This James guy is dangerous. So, promise me you will stay away for now."

I pause for a moment. "Yes, okay," I lie.

"And this Emma as well. I looked into all this to help you keep you informed about what you're dealing with. And everything tells me to stay away. So, you need to stay away."

"Fine, yes, I will." Double lie.

Craig has warned me previously about James's history. The two charges of assault that were dropped. The charge of intimidation that also mysteriously went quiet. And I've seen it myself in the videos from the house. My rational brain tells me to give this thing a wide berth, but I just can't.

There's a pause for a moment and—

Tell him about Phil and James.

The thought has been whirling around my mind all evening.

If Phil is… what? Seeing James? Meeting him? There is an innocent explanation. There has to be. Except innocent explanations don't usually come with thundercloud body language on cliff edges.

I decide to start with the bit that doesn't make me sound crazy. "Craig… how's Phil? I mean, really."

Craig levels me with the detective gaze. "He's fine."

"Fine-fine or British-fine?"

"British-fine, obviously."

We both laugh. It helps. "He's just been… out a lot," I say, careful. "A lot of dates."

"That's allowed," Craig says. "We're not a cautionary tale just yet."

"I know," I say quickly. "Just checking in. Because I care. And because I'm nosy."

Craig's expression loosens; the lines around his eyes go kind. "He's okay. We're okay. Work is intense. He's just getting out and about, enjoying himself. But I always know what he's up to, who he's with."

"Do you?" I say, not meaning it to come out with so much judgement.

"Why do you say that?" he stares at me, brow furrowing.

"Oh, no… I just… I think…" I fumble, unable to formulate normal person sentences.

"Is there something you're not telling me?" Craig asks, lightly, like a joke, but also not. I hate him a little for being so good at his job.

Tell him now.

I go to open my mouth.

"Hello?" Phil's voice. Warm, normal, Phil. He strolls in, cheeks pink from the cold, scarf looped like a magazine advert.

"That was quick," Craig says, kissing his cheek.

"Yeah, not quite what I thought it was going to be." Phil grins at me.

"So, no railing tonight then?" I ask.

Phil whacks me playfully over the back of the head. "You wish, handsome. Where's the wine?"

I clock a glint in Craig's eye. Something's on his mind.

The night continues. Craig pours another glass. Phil jokes about guillotines. We all laugh.

Just another normal night at Craig and Phil's

But underneath it all, I can feel a tension brewing.

Three people, one table, and too many truths waiting for someone to break first.

Chapter 46

TOM

We're lying side by side, the duvet tangled between us. The light outside has that flat, end-of-afternoon flare where everything looks hazy.

For a while, neither of us speaks. The room is silent aside from the tiny sound of Buster licking what I hope is his paw somewhere in the hall.

We don't mean to end up here.

It started with coffee. It always does. Coffee, and his half-smile when I opened the door. Then coffee becomes sitting on the sofa, and sitting becomes shoulders touching, and shoulders touching becomes, well, electricity.

And then, I'm in bed with Pete having a wonderful afternoon of sweaty, enthusiastic sex.

Pete stares at the ceiling like he's trying to memorise it. "Sorry, I didn't intend for this to happen," he says eventually.

"You're sorry?"

"Oh no, not at all. Just one of those things I felt obliged to say," he says, grinning.

Then he exhales. "It's nice," he says, eyes half-closed. "Being somewhere that feels normal for five minutes."

Pete hadn't mentioned the memory stick I gave back to him last time we met. The memory stick of videos that exposed the truth of his and James's relationship. I wanted to ask him to be sure that he got it back to the office before James realised. I presume if he had noticed, there would have been repercussions, and Pete wouldn't be calmly lying next to me right now, so I assume the danger has passed.

Pete isn't aware, however, that I've copied all the videos onto the desktop of my laptop. At some point, I'll broach this with him, but not today. Not when we are having this blissful moment together.

Pete's fingertips trace slow lines on my forearms, the hairs upright as he brushes over them. "Do you miss your dad?" he asks suddenly, but the words feel gentle.

I blink, caught off guard. "Why do you ask?"

"Curious, I suppose," he says.

I stare at the ceiling. "I mean, yes, of course I miss him. But… It's hard to miss him, a connection that was never really there?"

"So, you weren't close?"

"We were… complicated, he and I. He was the strong-and-silent type, and I was the talk-and-overthink type. Neither of us really understood the other. But near the end, I think we tried. We just ran out of time."

He nods, quiet. "That's the worst bit, isn't it? Time pretending it's endless until it's not."

There's a lump forming in my throat. "Yeah." I breathe out. "Mum died when I was nine. Car accident. After that, it was just Dad and me, and… we didn't know how to talk about her, so we didn't."

Pete looks at me for a long moment. "My mum died when I was young,too," he says softly.

Something shifts in the air between us. "Really?"

He nods. "I was eight. Some heart thing. She was in and out of the hospital a lot. And then she died."

"I'm sorry," I say, because there isn't anything better to offer.

He smiles faintly. "People always say that. I don't mind. It's nice that anyone still does."

He rolls onto his back, eyes on the ceiling. "After she died, my dad… disappeared. Not right away. But grief got him drunk, and drink got him mean. One night, he just didn't come back. I waited two days before someone knocked on the door."

My chest tightens. "Oh, Pete, what happened?"

He gives a humourless laugh. "Social services came eventually. I think a neighbour had seen me sitting in the window on my own for a few days. They said I was going somewhere safe. I think they believed it. At the time."

He goes quiet for a moment, like he's listening to the memory.

"The first foster house was fine," he says. "Normal, even. A woman called Margaret. She baked all the time and wore massive slippers.y Then she got sick and went into hospital, and I got moved."

His tone flattens as he continues. "After that, things never stabilised. I went from place to place. New house, new rules, new strangers. Some were decent, kind. Most weren't. You learn the difference very quickly. But even the decent ones never felt like home."

I swallow hard. "Pete…"

He shakes his head. "It's okay. It's a long time ago. I'm just… saying it out loud. Some of them were …" He trails off, eyes still on the ceiling. "Let's just say, some people take in kids because they think it'll make them look good. Doesn't always mean they should be near kids."

There's silence between us that falls so heavy that I pause for breath until Pete continues.

"By fourteen, I'd worked out how to disappear. Smile, nod, say please and thank you, don't make a fuss. The quieter you are, the less they notice you. That's how you survive."

I try to imagine being ten and knowing that. It makes my heart ache.

"So, when people talk about family," he says, "I don't think of parents. I picture anyone who stays, who commits, who chooses me."

There's something in that line that makes my stomach twist. *I picture anyone who stays.*

I stayed for Daniel, longer than I should have. I stayed because I thought leaving meant failing.

Pete keeps talking. "I met James years later, when I'd finally started to feel like an adult. He gave me everything I wanted. Stability, security. A face to come home to every night and someone to wake up next to me in the morning. There were some days where he'd spoil me rotten, and I felt like the luckiest man on earth."

His voice trails off, and I squeeze his hand.

"I thought I could handle it," he says finally. "He said he loved me. That I was difficult sometimes, but he loved me anyway. And I thought, well, love's supposed to hurt a bit, isn't it? Everything else in my life did."

My heart stumbles. *Love equals pain equals love.* That logic is carved into too many of us.

He laughs, but there's no joy in it.

"Did you ever find your dad again?" I ask.

"No," he says simply. "Part of me wanted to. Most of me didn't. But I rarely even think of him."

I keep staring at the ceiling. The shape of our loss is similar. The outline may differ, but that feeling of emptiness remains the same. My dad never left, but sometimes it felt like he wasn't there in the first place. And now, he never will be.

Pete turns onto his side again. "You must miss your mum," he says.

"I don't really remember her properly," I admit. "Bits and pieces. I definitely remember how her laugh sounded . Sometimes I think I remember how her perfume smelled. My brain kept some of the fragments but lost the person."

He nods slowly. "Yeah, same. I dream about mine sometimes. Like, I know it's her without actually seeing her face."

I nod, because I often experience that same feeling.

Pete pauses. "Sometimes I think grief isn't about missing the person, more missing a version of you that existed when you were both there."

"That's…" I exhale. "That's uncomfortably accurate."

He smiles faintly. "Sorry. I go a bit philosophical when I'm tired."

"Please, philosophise away," I say.

"That's not a word."

"It's absolutely a word."

He grins. "Okay, I will continue to philosophise."

"Please do. You make trauma sound like something manageable."

He chuckles. "It's not, though. I still panic if someone raises their voice. I still overthink every text message, which is why I don't send them."

"Ah, I wondered why you were such an old-school phone user."

"Yes, this is why," he chuckles lightly as he speaks. "I keep spare toothbrushes for guests I don't have, because I can't stand the idea of anyone feeling unwelcome. My therapist says it's 'adaptive coping.' I say it's retail trauma."

I laugh quietly. "That's the most British diagnosis I've ever heard."

He grins. "Very much so."

There's another pause, gentler this time. "Thanks for telling me that stuff," I say.

He shrugs, but there's a faint flush in his cheeks.

For a while, we just lie there, facing each other. His eyes flicker closed and open again, sleep luring him in. As I near my own slumber, those I've lost stir in my mind: Mum, Dad, Guy. They're not gone, not really. They just live in the spaces between my thoughts.

Before we both fall, I close my eyes, enjoying the calm.

Part of me wants to protect this quiet forever. Another part knows it can't last.

But for now, I let myself believe it can.

Chapter 47

SAM

Sam has had the feed up all afternoon.

The laptop is propped up on the kitchen island like he's about to live-stream a cook-along. Four camera windows: hallway, living room, study, bedroom. Live and exclusive from Tom's house.

He wasn't all that interested in the sex. Sweet, neat, barely a touch above vanilla. The kind of thing you could watch to a Coldplay soundtrack.

What catches him is the after. Pete turns onto his side, palm open in that over-sharing way of his, eyes alive. Tom is listening with an almost devotional focus.

There's no sound on the feed, but he doesn't need it. He reads body language like subtitles. He analyses each little movement, touch and expression as their post-coital talk continues.

It's hypnotic, really.

He's still watching when a voice whips him back into the room.

"What the fuck is this?"

James.

Sam doesn't startle easily. He snaps the laptop half-closed and turns. James stands there in gym clothes, damp hair slicked back, eyes sharp enough to cut marble.

"Just keeping an eye on things."

James's jaw tightens. "They're still together."

"Looks that way."

"He's trying to get rid of me," James mutters. "He's planning something."

“Paranoia is not the sexiest look on you,” Sam says, hoping humour will ground him.

“I know he’s up to something!”

“Or maybe, it’s jealousy?” Sam sips his tea.

“Don’t be fucking ridiculous.” James grabs the nearest glass and hurls it across the room. It shatters beautifully, making Sam’s pulse jump, despite his calm poise.

James storms out, the door slamming behind him.

“Fantastic,” Sam mutters. “Love that for my bare feet.” He exhales and re-opens the laptop. Pete’s now getting dressed, pulling on jeans, reaching for a shirt that’s clearly Tom’s. He leans down, kisses Tom and walks out of frame. Tom stays lying there, hand pressed flat to his stomach like he’s holding himself together.

Sam closes the laptop. He dries his hands, pockets his keys, and leaves.

It’s a good day for mistakes.

It’s a fifteen-minute drive when he gets to his destination.

Tom looks surprised when he opens the door, wearing a T-shirt, shorts, and socks, his expression halfway between wary and polite. “Sam?”

“Tom.” Sam smiles as if this is the most natural thing in the world. “I was driving by. Thought I’d pop in.”

Tom blinks. “How do you even know where I live?”

“Pete,” Sam says. It’s plausible. He could’ve found it that way.

Tom softens a little. Then frowns. “Right. What can I do for you?”

Sam leans against the doorframe. “Just thought I’d check in. See how you were doing. I drove past the other day, and there was this bloke hanging around. Dark hair, suit, trying to get in. Looked like he knew the place. Think he had keys.”

Tom freezes for a second, his breath catching in a way that tells Sam everything. Bingo.

That was, of course, a lie, but he’s still dying to find out who this guy is who keeps rummaging through his house when he’s out. Maybe the direct approach is the best way.

“Ex?” Sam asks, casually.

Tom exhales. “Something like that. It’s nothing.”

Nothing is never nothing. But Sam lets it slide, smiling like it’s all fine. “Still, be careful. World’s full of weirdos.”

“That it is,” Tom says, but he’s smiling now, softening.

Sam softens his voice, a tone more akin to a friend sharing humble advice. "Look, I know this is none of my business, but the house is tense right now, as I'm sure you've guessed."

Tom nods slowly.

"I know you and Pete have your thing going on, and normally I'd be all for it…" Sam's voice trails off.

"But…?"

"But…it might be an idea to keep your distance for a bit."

"Oh, really?" Tom frowns.

"Yeah, James, bless him, he can get stressed out and take things a little too far sometimes."

"So I hear," Tom says quickly.

"Oh?" Sam's ears prick up. "What has Pete been telling you?"

Sam notices Tom's breathing is deepening. "Not just Pete. I've heard some other things."

"Like?"

"The police investigations, two assault charges that got dropped, intimidation complaints. I know James has a history of this kind of thing."

Sam's head tilts, curious. "Police?"

"Yes, police," Tom confirms.

"That's not remotely true," Sam says. "James has never been investigated for anything. Not once. He's far too careful for that. Whoever told you that was lying. Or wanted to scare you off."

Tom frowns.

And Sam is telling the truth here. James has a temper, a dangerous temper, yes. But, Police investigations, assault charges? That is absolutely fiction.

"Oh," Tom says, looking bemused.

Who has been lying to you, Tom?

"That said, maybe you should listen to them regardless. I'm not trying to scare you," Sam lies. "I'm trying to stop you from getting burned. He's on a knife-edge. One more spark and…" He lets the sentence die.

"And what?"

"He could…snap."

Tom studies him. "And have you seen him snap before?"

Sam's eyes hold steady. "Yes."

He doesn't elaborate, but the memory slides through him like cold water. He knows very well what James is capable of. The aggression, the violence.

It has served Sam well in the past.

"For Pete's sake," Sam says quietly. "Keep your distance. You being around makes him nervous, and when James gets nervous, Pete pays for it."

"Well, maybe Pete should just get out," Tom says, heat edging into his voice.

There he is.

Sam laughs. "Oh no, that will never happen. Pete and James are forever." He stops laughing. "Or until one of them is six feet under."

Tom flinches at that. Sam notices but pretends not to.

"Anyway, I'll leave you to it," Sam says with a smile. He steps out into the cool evening. The door closes behind him, leaving him alone with the hum of the streetlights.

He gets into the car and then laughs softly, forehead resting against the steering wheel. That's the satisfaction of a plan beginning to take shape.

He wasn't sure about Tom at first.

But now. Now, it's time to really put him to the test.

Chapter 48

TOM

Sam's footsteps are still in my head when the front door clicks shut, and he's gone.

The house suddenly feels too quiet. My brain is a whirlwind, so much to process from such a short conversation, which felt like grenade after grenade.

Sam's words keep looping in my brain:

He's never been charged with anything. Whoever told you that was lying.

Craig had been very clear. James had been charged twice for assault. Investigated for intimidation. A whole catalogue of indications that painted James as exactly the sort of man who would control and abuse.

Either Sam's gaslighting me, or Craig got it wrong? But Craig doesn't get things wrong. Ever. Well, apart from the time when he confidently predicted Olly Alexander would smash Eurovision 2024. But he never gets important things wrong.

Whoever told you that was lying.

Would Craig lie to me? I trust him more than anyone. He's supported me through everything. My relationship with Daniel, the loss of my father. He was also a very prominent support in the late '90s when I tried to dye and perm my hair like Justin Timberlake, which ultimately ended up like a selection of microwaved Super Noodles on my head.

Of course, I trust Craig infinitely more than I would ever trust Sam. Either way, the not-knowing feels like a mosquito buzzing near my ear.

I stand in the middle of the living room, hands shoved into my pockets, and try to locate the logical centre of my brain. Buster scoffs at me from a sunbeam on the sofa, acting like he's personally disappointed.

One more spark and he could snap.

I grind my knuckle into my forehead as I think this through. James is dangerous; this is not new information. Although this was positioned as a friendly warning, it came across more as a threat. Was Sam telling me to stay clear? Or is James genuinely going to snap at any moment?

The thought of what that means for Pete is unbearable for me. More than ever now, I want to help Pete save himself from this. He needs to get out before it's too late.

Pete and James are forever.

I don't believe this. They can't be forever. No one can live in a relationship like this forever.

Or until one of them is six feet under.

These are the words that make me sick the most.

I look out to the garden, the haze of the sun warming my face, but it does little to calm me.

Then the final bombshell. Sam said he'd seen a bloke trying to get in, who fitted Daniel's description perfectly. What is he still doing around here? I've told him to stay clear. We've not spoken again since the "Emma is a fraud" revelation, which, okay, turned out to be true. But as Craig reminded me, that doesn't give him a key back into my life.

Keys. Another thought. Sam mentioned it looked like he had keys. No, Daniel definitely doesn't have keys, there's no way he can get in. Unless…

My jaw tightens. Surely not.

I find myself sliding open the back door and heading into the garden, bare feet on the dewy grass because, of course, I forgot shoes in the mad dash out.

The fake rock by the patio, my cheap, tasteful garden ornament that conceals the spare key, is among a pile of small rocks that create a boundary in the garden. I grab the rock and open it.

Empty.

I feel my stomach do somersaults, and the cream cheese bagel I shoved in my mouth moments before Sam arrived is now grasping up into my throat.

The idea that anyone has a key to my house and could be wandering through my things while I'm here and drinking tea in another room makes me more queasy.

But the fact that it's Daniel.

It's a movie-level panic: you know that sick, cinematic lurch when the protagonist realises they've been duped? I experience it now in high-definition shame and low-grade hysteria.

Locksmith. Change locks. Call Craig. Call the police. Call Sam and punch him through the phone for leaving me with more questions than answers.

All that, plus save Pete.

All sane options. All reasonable.

Too many priorities, but in the short term, all I want to do is keep my home safe. I need to get the locks changed. I rush to my office and flip open my laptop to search for locksmiths. It pings to life, but before I open the browser, I see the remaining CCTV videos on my desktop that I had copied over from the memory stick.

I hadn't told Pete that I had copied them over. I couldn't, not when we were having such a glorious afternoon together, pretending everything was normal. I didn't want to break that feeling.

But they're still here, and I'd only watched a selection yesterday.

Thoughts of changing the locks disappear from my mind as the remaining videos call to me. I know what to expect. More videos of James and Pete's cruel and vicious relationship. And while I know looking through the rest of these videos is immoral, a betrayal of trust, I have to see them all.

The first video is timestamped a year ago: late afternoon in the kitchen. James and Pete are at the breakfast bar, arguing. With my heart in my mouth, my attempt to lip-read becomes senseless, as in one swift move, James slams Pete up against the fridge by his throat.

The video makes me feel sick, so I click out and on to the next.

Video after video plays in a cascade, each one shows James's shadow looming over Pete as if it could swallow him. One clip shows James grabbing Pete's arm so hard it looks like it might break. Another clip shows plates shattering to the floor at Pete's feet. Another of James pushing Pete down on the sofa, the movement sharp and ugly.

I get to the last video.

The screen jolts into motion: a blur of limbs, shirts, chaos in the doorway. It takes me a second to understand what I'm seeing. Two figures. A fight. A mess of soundless violence.

I sit up so fast the chair shrieks across the floor. My pulse spikes, every nerve screaming, as I focus on the two men.

One is James.

And the other:

Chris.

They're not just fighting. They're decimating each other. Every movement is wild and desperate as they crash from against the cupboards, to the freezer, to the floor. Their heaving bodies create destruction with every lunge, as plates explode and cutlery flies across the tiles. It's chaos.

Blood flashes across the floor. I don't even know whose. Their bodies tangled, feral.

Chris manages to get on top, his face twisted in a mix of fury and survival. He lands a clean punch, right to James's jaw. The impact throws James back. I flinch as if I can feel it.

For a heartbeat, Chris has the upper hand. He draws back again, one more hit, maybe enough to end it.

Then James's hand moves. A flicker of metal catches the light.

A knife.

It happens in a blink.

The first strike lands at Chris's throat.

Chris's hands fly to his neck in a horrible, jerking motion.

The second blow follows instantly. A flash of red against white.

The third. The fourth.

By the fifth, I'm gripping the edge of my desk so hard my fingers ache. I can't breathe. The screen shows movement, then stillness.

Chris collapses forward, half onto James, blood soaking his shirt, his arm twitching once, twice.

Then nothing.

The video file ends.

And I just sit there, frozen, the world narrowing to the size of that flickering image.

Chapter 49

TOM

I don't move for a long time after the video ends.

The screen goes dark, and I just sit there, staring at my own reflection in it. A ghost of me looks back, pale and confused, and I see the fear in his eyes.

Chris is dead.

James killed him.

And I've just watched it happen.

Every instinct tells me to rewind, to watch it again, to confirm, as if confirmation would make it more bearable.

I don't. I don't need to. I know what I saw, and once is enough.

My stomach already feels like I've swallowed glass.

The house hangs in silence. I get up, pace the living room, then sit back down again. I can't stay still. My mind keeps flickering between thoughts like faulty Christmas lights.

James did it. James murdered Chris.

Pete lives with him.

Pete sleeps next to him.

The thought makes me nauseous. My hands are shaking, so I clasp them together like I'm praying, but prayer feels too hopeful for this moment.

I have to do something.

The obvious answer screams in my head: go to the police. It's the one rational thought trying to push through the storm. I've got the proof, every horrible second of it. But I can't just walk in alone. They'll want context. They'll want details. And I can't do any of that without Pete.

My having this video alone is a huge invasion of Pete's privacy. One, in hindsight, I'm comfortable with based on what I've just found. However, I need to talk this through with Pete before we go to the police. I can't go behind his back.

I need to do this with support. Together.

It sounds almost reasonable in my head, like something Craig would say: *Don't do anything rash, Tom. Keep your head.*

Craig.

God. I should call him.

He'd know what to do. He is the police. But the idea of explaining how I got this footage, how I broke into James's house and stole it…well, that would go down about as well as an arson confession at a fire station. And then it would be out of my hands, I'm sure. Craig would call his murder squad pals, and it would all snowball before I could speak to Pete.

No.

Pete first.

Then the police.

I want to shoot over to Pete's place right now. I look at the clock. It's 9.30pm. James will be home, and I need to get Pete alone. I think about calling him now, but I stop myself. No, James might be there when I call, and this needs to be a face-to-face conversation. Waiting until first thing in the morning is the best course of action, I assure myself.

I consciously breathe, trying to slow the panic rushing through me, but the adrenaline is not fading. I keep replaying Chris's final moments: it's all a blur of frantic limbs and blood, the glint of the knife, slashing back and forth like lightning. The vision plays on repeat as my stomach twists in disgust.

The laptop screen still glows faintly. I snap it shut and push it away like it's contagious.

I'm about to go to bed when my phone rings. Facebook Messenger.

Emma Christianson.

I just stare at the name for a full ten seconds before opening it.

Hey Tom. What did you find out? Can we meet? Tomorrow maybe? x

The message feels almost harmless, ordinary. But knowing what I know , and what she doesn't, it lands like a bullet to the chest.

Her brother isn't missing.

He's dead.

And the man who did it is still walking around free, sleeping next to Pete, eating toast in the same kitchen where he bled out.

I grip my phone tighter. I can't tell her. Not yet. She deserves the truth, but not through a screen. And not until I speak to Pete. Still, now I know, ignoring her feels cruel.

Nothing new to report, but let's catch up soon. Will message you tomorrow.

I hit send and throw my phone to the side. Even that short message fires a tense heat in my chest.

When I finally crawl into bed, exhaustion crashes over me like a wave, but sleep doesn't come easy. Every time I start to drift, I see flashes: Chris's face, the blood, James's blank expression after it's done.

I don't know what time I fall asleep. Sometime after two, I think. The house is quiet, the kind of quiet that feels heavy, like it's waiting for something.

Then there's movement.

It's faint at first. A sound like a shoe brushing carpet. I think it's part of a dream until I open my eyes.

Someone is standing at the end of my bed.

For a split second, I freeze. My brain can't make sense of it. The figure is dark, half-silhouetted by the streetlight leaking through the curtains.

I bolt upright as my heart lurches violently, the duvet tangled around my legs. "What the fuck—"

"It's me," a low voice says. "Tom, it's me." I recognise the voice instantly.

Daniel.

He takes a small step forward, hands raised like he's warding off panic.

"I just want to talk," he says.

"What are you doing in my house?!" My voice sounds wrong, too loud in the stillness.

Of course, I know how he got in the house. The spare key. I was adamant that I needed to change the locks. Just my luck that I got distracted watching a CCTV murder video of my boyfriend's ex.

How is this my life?

"Can we just talk?" he says simply.

"I should call the police." I reach for my phone on the bedside table.

Daniel moves fast towards me. "Don't."

"Get out of my house."

"Just listen—"

He grabs for my arm. It's not rough, not at first, but it's firm. I yank away, stumble half off the bed, reaching for the phone again. This time, he catches my wrist hard.

"Daniel, stop!"

He pushes forward, maybe trying to stop me, maybe just panicking.

"Tom!" he says, breathless, almost pleading. "Don't do this."

The weight of him knocks me back, and my head slams against the wall with a dull crack. Pain bursts behind my eyes.

The words blur. The room warps.

I don't remember falling to the floor, but I see his face above me, too close, a mix of desperation and fear, and then everything goes black.

Chapter 50

DANIEL

Daniel sits on Tom's cold bathroom floor, legs pulled up towards his chest, arms on his knees, back pressed to the wall. The wait for Tom to regain consciousness was longer than anticipated. The only sound is the repetitive drip of the basin tap, every drop torturing him like a countdown towards a deadline he's desperate to beat.

Tom is slumped in front of him, his body half-curled against the bathtub, wrists bound behind the back of the toilet with duct tape. His head hangs forward, chin to chest. Unconscious, but breathing.

Daniel watches him closely, looking for signs of movement. He reaches out and touches Tom's shoulder gently. "Tom?"

No answer.

He waits, counting under his breath. When the first flicker of movement comes in the form of a shallow inhale, Daniel exhales, relief and dread mixing in his chest. Tom's fingers begin to flicker, as do his eyelids.

"Good," he murmurs. "You're back."

Tom groans, disoriented. His head lolls, eyes half-opening. The confusion hits first, then fear becomes visible in his widening eyes.

"Daniel?" His voice is raw. "What the hell…what are you doing?"

"You're fine," he says. His tone is calm. "I just needed you to stop panciking so we could talk properly, like adults."

"Talk like adults?" Tom struggles against the tape. "You tied me up in my own bathroom."

"I had to," Daniel says. "You weren't listening."

Tom lets out a short, disbelieving laugh that dissolves into a cough. "Jesus Christ, Daniel, this isn't how people get heard."

Daniel ignores that. His heart is hammering, his palms slick.

"What has happened to you?" he says. "There was a time when you would do anything for me. But now, look at you, won't even give me the time of day. Yet, you'll become pals with a crook like Emma Christianson!"

"How do you know her?" Tom asks.

Daniel sighs. "I was her lawyer briefly. I was assigned to her a few months back when she was charged with arson," he explains. "Although it didn't last long, when I realised that she was a compulsive liar. She lied about everything and anything she could. Completely untrustworthy and not worth my time. Or yours, for that matter, but maybe that's just who you are these days."

Tom doesn't respond.

"Look, I don't want to hurt you," he says, and the words are true in the moment. "But I've run out of time. We can no longer do this civilly when you won't listen to me."

Tom tugs his arms, but the duct tape is holding him tight.

"I need my money, Tom."

Tom blinks at him, still dazed. "What?"

"I know your dad died." Daniel leans forward, searching Tom's face. "I know what that means. The inheritance. You've come into money, haven't you?"

"Yes, you know I have."

"I need my fair share of it," Daniel says calmly. "My settlement. And I need it now."

"What are you talking about? My dad died well after our divorce was finalised." Tom swallows hard. "You've completely lost it."

"No." Daniel's breathing quickens.

At first, Daniel had planned to do things properly. The formal route. He'd even drafted the beginnings of the application, his claim to financial relief as a former cohabitant under the Inheritance Act. The respectable, legitimate way to get what he was entitled to. But they are way beyond that. Now, it's just about making it through the night.

"I've done my research. I've seen the filings, the probate application. It's public record, Tom. Don't insult me."

Tom closes his eyes like he's praying for this to stop. "You've been digging through legal records?"

"I had to," Daniel says. "You wouldn't talk to me. You blocked my number, you ignored every message. What choice did I have?"

"Every other choice than this!" Tom snaps, voice breaking.

Daniel's jaw tightens. He looks down at Tom. "Four hundred thousand pounds," he says quietly. "That's what I need."

Tom laughs, a high, incredulous sound. "Four hundred thousand? Are you out of your mind? I don't have that kind of money!"

"Yes, you do."

"I don't."

Daniel crouches again, his face inches from Tom's. "Don't lie to me," he says, voice trembling now. "You inherited your father's estate. He was a multi-millionaire. I'm not an idiot. You think I didn't check? I've been looking through your files, your laptop. I know it's there somewhere. Maybe property investments. Or hidden accounts."

Tom shakes his head, desperation creeping in. "Daniel, listen to yourself. You're talking like...like a criminal."

Daniel laughs softly. "I'm not a criminal. I'm just getting a share of what's mine." He looks past Tom, eyes unfocused, as if explaining to someone else entirely. "When you walked out, you took everything. You left me with nothing but debts I couldn't pay."

"Your debts. From your gambling, not mine!" Tom screams back.

Daniel ignores that. "I was loyal to you, Tom. I fought for us. You shut the door and pretended I didn't exist."

"I didn't pretend—"

"Yes, you did!" Daniel's voice cracks. "You erased me. But this—" he gestures around, at the bathroom, the house, all of it—"this is mine too. You don't get to move on and build a life, and leave me out cold."

The silence that follows is heavy, broken only by their breathing.

"I need that money. And I need it tonight."

Daniel thinks about the men he owes and feels his stomach knot, the kind of dread that makes breathing feel like swallowing glass.

They're not loan sharks in the cliché sense, no tracksuits or baseball bats. Much worse. They wear well-fitted suits and drive expensive-looking cars. They call themselves investors, consultants, "private facilitators."

He met his debtors through an online gambling forum. They promised him fast cash as his losses mounted. At first, they were polite and professional, the money always transferred within the hour, no questions. Five grand here, ten grand there. Each time, he swore it was temporary, he'd win it back. And so often he did.

Until he didn't.

Now the balance sits at four hundred thousand pounds, and his time is up.

He's heard stories about what happens when people don't pay. A man in Bath was found in his car with two broken hands and a warning carved into his chest with a rusty knife. A man in Manchester had his leg sawn off below the knee while he was pinned down. Another had his ear and nose sliced off. Plenty of others who disappeared entirely or "relocated," though no one ever heard from them again.

He can't be next.

Daniel thought he was different, smarter than them. He had charm and legal know-how to buy him time. But people like this don't care about your qualifications, your smart talk, or your status. They just want back what is theirs.

Now every message from his phone deepens his anguish. He's suffocating in his life, continually gasping for breath. If he doesn't get his hands on this money, it's not about losing his flat or his credit card: it's about losing his limbs, at best. At worst, his life.

And Tom is his last, desperate roll of the dice.

Daniel pulls his phone from his pocket and scrolls through something. "I've been looking for proof," he says absently. "Emails from your solicitor, confirmation letters, bank balances. Tell me, tell me how much you have stashed away!"

Tom stares at him. "So, you have been breaking into my house?"

Daniel looks at him sharply. "Our house! You paid for this with that inheritance, half of that should be mine – half of this house is mine!"

Tom's voice rises. "That was my Dad's money, none of it is yours!"

Daniel slaps him. The sound is small, sharp, shocking even to himself.

Tom's head jerks to the side, his breath catching. The room tilts with silence again.

Daniel lowers his hand slowly. "I didn't want to do that." His voice is shaking. "But you need to stop talking to me like I'm crazy."

Tom blinks hard, fighting tears. "You are crazy."

His tone softens, cracks. "I just need help, Tom. I'm drowning."

Tom looks at him then, really looks, and for a moment, there's pity in his eyes. "I can't help you," he says quietly. "Not like this."

Something inside Daniel curdles. Pity is worse than hatred. Pity makes him feel small and powerless.

He crouches again, face close. "You could fix this. Right now. Just transfer the money to me now. I'll get your laptop."

"I don't have access to that kind of money!"

Daniel exhales sharply through his nose. "I don't believe you."

"I can get you something tonight." Daniel hears the desperation in his voice. "Maybe thirty at a push!"

"Thirty! Are you having a laugh with me! I know you have millions hidden away!"

"I don't!" Tom screams.

Daniel stands, pacing, thinking. He's running out of time. The men he owes gave him until midnight. It's nearly morning. He can almost feel the noose tightening.

His mind scrambles.

Tom is lying. He just needs some persuasion.

He spots the white towel hanging on the rack. Then his eyes slide to the shower head.

The thought comes before the morality does.

He turns on the tap, lets the water run warm, then hot, then back to cold. The hiss fills the small room, drowning out Tom's voice.

"Daniel, stop. What are you doing?"

Daniel doesn't answer. He grabs the towel, folds it twice, and steps closer.

"Daniel, don't—please."

"You're making this harder than it needs to be." His voice is almost gentle. "Just tell me you'll transfer me four hundred tonight, and this is over."

Tom just stares up at him, frozen in fear.

He presses the towel over Tom's face. Tom thrashes instantly, shouting, muffled. Daniel tightens his grip and lifts the showerhead.

Water pours down. The fabric darkens instantly, plastering to Tom's skin.

Tom jerks, sputters, chokes. The sound is awful, a frantic mix of muffled screams and gurgling. Daniel's arms tremble, but he doesn't stop. Not yet. Not until he's sure.

"Where is it?" he shouts over the water. "Tell me!"

Tom can't answer.

He can't breathe.

Chapter 51

TOM

Water rushes over my face, through the towel, into my mouth, up my nose. My lungs scream for air. My throat convulses. The hiss of the shower becomes the only sound I hear alongside my desperate, choked gasps.

I can't breathe.

I thrash against the tape, holding my wrists to the toilet, but there's no strength left, only panic. The instinct to survive overpowers everything, but my options to escape are zero. My thrashing body can only wait for the end to come.

And just when I think I'm going to pass out, when the burning in my chest turns white-hot and the edges of my vision blur, Daniel pulls the towel away.

I gasp a ragged, animal noise, as air floods into my lungs. I cough, splutter, twist onto my side, choking up water, bile, fragments of panic.

Daniel watches me, chest heaving, face pale and shining with sweat. His hands shake, but his wild eyes are fixed on me.

"You made me do that," he says quietly.

I can barely form words.

He shakes his head, crouching in front of me. "I needed you to listen."

"By drowning me?" I rasp. "You've lost your fucking mind."

He doesn't answer. Instead, he just stares.

My breath is still heaving. Desperately, I try to control it as the silence stretches between us, the drip-drip from the showerhead the only other sound.

“Daniel, listen to me,” I start, forcing my voice steady. “I don’t have what you think I have.”

His laugh is short and bitter. “Bullshit. Your dad dies, and suddenly you’ve got a new house, new furniture, a new car. Now, you’re on some long-term sabbatical, like you don’t even need to work. You think I don’t see it?”

“It’s not like that, Daniel.”

“Really? Then tell me how it is.”

My mind races with lies and stories I could fire back, but I know he’ll see through it. He knows my little tells: the way my voice rises, the twitch of my eye. Micro-behaviours he’s witnessed over ten years of marriage, now being used against me.

“I did get money,” I admit.

His eyes flash.

I don’t say it out loud, but after inheritance tax, it was about £1.6 million.

“Most of it went into this house,” I continue quickly. Again, not that I’m telling him this, but it was around nine hundred thousand, gone straight into the purchase. “The rest, it’s tied up. Locked away in schemes, investments, stuff I can’t access. Not tonight. I can’t get to it, Daniel.”

Again, this is true. Most of it is not readily accessible.

He tilts his head, studying me. “How much can you get?”

“I told you, thirty thousand. Maybe thirty-five at most.”

He gives a humourless smile. “You expect me to believe that?”

“It’s the truth.”

“Truth?” he snorts. “You don’t know what the truth is, Tom. You’re a liar, you always have been! A liar and a cheat.”

My throat tightens. I can’t find my voice.

Daniel crouches again, inches from my face. His breath smells faintly of whisky. “Sneaking off, behind my back. Your weekly hookups with lover boy in that sleazy hotel.”

I say nothing. Even now, the guilt kills me.

“I felt sick when I found out,” he continues. “When I got those videos.”

I have no idea what he’s talking about. “Videos?” I ask. “What videos?”

He shakes his head, eyes burning into me. “Videos of you and him, walking into that hotel on Park Street, every week.”

My heart stops for a beat.

The hotel on Park Street.

Our regular meeting point, outside of work. Mine and Guy's time together, alone.

Daniel knew about it.

"That's how you found out?" I whisper.

"They came from some mystery number. And it was clear as day what was going on. It still makes me sick to think of you and him together, behind my back."

My brain is a whirlwind. I never knew how Daniel had found out about Guy and me, but now, the truth is coming out.

"Why didn't you say?" I stutter.

"I didn't need to. You just admitted it as soon as I challenged you."

"Challenge" is a light word. The last time we talked about this was the night Daniel punched me in the face, the first time he was violent, and the last time we called ourselves a couple.

Those videos broke us apart.

"Who sent them to you?" I have to ask.

"Well, for a long time, I had no idea. Figured it was a friend or his wife."

Evelyn.

"Yeah," Daniel continues, "I found out he had a wife too. Both as shameful as each other."

My mouth goes dry. "Who sent it?"

"It was from an unrecognised number, but it hit me the other day, when I was looking through your laptop, it would be worth a check. It didn't take long to match it to one of your contacts."

"Who?" I demand a third time.

Daniel gives me a self-righteous smile. "Craig," Daniel says. "Your friend. The copper."

It hits me like a punch to the stomach. I taste bile in my throat.

That can't be true. My brain rejects it outright. Craig wouldn't…he couldn't.

But Daniel's eyes are steady, convinced.

"Why would Craig—"

"No idea," Daniel snaps. "Maybe he thought I deserved to see what you were doing behind my back."

Why, why would Craig do that?

"But it doesn't matter now, though, does it?" Daniel says with venom.

"Daniel..." I whisper.

“Dead as a dodo. Sliced up and left on the pavement like the trash he is. He got what was coming to him,” he hisses.

There’s something in his voice that makes me look up. He’s staring past me, eyes unfocused, almost… detached.

I’m struggling to process this. What is Daniel telling me?

He got what was coming to him.

“What do you mean? What did you do?” I plead.

“What did I do?!” He slaps me again, harder this time. My head cracks against the porcelain. “You were the one sneaking around, lying, betraying me! You broke us, Tom. You made me do everything that came after!”

I taste blood. My ears ring.

He crouches again, grabs the towel. “Let’s try this one more time, yeah?”

“No—please, don’t—”

The towel comes down again. The water hits.

This time, I don’t even fight. My body convulses once, twice. The world dissolves into a blur of sound and colour, the hiss of water, the burning in my lungs, the black spots blooming behind my eyes.

“Where is my money?!” Daniel screams.

Just as I’m about to pass out, the towel is off me again. I gasp as much air as I can. “Daniel… please,” I splutter. “I don’t have that much. Give me a few days, and I can help you.”

I flinch as he grabs the towel again.

“Daniel, please,” I gasp. “You don’t have to—”

He doesn’t listen.

The towel hits my face again, wet and heavy. The water starts instantly. Cold this time. I can’t scream. The sound turns into bubbles, trapped under fabric. My lungs seize. My body jerks violently. I try to tilt my head, but his grip is like iron across me. I thrash my legs to kick him away, but he rests his weight on top of them to pin me down.

With my vision on the edge of darkness, he lifts the towel away, and I vomit water across the tiles. I gasp for breath, my mouth wide open, the veins in my neck red and throbbing.

Daniel crouches close, breathing hard, eyes wild but glistening. “Just tell me where it is,” he says softly, almost pleading now. “Please, Tom. Just tell me, and this ends.”

“There’s nothing to tell.”

“Liar!”

Daniel storms out of the bathroom. For a moment, all I can hear is my own ragged breathing. Water still drips from the shower, pooling under my knees. The air smells like damp fear and iron.

Downstairs, a door slams. Footsteps. Then silence. Maybe he's gone. Maybe it's over.

But I know better.

The house is filled with the kind of quiet that comes before a scream. My pulse thunders in my ears. And then it starts again: the heavy tread on the stairs, faster this time, heavier.

When Daniel bursts back into the bathroom, he looks like someone else. His pupils blown wide, his face slick with sweat.

Possessed.

In his hand: a teaspoon.

For a second, my mind refuses to register it. The banality of it. A kitchen spoon, shining under the harsh light. But then I see how tightly he's gripping it, the tremor in his wrist, and suddenly it's worse than any knife.

He drops to his knees in front of me, grabs my throat, jerking my head back so hard my neck cracks. His breath is sour, inches from my face.

"This is your last chance," he spits. "Tell me you can transfer the money tonight."

"Daniel, please—"

He raises the spoon.

"Or I'll take your eye out."

The words hit like a gunshot. My vision tunnels.

The metal is cold when it touches my skin. He presses the rounded tip into the flesh just below my eyelid, enough to make the world blur. My body tries to flinch, but the tape holds me fast.

"Tell me!" he shouts. His voice cracks, part rage, part despair.

"I can't," I choke out. "Daniel, I can't—"

The spoon presses harder. My eye floods with tears, and somewhere deep in the dark part of me that still thinks logically, I realise he will actually do it.

Then his grip tightens.

And the world narrows to that small, terrible point of pressure as he pushes the spoon in.

Chapter 52

SAM

The vase on the windowsill is the nearest heavy thing, and violent improvisation is a practised skill of Sam's.

He swings.

The vase connects with a wet, indisputable *thunk* against the man's temple. He drops the spoon as if it has burned him. For a dizzy second, he falls back, mouth open, eyes widening.

Tom gasps for breath as his attacker's hand is released from his throat.

The assailant recovers faster than a person should. He lunges like a dog with a taste for blood, grabbing at Sam with frantic anger, fingers clawing for anything to hold. The two of them collapse backwards, a tangle of limbs and rage on the landing. Sam feels a knee slam into his ribs, a deep breath exiting his lungs in a flash. The adrenaline comes next, coursing through his body. Instinct takes over, and he hits back.

They roll across the wood floor. His attacker lands a punch that stings across Sam's jaw. Sam is faster, cleverer in the sorts of scrapes that require improvisation and answers with the heel of his hand to the face. He hooks an ankle, and the man overbalances. Sam plants a foot and gives him a hard shove.

For a split second, the man's eye betrays him, an understanding that this is game over, before he tumbles down the stairs in a horrible, ungainly flop. The sound of him hitting wood is grotesque and final: a thud and then silence.

Sam is up instantly, standing on the landing with his heart in his palms, listening for a startled groan or any signs of movement.

Nothing. The body lies silently at the bottom of the stairs.

Sam massages his ribs, still stinging from the blow they received. He's been in more fights than he can count. He grew up around people who solved problems with fists first and feelings later. He learned early that you don't always win, but you make sure they remember you were there.

Violence isn't new to him. It's muscle memory.

After a final look at the crumpled body at the foot of the stairs, Sam rushes back to the bathroom. "You okay?" he asks.

Tom is still coughing and just nods through it.

Sam scrabbles through the bathroom cabinet like a man picking through pockets after a fight, until his fingers close around a pair of tiny nail scissors. He slices through the tape around Tom's wrists in one decisive sweep. The skin underneath is red and raw, his hands trembling.

Tom slumps backwards against the tiles, still coughing. Sam pauses, allowing him to catch his breath. His eyes are enormous. "You… how did you—" His voice breaks. "Why are you here?"

Sam thinks fast. The truth that he'd been watching the CCTV, that he'd seen his attacker knock him out in the bedroom, can't be shared.

"I came back," he says instead. "James and Pete had a rough day. I came to give you the heads up."

"What happened?" Tom fires back.

"That doesn't matter now. How are you feeling?"

Tom's face crumples from confusion into gratitude. "Thank you," he manages.

"Who was that?" Sam asks.

"Daniel…my ex-husband," Tom admits. "He's been following me, coming into my house. He's after money. You were right earlier when you said you saw him trying to get in. I think he has my spare key."

"Shit, you might need to get the locks changed then."

Tom almost laughs. "You think?"

So, it was an ex. Exactly the kind of complication we don't need right now.

Sam holds out a hand and pulls Tom up. They move to the landing together and peer down.

The floor is empty.

"Where is he?" Tom whispers, panic lacing his voice now.

“He was here,” Sam confirms. “He was at the bottom of the stairs.”

“I need to call the police,” Tom says, because that is what you are supposed to do when someone assaults you. His hands are still shaking; his voice will not be steadied by the legalities Sam is about to articulate.

“No,” Sam says quickly. The word is small, but clear.

Tom blinks. “What?”

“I don’t want the police here while I’m here,” Sam says. He watches Tom register his look, the way his brows pull together like he’s trying to problem-solve a foreign language. “I’ve had a… history with the police before. It’s complicated.”

Tom’s jaw tenses. “Okay… but I need to call them.”

“Yeah, I know. I just don’t want to be involved.”

Tom scrunches his face, still processing what’s unfolded tonight.

“I’ll go, then you can call them. You okay to be alone?” Sam asks.

Tom nods, the movement small. “Thank you.”

They both go downstairs for one final check to make sure Daniel is not still in the house, then Sam turns and leaves as quickly as he can out the front door. Keeping an eye out for any movement around him, he darts to his car and drives away.

That was a detour Sam hadn’t planned for tonight.

When he saw events unfolding on the CCTV, Sam knew he had to intervene. He’s not some cape-wearing saviour; he doesn’t believe in being a hero. But he knows when a situation needs handling, and Tom dead on a bathroom floor would have been very bad for business.

Tom needs to stay upright and focused. That’s what makes him useful.

Daniel was noise, a dangerous noise, and Sam doesn’t tolerate interference.

Not from ex-husbands, not from anyone.

Whatever is in motion, Tom still has a part to play.

And Sam intends to keep the stage clear.

Chapter 53

TOM

As Sam disappears up the road, I close the door, my hand still softly shaking. I'm not sure if it's the fear or the fact that I'm still in soaking clothes.

I keep replaying it: the water, the towel, Daniel's hands around my throat. Every second loops like a twisted training video.

I should be one eye down, maybe two. Maybe dead. If Sam hadn't turned up when he did—

I stop that thought before it finishes because the ending is obvious and horrifying. Sam saved my life. I can't even remember why he was here, but if he hadn't been…

And Daniel. Jesus, Daniel.

I thought I knew what unhinged looked like. I've seen his anger, his cruelty and control, but this was something else entirely. Something cracked and desperate.

I knew about his gambling problem when we were together, and the debts. Since we split, things have clearly escalated. He got involved with dangerous people, enough to drive him to this.

But what is sticking with me is what he said about Guy.

My stomach lurches.

He got what was coming to him.

That's what he said.

I don't want to consider what Daniel was suggesting. Could he be responsible for Guy's death? I wouldn't want to believe it. But after tonight, Daniel's violent, unhinged behaviour, it seems more than possible.

And the videos of Guy and me together, going to our hotel. I never knew how Daniel found out. I always wondered if it was Evelyn, Guy's wife, that she secretly always knew, her phone calls and endless texts about Guy's murder just a way of punishing me further for my infidelity.

But… Craig?

Craig. My best friend. My constant. The man who has been in my corner through everything. My relationship with Daniel, my father's death, and Guy's murder. I've trusted him implicitly for years.

He wouldn't do that. Would he?

And yet, Sam said Craig lied. Lied about James being investigated. And Daniel said Craig sent the video. And my phone had blocked Daniel. The only person with the opportunity to block him was…Craig.

My head is pounding.

I grab my phone. The screen glows brightly against the dark of the living room. I scroll to Craig's name and hit call before I can talk myself out of it.

He answers on the second ring. "Tom? What's wrong?" His voice is calm but alert, that professional police tone that says he's in control before I even start.

"He broke in," I say. My voice comes out as a whisper. "Daniel. He broke into my house. He tied me up, Craig. He—" I can't say the word waterboarded. It feels absurd, cinematic. "He was going to kill me. Sam was here. He—he saved me."

There's a sharp inhale. "What?"

"He's gone now," I continue. "Daniel. He's—he fell down the stairs, I think, but when we looked again, he was gone."

"Okay. Okay, listen to me," Craig says quickly. "You need to stay where you are. Don't go outside. I'll call it in right now. We'll get a unit round, and I'll be there in fifteen minutes."

But something inside me hardens "No."

"Tom—"

"No, Craig." The words fire out faster now, driven by anger and betrayal. "I need you to answer a question first. Did you send Daniel videos of Guy and me?"

Craig doesn't answer. Not right away. And that silence, just a heartbeat too long, detonates inside me.

"Oh, my God," I whisper. "You did."

"Tom—"

"You did! He told me! He said you sent it! That's how he knew! That's how he found out!"

His voice changes, quiet, deliberate. "Tom, I did what I had to do to—"

My heart spikes. "What you had to do? You gave him proof!"

"I was protecting you," Craig says. "You weren't safe with him. You couldn't see it, but I could. You think I enjoyed it? I did what I thought would make him go."

My laugh comes out wrong, a dry, shocked sound full of disbelief. "You think that helped? You think sending him a video of me with another man helped?"

"You were never going to leave him, Tom, until I showed you what he was capable of," Craig says, his voice growing tighter.

It was the revelation of the videos, which pushed Daniel to be violent, leading to the final breakdown in our relationship "So, you wanted him to find out so he would hit me?!"

"No! I didn't know he would go that far, but you were never going to leave him. This was the best thing for you."

"I nearly had my eye pulled out with a teaspoon. None of this is the best thing for me!"

"Jesus, Tom, let me come over now?"

I'm pacing without realising. The floorboards creak. My body doesn't know where to put the anger. It's burning holes through my skin. "You went into my phone, too, didn't you? You blocked him."

Craig sighs. "Yes. I had to."

"You *had* to?"

"He was trying to get back into your life again, Tom. After everything. After what he did to you. I couldn't just watch you fall back into it. He manipulates you. You're not yourself around him. I had to make it stop."

"By spying on me?"

"By keeping you safe."

"Safe?" I laugh again, though it sounds more like a choke. "You call this safe? He tied me up, Craig! He nearly killed me. And I think he killed Guy, too."

"What? Guy?"

"He more or less confessed to it! Said Guy got what was coming to him! And that was your doing, Craig! Daniel didn't know who Guy was until you sent him those videos!"

"Tom—"

"And now he's dead, and I don't think I can ever forgive you for that."

There's another heavy silence before he continues, Craig's voice now calm and clear. "I'm still sending the police, Tom. You need to stay put. Do you understand me? Don't go anywhere. Don't call anyone else. Just stay in the house."

I swallow hard, my throat dry and sore. "I don't want your help," I say finally. "Not anymore."

"Tom—"

"I mean it, Craig. Stay away."

I hang up before he can answer.

For a moment, there's only silence. My reflection stares back at me in the dark TV screen, something halfway between fury and shock.

The silence is shattered by the sound of my doorbell, the shrill ring making me jump.

I'm frozen, terrified at who could be on the other side of the door.

The doorbell rings again.

I look at my watch: 00:02

Midnight visitors don't bring good news.

Chapter 54

PHIL

Phil's breath creates a fog ahead of him as he walks, hands deep in the pockets of his coat. The night is sharp with a biting cold. It's late, and it's far too late to be walking the backstreets of Bristol. But Phil needs to clear his head before he gets home.

He told his husband, Craig, that he was on another day. Not the most creative of lies, but they are the ones that work the best. Something about meeting a guy from Scruff who collects Star Wars LEGO and has a questionable taste for craft beer. As expected, no questions asked.

That's the beauty of a polyamorous relationship: you don't have to lie.

Until you do.

He hates it. The deception sits uncomfortably in his chest, getting heavier with each new lie. But some things can't be explained. Not yet anyway.

The truth could destroy everything.

The street is quiet, except for the occasional hiss of passing cars. Bright lights paint the damp pavement orange, his shadow chasing him down the street. He takes a turn down a narrow lane, cutting through towards the main road. He knows every shortcut by heart, having done it a thousand times.

Phil hadn't planned to see James tonight. But things had escalated at James's house, and they had to reconvene. Every time they met, it came with a quiet kind of dread that he carried home. A dread he needed to walk off before he stepped through the door at home.

The wheels of their plan were in motion, but it demanded precision, or this whole thing could fall apart.

For the last half mile of his walk, Phil has been telling himself he's done everything as agreed. Ever call, every message, every meeting, all followed the plan to the letter. He's been painfully careful with the detail because, with James, precision isn't optional.

And things are at a knife-edge now.

But no one can know what they're planning. Not Craig. Not anyone. Because if they did, if anyone even suspected, it wouldn't just be the plan that went up in flames.

And with so much at stake, there can be no loose ends.

His phone rings. Craig.

He hesitates before answering. "Hey."

"Where are you?" Craig's voice is the tight, serious work voice that means something's happened.

"About five minutes away. Why?"

"It's Tom," Craig says. "Daniel broke in. Assaulted him."

Phil stops walking. The cold air feels denser suddenly. "What?"

"He's okay. Well, not okay, but alive. I'm about to call it in and go over."

Phil swallows hard. "Jesus, Craig. Is he ok?"

"No, not really. It's a long story. I'll fill you in when I'm home, although not sure when that will be."

"Okay, do you want me to come with you?"

"No, no, get to bed," Craig says. "Stay home, I'll message when I know more."

"Yeah. Okay."

But before he can say anything else, the sound comes.

Tyres.

Fast.

Behind him.

A flash of headlights arcs across the pavement. The roar of an engine.

He turns instinctively, raising a hand against the glare.

And the car is already there, hurtling towards him, too close, too fast.

The bumper catches his hip, a violent, stunning blow that lifts him off his feet. The world spins like chaos. The impact knocks the phone from his hand, Craig's voice still crackling faintly through the speaker.

Phil hits the bonnet, the wind slamming out of him, then tumbles over the roof, down, hard onto the pavement. Pain blooms sharply through his ribs, his wrist, the side of his face.

For a second, there's no sound but his pulse, a thumping between his ears.

Then, the car screeches around the corner, its red taillights disappearing into the night.

Phil lies there, face aching, cheek against the wet road, his lungs burning with each breath. Everything hurts. His vision blurs at the edges as the pain swoops in.

On the ground beside him, his phone is still on. Craig's voice, tinny with panic:

"Phil? Phil! What the hell was that? Phil, answer me!"

Darkness.

Chapter 55

TOM

“Hello?” I say, through the door.

“Tom?” a female voice replies.

Emma.

I open the door with the chain still on because tonight has already featured waterboarding, a head injury, and an unexpected cameo from a teaspoon. I’m not taking chances.

“Tom!” Emma breathes, hair wild, cheeks flushed, like she’s jogged here through a hurricane. “Thank God.”

Of course, it’s Emma. Midnight and panic are absolutely her brand.

I slip the chain and let her in. She scans my flat like danger might be lurking. "Sorry for coming so late. I messaged you, but you didn’t reply. And then Pete—" She stops, hand to chest. "Can I sit? I’m suddenly very aware my heart’s pounding."

“Join the club,” I say, closing the door.

We move to the living room. I’m aware I look a state, dressed in a soaked shirt, damp, frazzled hair, bruise blooming beneath my eye. I perch on the arm of a chair because sitting properly feels like a commitment.

“What’s happened?” I ask.

“Pete called me,” Emma says, her voice rigid. “About twenty minutes ago. He sounded panicked, almost hysterical. He said James was ‘going insane’. Those were his exact words. Then, there was more shouting, and the line went dead.”

I’m already reaching for my phone. “We need to call the police.”

“No,” she says immediately, too quickly.

My thumb hovers. "Why not?"

"Because I'm not on good terms with them," she says, with the airy defensiveness of someone describing a bad Tinder date rather than a public institution.

"Oh, you too," I say, thinking of my similar conversation with Sam earlier this evening, and then the irritation bubbles up. "No one seems to want to get the police involved these days, even though it is literally the most sensible thing to do."

Emma's chin lifts. "Yes, well, I have a bit of…history with them."

"Yes, so I hear. Two years for fraud, wasn't it?"

Her eyes widen, the truth hitting her like a slap. She pauses, then replies. "Look, yes, I've done stupid things. Some desperate things. I grew up very cushioned, and then the cushion was ripped away, and turns out I don't have the soft skills for poverty. I made bad choices to keep myself… afloat." She flutters a hand. "That's not who I am now."

"Right, but also, haven't you just been charged with arson?" I add.

She actually recoils. "No. Well, yes. But I absolutely didn't do it. I have an alibi. I'm getting it sorted."

I can just nod at this point. Emma's criminal past and present are the least of my worries.

"I know what you think of me," she continues, softer. "Unstable, erratic, the human embodiment of a car alarm. Fine. But I love my brother, and I know Pete knows more than he's saying. If James is terrorising him, he won't talk to anyone. If we get Pete safe, he will. It's the only way I find out what happened to Chris." She swallows. "Please, Tom. Help me help him."

The words knot in my throat. I want to blurt the truth: Chris isn't a mystery to find. He's a body in a video. A knife to the neck from James.

But I don't.

Not without Pete. Not after what I saw. Not when telling her right now would be like smashing a stained-glass window with my bare hands.

I try for practical instead. "If James is as dangerous as you say—"

"As I know," she corrects, a little fierce. "And as you've started to realise."

"—then going there without the police is stupid."

"Stupid," she agrees. "But necessary." Her eyes shine with that manic determination I used to admire in contestants on The Apprentice right before they said something stupid. "If James is in a rage and thinks Pete's called for help, we can't afford uniforms on the doorstep. He'll lock down, deny everything, cut the power, whatever he does. If we go now, we might actually reach Pete."

"And what?" I ask. "Knock? Ask politely if we can collect our terrified friend from the bathroom?"

She leans forward. "You've been in that house. You know the layout. You can get us in. We don't need the whole cavalry, just ten quiet minutes with Pete."

Every sensible part of me is shouting no. Call the police.

But calling the police would mean staying here, and staying here means replaying the bathroom, the towel, the sound of Daniel's breath in my ear. It means changing locks and statements and escalating things with Daniel to a whole place I'm not ready for tonight.

Daniel hurt me tonight. But he also taught me a brutal lesson: timing can mean the difference between having your eyeball in or out of your body. Thank god again for Sam intervening. Sitting here reminds me that every second of inaction counts.

Emma's plan is dangerous and illogical and probably exactly how people end up on the wrong side of a headline, but it is action. It is doing something before someone else can do something to Pete or to me.

If I'm going to be scared, I'd rather be scared on my feet than waiting for another silhouette at the foot of my bed.

"Please," she says, softly. "If I thought I could do it alone, I would. But I can't."

I breathe out, resigned to my fate. "Give me two minutes."

I head to the study to grab my keys, and I stop.

The desk looks wrong. Not messy. Empty. I stare at the space where the laptop should be, and the cold creeps up my spine like a tape measure.

No laptop.

Daniel must have taken it earlier, while I was unconscious or when he fled the house. Every nerve inside me screams as it hits me: the video of James killing Chris was on there.

And now: gone.

"Everything okay?" Emma calls from the hall.

Instead of responding, I think about the CCTV videos on the desktop. Would he look at those? No, he's looking for money. He's probably trying to break into my bank accounts as we speak. I need to call the police, report this mess, change the locks. Shit, so much to get on top of, but this can wait for an hour, until we bring Pete back safely to mine.

There's no point explaining to her about the laptop, Daniel, our history, the events of tonight. It's not a quick story, and time is short. Instead, I grab my keys, throw on my trainers and head for the door. "Let's go."

As we head to the door, Buster watches us from the stairs like a landlord.

"I'll drive," I say.

"I brought my car," she replies. "Separate vehicles, fewer chances of being boxed in. And I'm not great at… collaborative parallel parking."

Fair. We head out the door, getting into our respective cars and drive into the night.

Chapter 56

EMMA

Emma leaves Tom's house and heads to her car. The air is wet with drizzle, and it stings her cheeks as she walks down the quiet Bristol street. Streetlights stretch long shadows across the pavement, her heels clicking like punctuation marks with every step.

She slips into her car and pulls away through the mist into the night.

Her mind loops through the conversation with Tom. He looked shattered, and with good reason. But she had to push him not to call the police and join her. Pete could be in real danger, and she couldn't let him stall with his caution. There isn't time for careful anymore.

The car hums beneath her as she drives through the half-empty streets, and her thoughts slide backwards, uninvited.

She hadn't been born into desperation. The Christiansons were wealthy and respected, the sort of family who sent smug Christmas cards with matching sweaters and charitable donations listed beneath their signatures. Her father, Leonard, was a charming and persuasive investment adviser, hugely successful and entirely allergic to regulation. When the investigation came, it came quietly: a handful of frozen accounts, whispered settlements, a "career pause" that became permanent.

Emma was seventeen when she realised money was oxygen and that her family was learning to live without it.

She had to learn the vocabulary of survival, a careful mix of networking, embellishing and bluffing. By her late twenties, she was consulting for small charities: raising funds, writing proposals, making people feel seen. She was very good at making people feel seen.

What she was really doing was siphoning funds to herself: grants that never existed, donations transferred into bogus bank accounts, which ended up in her pockets.

It wasn't greed, she told herself. It was a necessity. Just creative accounting, a victimless crime.

Until one of the charities folded. Until the auditors arrived. Until her bright-eyed, ambitious colleague, Fiona, opened her mouth and handed Emma's name over like a gift.

Prison was less dramatic than she'd imagined. The kind of place that teaches you about calm and rage in equal measure. She served twenty-four months.

She didn't plan to see Fiona again after her release. But the Gods of coincidence were working against her that Saturday afternoon as she wandered into a cafe in Borough Market. There she was ordering tea and a scone like she hadn't single-handedly ripped Emma's life apart. They'd argued loudly, and some regretful words were shared between them.

A few days later, Fiona's house burned down. Fiona's husband had died. The police called it arson. And soon, Emma Christianson became the name on everyone's lips linked to a crime of alleged revenge.

There was some evidence, circumstantial at best, that pointed the finger at Emma. The fact that her last words to Fiona in the packed cafe were, "I hope you and that fucking ugly husband of yours die and burn in hell," didn't exactly work in her favour. But it was enough to get her charged. And more than enough people to testify against her.

She has an alibi, though. Well, nearly.

She checks the date on her phone as she so regularly does.

Thirteen days left.

Thirteen days until her trial begins. That's how long she has until she has to get the evidence to prove her innocence.

And this is why she needs to find Chris.

Their relationship had always been stormy at best, equal parts devotion and destruction. They did love each other in that chaotic, complicated family way, but with opposing personalities and a traumatic childhood history, this was never easy. Emma was the family hurricane, always scheming, never pausing for a breath. Chris was stillness and calm. He grounded her, but also infuriated her with his moral compass, constantly pointing to disappointment.

They hadn't spoken for four years. Chris didn't even know she'd been in prison until long after she'd served her time. But desperation has its own gravity, and one night, when her bank account was gasping, Emma found herself driving to find him.

She told herself it was about making peace and building bridges, but she already knew Chris had money. Money real enough to help her. For weeks, she watched from a distance, sitting in her car, tracking his daily movements that led her to the house. The house she later learnt was James & Pete's.

That night, she knocked on the door, and a young man answered. Pete. Chris wasn't home. So she smiled, said she was his sister and accepted an awkward but brief invitation inside.

That was the night of the fire.

When Chris found out about her visit, he reached out. They began texting, cautiously rebuilding their fragile relationship.

When she was hurled into the police station the following week and charged with arson, her only alibi was her visit to that house. They apparently tried to contact Pete a few times, but he never responded. Chris was her best way in. Her only chance to convince Pete.

Then Chris disappeared.

No trace. No explanation. Just gone. As was her one chance at proving she didn't light that match

Since then, she'd tried everything. Messaging Pete, begging him to help. Pleading that she only needed him to say they'd spoken that night, to confirm she'd been there before the fire started. But Pete was scared. He said James would never allow it, didn't want him involved, wanted him to stay away from the police.

If only James were out of the picture.

Now, as she drives through the quiet streets, that conversation replays over and over. If she can't find Chris, she needs Pete. Or at least, she needs James out of the way. Without him, she might finally get to the truth.

And to her freedom.

Yes, she wants to find her brother. Of course she does. But beneath the guilt and nostalgia, there's a deeper truth she can't escape.

She doesn't just want her brother.

She needs her alibi.

And time is running out.

Chapter 57

DANIEL

Daniel sits in the car, engine off, the only sound the low hiss of rain on the windscreen. His body throbs with pain. His ribs and shoulder ache, and there is a dull pulse behind his eyes from where he hit the stairs. He grips the steering wheel, trying to steady his breathing, but his chest still rattles.

The laptop sits on the passenger seat. His last hope.

He's already past his midnight deadline. The people he owes don't do grace periods. They do sharp, physical reminders.

He checks his phone again. No new messages, but he knows they're coming. They know where he lives. They know his car. They'll be looking in all the right places. If Tom's called the police, and he will have, then there'll be sirens in the mix too. The debt collectors and the law, a tag team designed to crush whatever's left of him.

He looks at the laptop again and rubs his jaw. This was his desperate last attempt: to spend the last few hours trying to get into Tom's online banking. He hadn't tried before because he didn't want it flagged if he got it wrong. But we're beyond that now.

Tom inherited over a million. Daniel knows it. He was married to him. He's entitled to a share. Legally, ethically. That's what he told himself at first.

But before he even got started with his banking, he noticed the video files. A folder on the desktop that wasn't there last time he looked.

He wasn't really interested in them, but curiosity is a weakness he's never learned to master. He clicked. And then clicked again.

What he saw made his stomach turn.

The first few were small: arguments, shouting, a shove, a thrown glass. Then worse: violence, fear. Always the same tall, angry man and another man taking the hits. But the final video… that one he watched twice.

The fight in the kitchen. The chaos. The man — the victim — trying to fight back, failing. And the knife. Over and over.

Daniel had seen death before, but not like that.

He recognised the attacker. Not the name, but the face. He'd seen him leave the same house he'd watched Tom and his new boyfriend come out of as he followed them.

So, this is what Tom's caught up in. Wealth, deceit, violence.

And maybe, just maybe, opportunity.

He can use this. A video of a man being murdered. That's leverage. That's worth something. If the people in that house are mixed up in it, they'll pay to make it go away.

He doesn't need much. Just enough to disappear. Five hundred thousand. That's the figure echoing in his skull. Enough to clear the debts and start over somewhere warm.

He leans back and stares out the windscreen.

He's parked outside their house. It's a handsome place. He can smell the money from here.

He reaches into the glove compartment and pulls out the gun. He bought it from one of the men who lent him money, before their relationship soured. He'd gone back to his house to grab it. After what happened at Tom's earlier, it was clear he needed some added protection.

He doesn't plan to use it. Not really. But he's also out of time, and desperation can bring out new sides of you.

He imagines how it'll go. Knock on the door. Calm voice. "We need to talk." Show them the video. Let them see the problem. Let them understand that unless he gets what he wants, that footage will find its way into the public. Simple business.

He's good at sounding reasonable, even when he's drowning.

Then he closes the laptop, tucks it under his arm, and opens the car door. The rain hits like cold needles. He pulls up his collar and starts walking toward the house.

His steps are slow and deliberate. The gun feels heavier with every one.

He hesitates at the gate. This is it. The final roll of the dice. The house looms over him, silent, unaware that its walls are about to hold one more desperate act.

Chapter 58

TOM

Rain batters the windscreen so hard that it sounds like a round of applause from hell. As I drive down the road, I can barely see ahead of me, streaks of white lines appearing for a moment as the wipers pass. My phone, connected to my car, rings, illuminating the screen of my dashboard.

Pete.

I answer it with an anguished tap. "Pete? What's going on?"

His voice is frantic. "Tom—Tom, I don't know what to do."

"What's happening? Are you okay?"

"He's completely lost it. I've never seen him this bad."

"Where are you?"

"In the bathroom," he pants. "I've locked the door. He's downstairs. I can hear him. He's smashing things."

My heart spikes. "Pete, listen to me, stay in there. I'm on my way."

"No!" His voice cracks. "If he sees you, he'll kill you."

"Emma called," I say quickly. "She told me. I was already heading over. Just hold on."

"I think he's broken my rib," Pete whispers. His breath comes in short, painful bursts. "I can't breathe properly."

The words hit like a glass of ice water to the face. "Oh my God, Pete. You need to get out of there."

"I can't. I can't get past him. And I can't jump the window, it's too high. Tom, he's gone mental."

"Okay, okay, listen," I say, forcing myself to stay calm. "I need to call the police. If your rib is broken, you need medical attention. I know what James is capable of. He could kill you, too."

There's a pause. "What do you mean?"

"I saw it," I admit. "On the CCTV. I know he killed Chris."

Silence. For a few seconds, all I hear is the rain and the engine.

Then Pete says, barely audible, "You what?"

"I saw the video, Pete. He stabbed him. In your kitchen."

A broken sound escapes him, part sob, part disbelief. "Jesus Christ… You shouldn't have seen that. I thought you told me you hadn't watched them."

"I know, I'm sorry I lied. I copied them onto my laptop. I had to! I was trying to help you! But listen, we can go to the police. We can end this. Together."

"No," Pete says quickly. "No, we can't."

"Of course we can. He murdered someone, Pete. There's clear proof of it."

"I helped him," he blurts out.

My stomach twists. "What?"

"I helped him bury Chris." His voice fractures, shaking apart. "After it happened. I didn't have a choice, Tom. He made me do it. He said if I told anyone, he'd kill me."

For a moment, I can't breathe. "Pete…"

"He said we'd both go down for it. He had messages, photos, stuff that makes it look like I planned it."

"Look, if he coerced you into it, the police will understand when they see the videos of how he's been treating you—"

"No! I'll go down for it too. I can't go to prison!" He's sobbing now. The sound of him crying while trying to keep his voice low makes something inside me tear open.

"Pete, listen to me," I say, eyes fixed on the wet blur of the road. "You were scared. You didn't have a choice. The police will understand that."

"You don't get it," he says. "He's clever. He said if I leave, he'll make sure I take the fall."

Although I don't agree with him, now's not the time to debate this. The priority is to get Pete out of the house. Dealing with the police can be our next issue.

The phone rustles like he's moving. I hear something slam against the door from the other side.

"Pete?!"

"He's outside," Pete whispers. "He's shouting. He knows I'm in here."

My heart lurches. "Stay quiet. Don't say anything."

The sound that comes through next freezes me: James's voice, faint but furious, shouting Pete's name over and over, words too muffled to make out.

Then a heavy bang. The thud of a door taking a hit. Another.

"I'm going to fucking kill you!" I hear through the phone.

"Tom," Pete says, barely breathing. "He's going to break it."

"I'm nearly there," I lie. "Just hang on."

There's a crash, something splintering, maybe the bathroom cabinet, maybe the doorframe.

"Pete, talk to me. Are you okay?"

"Tom, please don't come in. He'll kill you, too."

A loud crash cuts me off. The sound of shattering glass, a scream.

Then silence.

"Pete?!"

Nothing.

I shout his name, but the line's gone dead.

I should call the police.

No. I'll get there first. Then I'll call.

The rain comes down harder, hammering the roof, blurring everything. I jam the car into gear and speed off.

For a split second, my dad's face flashes in my mind: the hospital room, the machines, the moment I stepped out for a coffee and came back too late.

Not again.

I won't lose someone else because I hesitated.

Chapter 59

TOM

I park a street over and kill the engine. My hands are shaking so badly as I pull the handle to open the car door. I get out, pull my hood up, and run to the lane at the side of the house.

Fifteen minutes since Pete hung up. Fifteen minutes of worst-case scenarios looping like a broken trailer in my skull. In the moment, I don't think to call the police. Instead, I run down the path, cut through the trees into James and Pete's back garden, as I did on my last visit.

My heart is in my mouth as I approach the back door, which is locked. My fingers find the spare key, still tucked under the plant pot, and I slowly unlock the door and enter.

Inside, it's unnervingly quiet.

Then, a sound tears through it.

A voice, raw and shredded. "I can't take this anymore!" A slam. Something metal skitters.

James.

Another ragged shout. "I've had enough!"

My legs are moving before my brain agrees. I move down the hall and stop dead just before the kitchen: the place is wrecked. A chair on its side. A drawer yanked open, cutlery splayed like a silver explosion.

Red smears of blood on the floor. Too many.

My stomach flips. Who's bleeding?

Another voice from the kitchen, this time Pete. "Please," he says. "We can find a way to make this work."

"Don't beg," James snarls back. "Don't you dare beg me now."

I move, peering into the kitchen. Pete is slumped in the far corner by the radiator, arms wrapped around his ribs, face grey. James is half-turned toward him, half-turned toward his own reflection, like a man arguing with two realities at once. He's shaking. He looks both furious and broken, fuelled by rage.

He sees me in the mirror first. Our eyes meet in that warped, splintered glass. For a beat, nobody breathes.

Then he turns, very slow, like a storm changing direction.

"What are you doing in our house?" he asks softly, which is worse than shouting.

"I'm taking him away," I say. The words leave my mouth without permission. "This ends tonight."

I didn't notice it immediately, but James is holding a knife.

I freeze.

James smiles, and there is nothing human in it. "You have no idea who you're dealing with."

Pete makes a small sound, tries to stand, can't. I want to dart towards him, but there's an angry James and a knife blocking my way.

"Pete—"

"You don't know him," James says. "Not like I do."

"I know enough," I say, and my voice shakes, but I don't care. "I know you hurt him. And I know about Chris."

There's a flicker in his eyes as the name lands. He could deny it. He doesn't.

"I've seen the video," I say. "In the kitchen. I know you killed him."

I'm not sure antagonising him like this is the best idea. My rough, unthought-through plan revolves around winding him up so he comes at me with the knife rather than Pete. I have room to run, giving Pete a chance to reach safety.

"You don't have a fucking clue what you're dealing with," James hisses.

"I think you're a fucking psychopath!"

"You don't know anything about me!"

"I know you're a monster!" I scream at him. "And Pete deserves better than you."

James stares at me. "You're so fucking naïve!" he screams, turning to Pete. "I just want him dead!"

And with that, rather than coming at me, James lunges at Pete, knife in hand. All Pete can do, backed into the wall, is throw his hands up as cover.

Instinct detonates. I launch. I catch the back of James's shirt and wrench him off balance. The knife hand slices a hair's breadth past Pete. James stumbles, his heel hooks the tiles, and he collapses back into me. Our weight drives me backwards, and I hit the floor with James on top of me, hard enough to wind me.

The knife skitters out of his grip and clatters to the side as he rolls. I roll with him, legs tangling, and shove my weight across his chest to pin him. His body is a machine of muscle and panic. He thrashes, digging elbows, trying to wrench free. My legs clasp around him, holding him to the floor. My left arm snakes up and finds his throat, and I clamp around it because if I don't choke him, he will kill me and then Pete. He chokes, eyes wide and red-rimmed, and the sound he makes is half-human, half-animal.

We wrestle for the knife as if two magnets had been thrown onto a table. His spare hand darts, fingers like claws, and finds the blade first.

For a breathless instant, he has it, fingers closing on cold metal. He pulls his arm back, aiming at me, at my side.

Then, movement from nowhere.

Emma.

She hits him like a freight train.

She dives across him and slams her weight down, her fingers looping around his wrist. James snarls and tries to throw her off; the three of us become a knot of limbs and sound.

Straddling him, Emma's hands are on his arms, and for a second, I think she will be ripped away. She grits her teeth, pins, and forces him down. In the churn of limbs, her hand finds the blade, or the blade finds her.

Either way, it drives forward.

A wet, horrific rasp ruptures the air. James' body loosens as a wordless cry rips free of him.

Warmth spills across my body.

He doesn't shout again. His thrashing stumbles and dies. I am still wrapped around him, feeling the sudden, ridiculous lightness as his body goes slack against mine.

Emma scrambles back on her knees, eyes wide and wet, breathing like someone who's just sprinted across a football pitch.

I push myself up, hands slick. I step away, and together, Emma and I look down at the man lying below us.

Blood seeps around us as the kitchen clock ticks like a countdown.

James is dead.

Chapter 60

TOM

I don't know how long I stand there. As if I've disconnected from my body, I'm frozen in the kitchen, the edges of my vision blurring.

I can't move.

Every sound has stopped, replaced by a terrifying, crisp silence.

James is on the floor, a heap of flesh, his arms and legs spread out. His eyes are still open, staring at the ceiling.

There's blood — so much blood — pooling and spreading, tracing the cracks between the tiles, creeping toward my shoes. My heartbeat pulsates with such velocity that it feels like it's breaking free from my chest.

I realise, with a hollow sort of clarity, that there's no coming back from this — for him, or for any of us.

Emma has become a tornado of motion. She's on the other side of the room, hands to her face, then twisting her hair, then a sudden, ferocious stillness when she realises the practicalities of the moment. She keeps glancing at James's body with that expression that's a mixture of terror and calculation.

I turn to Pete, who's pressed into the corner of the kitchen. His eyes are unfocused as if someone has left a light on inside his head, but the thoughts have departed. He's breathing, but it's shallow, almost calm, having tumbled deep into shock.

I don't know what to do about James's body. But Pete, Pete, I can help. I rush to him. "Are you ok?"

He doesn't respond, his eyes still glazed over. I grip his arm and lift him. I guide him to the sofa and sit him down like he's a person I'm borrowing for a minute.

"Wine," he says. One word. Not a request. A flat instruction.

Rather than question his request, I move on autopilot. I grab a glass and the bottle of red already open on the side. Pouring him a large glass. I hand it to him because it's something to do, a gesture that says I am still here. He takes it, brings it to his lips, and for the first time, his fingers actually register as fingers, gripping the stem like someone trying to remember how to function normally.

I turn to Emma. "Are you okay?"

She nods.

"We need to call the police," I say. Of course I do.

"No," Emma says, flat and fast. She turns and looks at me as if I've suggested we bring in a circus. "We can't call the police."

My shoulders give a small, reflexive shrug of disbelief. "What? What do you mean? He's dead, we have to."

"We pinned him down. Tom, we need to—"

"It was self-defence. He was coming for all of us. He had a knife."

"It will look like murder," she tells me.

"It wasn't murder!"

"We pinned him down and stabbed him."

"You stabbed him!" I fire back, instantly regretting it. This isn't the time to turn against each other.

"It was an accident!" Emma fires back.

"Exactly!"

Her eyes glitter with tears, but there's an edge to them that is not sorrow so much as a cold arithmetic.

"They won't see it that way. Not with me, I know what they will say."

"They will when they see what James is like," I say, remembering the videos I have.

"What do you mean?"

"There are videos from the CCTV around the house. Of James being aggressive and violent. It paints a picture of who he is."

"So, you did get access to the CCTV?

"Yes, on the laptop upstairs."

"So, what we did, that would be recorded too?" she asks.

I hadn't thought of this, but now, yes, it must have. I nod. "I think so."

Emma's face hardens. "We need to see it before we call the police. We need to know what it really looks like when we play it back, so it definitely appears to be self-defence. And if not, we can delete it."

"Okay," I reluctantly agree. I hesitate to leave Pete alone, but I have no choice. "Come with me."

We rush out of the kitchen to the study. The laptop is closed. The Mac's sleep light is a smug little dot. I open it, and the password prompt is waiting.

"Do you know the password?" Emma asks.

"No, I need Pete's Apple Watch to unlock it for me. That's how I got in last time."

I run to the bedroom to find his charging dock. It isn't there. I check the drawers in the room. Nothing.

"I can't get in. Only Pete can open it," I admit.

With that, Emma spins and runs back to the kitchen.

When I join them, Emma is closer to Pete, her words a continuous, frantic whisper. Her hands are on his knees. "Pete, please, let us get into the CCTV. I need to get in."

Pete isn't responding. He's just sipping his wine.

"Please, please Pete," she keeps saying.

"Emma—" I try to cut in.

"Or tell me about Chris. Tell me where he is. Where is Chris?"

"Emma, not now," I say as I step closer. "We can talk about Chris another time."

She ignores me. "You can tell me now, Pete. Now that James is gone. You always said if James wasn't around, you'd help me. Please, where's my brother?"

"Emma, this isn't the time. We need to call the—"

Pete turns to her suddenly. "You really want to know?"

"Yes, tell me! Where is he?"

No, no, I think. No, not now. I know what happened to Chris. He's dead at the hands of James. I saw it with my own eyes. Now, with another body lying on the same kitchen floor, is not the time for the revelation that Emma's brother is dead.

What is Pete thinking?

"Okay," Pete says simply.

Pete's face goes blank for a long breath. Then he reaches for the TV remote, bringing the sixty-inch television mounted on the wall to life. Everything in the room goes quiet, as if the house itself is inhaling. Pete taps on his phone for a second before a video starts streaming in front of us.

"No, Pete…" is all I manage.

I know the video. I've seen how it plays out. But watching it again, now with Emma watching too, is like some real-time YouTube reaction video.

James and Chris.

The fight.

The struggle.

The stab to the neck. And the second. Third. Fourth.

The blood. The blood everywhere.

Then the silence.

Emma is the first to make a sound, a sharp intake like someone has punched her in the stomach. Her hands bury her face. She falls to her knees, hands scrabbling at the carpet as if she can drag the picture back together. "No," she wails. "No, no, no."

I can't breathe. My chest tightens.

Emma looks up at Pete. "You told me he was alive," she says, as tears stream down her face.

Pete's empty face doesn't change as he stares at the blank screen. He's so calm.

Emma scrambles up and throws herself at him, voice raw: "Why did you tell me he was alive? Why did you keep saying it? Why—"

He's very quiet. His fingers flex around the arm of the sofa. "I hedged," he says. The room goes very still, like the moment before a storm. "I hedged my bets."

"What does that even mean?" Emma cries.

"Because you needed to believe that James had to be out of the way for you to find out where Chris was." Pete calmly turns to me. "And you needed to believe that James was going to kill me."

I shake my head, confused. "What?"

"I needed James gone. And between the two of you, I always thought one of you would do it eventually."

Pete takes another sip of wine. "And now that he's dead," he says softly, "we can get down to business."

Chapter 61

TOM

I stare at him.

"What do you mean… business?" The word doesn't fit in the same room as the body cooling twenty feet away.

"Honesty." He folds his hands in his lap, gaze steady at last, as though the signal has come back. "I think we all deserve some."

"Honesty?" Emma snaps. "You've been lying to me all this time."

Pete cocks his head. "And you kept coming. You wanted a truth you could live with. I gave you one."

I swallow what tastes like coins. "Pete, I think you're in shock."

"No," he says, with the soft patience of a teacher. "I'm thinking very clearly. The wine helped."

"Why did he kill Chris?" Emma's voice cracks on the name. "Why did James do that?"

Pete looks at the blank screen and smiles a small, nostalgic smile that turns my stomach. "Because he loved me. He was protecting me. Because Chris was so violent to me. He was planning to kill me!" Pete cries, like he's in panto.

Emma shakes her head violently. "What, what are you talking about? Chris would never hurt a fly!"

"You're right — but sshh," he holds his index finger to his lips. "That's our little secret."

"Pete, what are you saying?" I ask, my mind whirling.

"Chris loved me too," Pete continues, mild as milk. "He kept me well. For a long time. He was generous." He glances around the room. "He bought us this house."

Emma's eyes go wide. "This is Chris's house?"

"Was," Pete corrects, almost apologetic. "He signed it over to me when things got… complicated."

"Complicated?" My voice scrapes like hoarse glass. "You told me you and James have been together for years — married—"

"An embellishment," Pete says lightly. "James and I were together. Yes. But Chris came first." His gaze drifts to the doorway, the smear of blood darkening by the threshold.

"After the fraud investigation at his work, he was made the scapegoat and lost his job, couldn't get another one anywhere. There was talk of the Serious Fraud Office seizing his assets, so he signed the house over to me." Pete continues, "he had some investments that he cashed in, but with no more income coming in and legal bills to be paid, those disappeared fairly quickly and soon enough, everything was gone. And I mean literally everything."

Pete takes another sip of wine. "When it started falling apart, he wanted to sell, leave, reinvent. Go into hiding. New name. New country. On the run like some common criminal, the whole cliché. But this—" he gestures lazily around the high ceilings, the good furniture, the curated life— "this fits me. I don't run."

Emma sways, catching herself on the arm of the sofa. "So, you convinced James to kill him?" she whispers, each word a splinter.

Pete's eyes sharpen. "I needed James to choose me. And I needed him to stick around."

The room tips. I catch the back of a chair. "Pete…"

"James was a sweet guy. We started dating. Chris knew: he was into polyamory too, so that wasn't a big deal. But when I knew Chris was really leaving, that there was no more money, I had to make plans. I knew I couldn't fund living in this big house on my own. James made the perfect replacement. He had very big pockets, just wanted to look after me."

I blink. "So just break up with Chris. Why kill him?"

The smile on Pete's face drops. "Because they all leave eventually! Chris said he would be here for me forever, look after me forever. They all say that. Parents, fosterers, men with promises. Then they leave." He steeples his fingers. "I just needed assurance. Commitment. Security. A guarantee."

My mouth is dry. "So, you made James believe Chris was going to hurt you."

"I showed him things." He glances at Emma. "Your brother loved late-night catastrophising. Very literary. It didn't take much to frame that…anxiety." He lifts one shoulder. "A staged break-in. A shadow at the window. A cut on my arm I told him I got when Chris grabbed me. Bruises around my neck. Paranoia, fear, love — they do the heavy lifting. Men like James don't need much push to become saviours. Or executioners."

Emma's face crumples. "You coerced him into killing my brother."

Pete considers this and then tilts his head. "Coerced is a serious word. I would say… I simply accelerated an inevitable choice. Chris was going to leave me. James was going to leave me eventually, too. I just… adjusted the timing."

"You blackmailed him," I say. My voice sounds like it belongs to somebody older. "Afterwards. With the video of him killing Chris."

"I hate the word blackmail," he says simply. " I prefer 'insurance policy.' A sign of commitment. He agreed that night to look after me. To keep me. And he did, for a while. We made it work as best we could. He did have a temper, yes. He fought back sometimes, he'd get angry, frustrated with the situation, but nothing I couldn't handle."

"But you still wanted rid of him?"

"He turned out just like the rest," Pete sighs. "Men with money like to imagine they're free." His mouth tightens. "Recently, he'd been siphoning funds. Little streams to other accounts. Researching identities. Another one getting ready to run away to a simpler life. As I said, they all want to leave in the end."

"You found out," I breathe.

"I know everything in this house," Pete says. "That's the point of houses. They tell you if you listen."

"So, you tricked us. Made us believe he was violent to you?" Emma says, in disbelief.

"But he was, I saw the videos," I add.

"Like I said, he had a bit of a temper, yes. A simmering rage that would come out every now and then. Kind of understandable under the circumstances. But when you came along, I'd slip him a little something to ramp it up a tad."

"You drugged him," I say.

"A little something in his evening glass," Pete concedes, as if confessing to sprinkling oregano in a bolognese. "To increase the paranoia, the aggression. Worked much better than anticipated. Some temper tantrums, smashing plates. I can take a few punches to the face, had plenty in my time."

Emma points at him with a shaking hand. "You are a monster."

He considers it, smiles sadly. "I'm a realist."

"And us?" I ask, because my voice needs to do something besides tremble. "This — me. What was I? Another replacement?"

He looks at me properly for the first time, and the warmth that used to live in that gaze has cooled to something clinical. "You were a joy," he says. "*Are* a joy." He laughs quietly. "I've loved every second of being with you. There's no reason that can't carry on."

My body feels transparent. My blood knows what my brain won't say: he's been moving us like pieces, and we are already where he wants us.

Emma lets out a low, horrified sound. "You had us kill him."

Pete's smile flickers. "You had choices," he says softly. "And so did he. Tonight was always going one of two ways." He leans back. "Now that it has gone the right way, we can plan."

"Plan?" The word claws me. "For what?"

"For the future." He says it like a toast.

I stare at him. "You think I could ever—"

"Tom," he says gently, almost kind, "you already have."

My head is full of buzzing. I can't tell if it's the fridge or my nerves.

"Tom, I love spending time with you. We have a genuine connection." A surge of air flies out of my mouth in disbelief as I can't find the words to respond, as Pete continues. "These past months have been a blessing. You've brought so much joy to my life, so much happiness. We can continue how it's been."

Pete takes another sip of his wine. "We could be happy, comfortable, just the three of us?"

"Three of us?" Emma screams. "Are you insane? Are you expecting me to be a part of some psychotic threesome?"

Pete chuckles. "Oh no. I didn't mean you. I meant Tom and me. And my boyfriend."

Pete nods to the doorway.

And there he is: the other boyfriend.

Sam.

He doesn't speak. He doesn't have to. The gun in his hand does the talking.

Chapter 62

TOM

I feel like I'm drowning.

Sam's shoes make no sound on the tiles when he crosses the room. The gun hangs casually in his hand, like he's holding his phone. He doesn't look at the body. He doesn't react when he sees the body.

Boyfriend.

"You're a couple?" I ask.

"Yes, very much so," he says, as if we're discussing an old holiday. "Eighteen years. Since we were teenagers. We met in one of our foster homes."

The words land with the weight of a small anvil being dropped on my chest. "You and Pete?" I ask because I'm grasping for anything that even smells like an explanation.

Sam nods. There's a sense of im the action.

He looks at me, his eyes wide. "You don't get it," he says. "Pete and I — we didn't get families. We got new houses every few months. New rules. New faces pretending they'd keep us. We learned early: nobody stays unless you make them." He glances at Pete like it's the simplest truth in the world. "We had nothing but each other. No safety nets. No inheritance. No second chances. So we built our own. Made our own rules. Made sure nobody could throw us away again."

He shrugs, like it's just logic. "We've survived because we stay together. Always."

I don't know whether to be horrified or fascinated.

"You did this before," I hear myself say. It's not a question.

"A few times." He answers like a man checking off a list. Not proud, not ashamed. "It's proved an efficient way of securing our future."

Pete smiles at his partner. "We did what we had to. To survive."

"But I saw you, you and James… together," I say to Sam. Even in this moment, I can't bring myself to say the word "sex".

Sam nods. "Well, James liked to take his frustrations out on me. He wasn't going to get it anywhere else, so he just went with it in the end. And I very much let him." He smiles, "I like my men to get real rough."

"And I've always been more vanilla," Pete says, looking to me. "As you know."

"That's the brilliance of open relationships. What one partner can't give you, you can get from another," Pete says, like he's explaining the benefits of a Tesco Clubcard.

There's a pause, a break, while we all process this revelation.

Pete places his wine on the side table and stands up.

"So," he starts. "Now, we all know where we stand, let's talk this through like adults."

Before I can respond, Pete taps on his phone and looks up at the TV. The screen fills again with the same bright, clinical light, the same cluttered kitchen. The fight, the knife, the blood.

Except this time it's not James and Chris. It's James…and me.

Then the angle that makes everything worse: Tom — me — behind James on the floor, arms wrapped around his torso, face a knot of exertion. Emma over him, knife in hand, the stabbing motion clear and repeated.

The thing that had felt like self-defence in the heat of it becomes something else when it's replayed in pixels.

"See?" Pete says, his voice as calm as a man describing the weather. "It's a lot clearer now. You aren't defending anymore: you're restraining. She's the one doing the killing."

My stomach drops out of me. There is a hollow place where argument lives. "That's not how it—" My voice is thin. "It happened fast. He lunged—"

"He lunged," Pete repeats, not unkindly. "But you had the knife away from him first. You had the control." He leans forward, fingers steepled. "We could take this to the police, Tom. We could tell them every word and let the law sort it out."

I feel like someone's speaking through a wall. "I was holding him down to stop him," I say. "I thought he would have killed Pete."

"You've seen it back now," Pete says softly. "It's not a good look."

It is not a good look. The camera is merciless, as is the truth of what happened. When you see it played back, there is very little left to say that sounds like a defence.

Pete turns the remote toward me like a judge passing sentence. "So, let's just all calm down. We can all live happily together in this house. We have fun, don't we?" he says, all too casually. "And that can continue, but I just need access to your bank accounts."

The demand hangs in the air, not phrased as a threat but with every millimetre of implication it needs. Blackmail with more polish than the word deserves.

"I'm not going to blow it all in one go," Pete says, as if to reassure me. "I'm not reckless. Just enough for us to live long-term as we have been. Which will mean you coming off your sabbatical and going back to work, but that's no big deal. Then we can all live comfortably."

Sam's eyes flick to Emma. "With some extra top-up funds from you." She's sitting on the floor, knees pulled to her chest, wet tracks down her cheeks. She looks like she's about to break like a biscuit.

Pete also looks at Emma. "I know you need an alibi for the night of the fire. You can have it. There's the video of you here as well, timestamped and everything. Easy. I'll just need your funds, too."

"I don't have any money," she whispers.

Pete laughs. "Of course, you do. I know your family background. Chris told me all about it. I know how much money he started with. You don't just lose that kind of generational wealth."

Emma is the one to laugh this time. "Then, you really don't know me at all. I lost the money years ago. Blew it on all kinds of shit. The expensive clothes, the car, the jewellery, all I have left now is stuff. But I have no real money. I live month to month like anyone else. Why do you think I spent two years inside for fraud?"

"I see," Pete says. His tone is steady and clinical.

Pete looks at Sam, then back to Emma.

"Then, you're a complication," Pete says, almost apologetically. "If you can't contribute, then you're a liability."

Sam shifts, hands wrapped around the gun like it's a habit rather than a weapon. He steps towards Emma, and there's a moment when I think he's going to shoot her.

I hold my breath.

Instead, Sam places the firearm in front of Pete with the kind of deliberate calm that makes my bones go very cold.

Pete takes the gun as if taking a glass of water. He lifts the weapon, hovering it between us.

"So, you're going to shoot me?" Emma says.

Pete shakes his head. "No, shooting is a last resort."

"Far too messy," Sam adds.

"And there's already been far too much blood to clean up tonight," Pete says. "This is just to keep the order."

Pete directs the gun at me.

My body turns to stone.

Then Sam moves.

He closes on Emma with no theatrics, a shepherding motion that has no tenderness. She has little time, backing into the kitchen worktop as he wraps his hands around her throat so tightly in an inevitable motion. Emma's hands scrabble at his grip, nails raking the skin of his wrist. She gurgles, a horrifying, wet sound.

"Sam—no—" I find my voice, and it sounds as if it belongs to a stranger. I look at Pete, who keeps the gun firmly aimed at me.

Sam's jaw works. His face does not change in any way that shows what he is doing. The room shrinks to the two of them: Sam's hands around her throat, Emma's fingers in the air, wild and useless.

Pete watches, inscrutable, as if this is a negotiation and he is intently taking notes. Emma's legs kick, and for a moment, I see that she is still fighting. Her eyes meet mine once, like a final plea for help.

"Stop!" I roar, the word cracks like a whip. I want to run toward them, to stop this madness, but my legs feel like meringue with the gun pointed at me.

Sam's grip tightens, showing no mercy. "It's cleaner," he says. His voice is flat like he's telling me to reboot a laptop. "Quicker."

Emma's nails find his forearm, but it's all in vain.

He leans in.

Then she's still.

Her hands fall, slack. Her face turns away in a way that makes me think she could be asleep, but she's not.

Sam releases her as if setting down a tool, and she crumples at his feet. He steps back and looks at me, calm as a surgeon wiping hands.

"Done," he says.

Chapter 63

TOM

Emma is dead.

The room is too quiet for how violently she just left it. Her body is still on the floor, eyes half-open, mouth frozen mid-plea. I can't look at her. I can't look away either.

I don't even realise I'm shaking until I hear my own raw, broken voice. "You didn't need to do that! You didn't need to kill her!"

Pete sighs like I'm being unreasonable. "Tom, come on. Don't be dramatic."

"Dramatic? *You killed her*!" I shout, voice cracking.

Sam gives a little shrug, like he's a customer service assistant explaining why the item is out of stock.

"She didn't deserve to die," I say.

"Oh, come on, Tom, let's not pretend that she was Mother Teresa," Pete rolls his eyes. "She didn't give a fuck about her brother for years. Chris told me what their relationship was really like. She was selfish and manipulative. She was only interested in Chris when it served her purpose. She just wanted an alibi to get her off that arson charge."

My stomach turns. This is no defence. But also, I'm losing the fight to challenge back. "I don't understand any of this. Why? Why *me*?"

Pete leans back into the sofa like he's about to deliver a TED Talk. "Because you're perfect, Tom. Warm, lovely, funny. But also lonely, desperate to be loved—"

"I wasn't—"

"And very, very rich."

My throat closes. “What?”

“I mean that massive house for just you and your cat in Clifton is a bit of a giveaway. But I knew all about your inheritance before we first met.”

“What? How?”

He almost smiles. “Guy told me.”

The name hits me like a knife in the chest. “Guy? What—?”

Pete tilts his head gently, patronising. “You didn’t think our meeting was just luck, did you? Yeah, Guy told us all about it. Sam met him first, actually. Grindr. Had a little thing going for a while.”

Sam nods. “We used to meet on Tuesdays. I think your night was Thursday, wasn’t it?”

My eyes widen. “What?” I whisper.

“We’d meet up, we’d chat. You know what Guy was like, loved to open up. He mentioned your inheritance one night,” he continues, casual as weather. “Just in passing. Said he was dating some guy who’d come into millions. We realised very quickly what we could do with it.”

“But he was also talking about leaving his wife for you,” Pete adds. “And we couldn’t have you having a happy ending with him.”

A sound leaves me — part sob, part disbelief. “You — you killed him. You killed Guy?”

Sam exhales, bored with my grief. “We removed an obstacle. We’re good at that. We just needed you feeling a bit… vulnerable.”

Pete gestures around us, calm, logical. “Tom, look at the pattern. James. Emma. Guy. All people getting in the way of what we’re trying to build. James was working with some lawyer friend to help him escape. They’d have their secret meetings, about the hidden accounts, funnelling my money, the new identity—”

“Phil…” I whisper.

“Yes, Phil! How did you know?”

I don’t respond. I don’t need to tell them about me following James. Or how Phil is my best friend’s husband.

“Anyway, it doesn’t matter now anyway,” Pete waves his hand like he’s waving away a fly. “He’s also been sorted now.”

My heart skips a beat. “How? What did you do?”

Sam laughs. “Let’s just say I had to wipe a Phil-shaped faceprint off the windscreen of my car.”

No. Not Phil, too.

Sam wipes an invisible dust speck off his sleeve. "I took care of it this afternoon. Should look like a basic hit-and-run if no one looks too hard."

My vision blurs. "Phil is dead?"

Pete sighs like I'm ruining the mood. "He was a liability. But still, better clean than complicated."

I can't breathe. Three people are dead tonight. All orbiting me, and I didn't even know the planet was on fire.

Pete stands and moves closer to me, his voice soft like he's reassuring a child. "Tom, this is where you stop crying and start thinking about your future. Our future. This could be something beautiful. Love. Safety. Wealth. No more people disappointing you or letting you down. Just the three of us.

In the middle of all this — Emma dead on the floor, James cooling in a pool of blood, Pete smiling like a snake with a wine glass — it hits me like a punch to the throat: Guy is gone. They murdered him. And I never even got to say goodbye. I keep seeing him the way he used to look at me in those stupid hotel rooms, soft-eyed, amused. I loved him. Properly loved him. The kind of love that makes you imagine a future before you remember you're not built for one. And now he's just...erased. A loose end cut, because he mentioned something in passing about the man he loved.

My gaze drops to Emma's body. And then to James.

I walk slowly over to James's body. Pete keeps his gun focused on me as I turn away from him. I crouch down by the corpse in front of me, of a man I helped kill. A man I thought was a monster, but was just another fool wanting to protect Pete.

Sam moves behind me, resting a hand on my shoulder. "Come on, Tom. This could all work out perfectly. For all of us."

Not a chance.

A switch flips in me.

Something primal. Something final.

I take one step back, and my hand lands on the knife from the floor, the same one Emma pulled from James's neck.

I don't remember lifting it. I just know suddenly it's in my hand, and my hand is at Sam's throat, me behind him like he's a shield.

Pete flicks the gun up to me, but Sam is too close to risk firing.

His eyes widen, but he doesn't move. He studies me like a puzzle.

Pete's voice drops, almost delighted. "There he is. The version of you I always knew was hiding."

My arm is shaking, blade pressed to Sam's skin. I don't even know what I'm going to do.

But I know what I won't do.

I won't be their next body.

Chapter 64

SAM

Sam feels the cold pressure where Tom's blade presses into his throat, but his mind stays absolutely clear and focused.

He doesn't panic.

Panic is for people who haven't had to survive the brutal lessons of a cruel world. He learnt this in the foster houses that taught you to hold your breath when a door opened, or to sleep with one eye open at night. He learned this with Pete, where, together, they scraped together a semblance of a family in a cold and uncaring world.

"Come on, Tom," Sam says. "I saved your life earlier today, remember?" He feels the pressure of the blade against his skin soften for a moment, but quickly returns.

Tom doesn't respond.

"He was going to kill you. He was about to take your eye out before I swooped in and saved you," Sam says, calmly.

Pete doesn't say anything, just stands, pointing the gun. He knows when to take a back seat. He can see, despite appearances, that Sam has a way in to Tom, one that can help him off this ledge they're both perched upon.

"You owe me," Sam says.

"I don't owe you anything," Tom hisses back.

Sam can feel Tom's breath on the back of his neck. His eyes flick the room, doing a rapid-fire inventory of options: the heavy ceramic vase on the sideboard that would make a satisfying blunt instrument, the mantel clock he could smash to make a bloody diversion, the coat stand with jagged hooks.

All theoretical options, but none close by.

"Look, I'm just saying, if I hadn't seen him break into your house and come over, your eyeballs would have been spooned across the bathroom by now."

"What do you mean 'seen him'?" Tom fires back.

"We were just keeping an eye on you. We wanted to get to know you properly." Sam says calmly.

"What? Like cameras?"

Sam dodges the question. "You know he won't hurt you again, right? You know he's gone for good."

Tom stays quiet, but again, the pressure on his neck eases for a second.

"He came around earlier, just before you did. Worst possible timing. He had your laptop, some incriminating videos, and said he was going to the police unless we gave him money," Sam admits.

"I don't believe you," Tom says, but Sam knows he does.

"It's true," Pete adds. "But we silenced him."

"You're lying…" Tom breathes.

But he isn't lying.

Daniel thought he was walking into a negotiation.

That was his first mistake.

He turned up waving Tom's laptop like a golden ticket, convinced that a few video files made him king of the room. Then produced the gun, which was his next mistake. He said words like *leverage* and *settlement*, and *we can do this quietly*, as if he hadn't already crossed a line you don't come back from. Pete let him talk. Pete's good at that, letting people think they're steering the ship right up until they realise they're already in the water.

By the time Daniel figured out he wasn't the one holding power, it was too late.

Another obstacle permanently removed.

And it also left them with a gun, which has proved useful up to this point.

"He's out of your life for good now," Sam says. "Because of us."

"We did it for you. Because we care for you," Pete says. The way he can flip on those puppy-dog eyes on demand is a true gift, Sam thinks.

Sam's heart thuds a steady, practical tempo, and he measures distances in steps, plots trajectories for improvised weapons, imagines the arc of a chair hurled as a barrier. There's a phone on the coffee table, but it's face down and locked.

With slow, shallow breaths, he decides on movement first. Then distraction. Then the vase.

He just needs Tom to move about ten steps over.

"His body's in the garage. I can show you," Sam says.

Then Sam feels it.

A pen in his pocket. A cheap plastic one, he put it there earlier. Now it feels like a weapon. He slides his fingers against the barrel, feeling its small coolness.

Change of plan.

"No, I don't want to see anything," Tom says. "I just want to leave."

That's not going to happen, Sam thinks.

"And I'm going out the front door, right now," Tom says, trying to stay calm, but Sam can feel the vibrations of his shaking hand through the blade.

Sam fingers the pen loose, then grips it tightly.

The stab is quick, a spike of pain put into Tom's leg through denim, right where the femoral nerve blooms and convulses. Tom jerks. The hand at Sam's throat loosens by the fraction Sam needs.

Tom reacts too fast. The blade comes away from Sam's throat, but in the panic to pull away, the knife comes down and finds flesh.

Sam feels it, hot and sharp, somewhere under his ribs, excruciating. Air rushes from his lungs as if the whole room has exhaled. Tom stumbles forward like someone shoved from behind. With his momentum, Sam is pushed forward too, stumbling hard toward Pete.

Sam sees the look in his eyes. A half-second of panic before instinct takes over. The gun goes off. No warning, no hesitation. Just a crack of sound that feels like ten thousand doors slamming shut.

The impact isn't pain at first. It's force. A punch from the inside, stealing the breath from Sam's lungs as the bullet rips through him. He staggers, but the world has already started tilting, colours draining, sound thinning to a high, distant ring.

Time becomes unreliable. Either a heartbeat or a whole lifetime passes.

Tom is gone, sprinted out of the room, footsteps fading like someone abandoning a burning house. Sam doesn't chase him. He can't. His legs are no longer part of the plan.

He looks up at Pete instead.

Pete stands there, gun trembling, eyes wide and wet with regret and fury, all fighting for space in his expression.

Sam’s body gives up first. His head drops, vision greying at the edges, the world folding gently inward.

And then the light inside him flickers, once… twice… and goes out.

Chapter 65

TOM

I don't think. I just run.

My legs move before my mind catches up, slipping in blood, skidding across the tiles, lungs full of the metallic stink of gunpowder and death. Sam's body is still warm on the floor behind me, but I can't look back to process any of it: not Emma, not James, not the fact that the house is just a maze of corpses now.

I just need to get out.

The back door. The garden. The street. Freedom.

I'm two steps from the kitchen door when the first deafening gunshot cracks behind me, ripping through the air, splintering the wood frame inches from my hand.

I drop out of pure instinct. The second shot hits the counter I was just beside. Plates explode, and glass rains over me. Pete's voice tears through the room:

"You killed him! You killed him!"

He sounds broken, but the strength in it is terrifying. I can feel his rage like heat on my back.

I crawl, fingers slipping on the floor, reaching for the handle, pushing the door, but another shot forces me in the opposite direction, away from the exit. He's herding me like prey.

The only path left is the side door, the one that leads to the garage.

I sprint.

Another shot echoes. No time. I slam into the door, burst through, and my feet hit concrete. The smell changes: cold, oil, dust, and—

Daniel.

He's on the floor, propped against the wall like a puppet with its strings cut. His throat is a gaping red smile, eyes open but empty. Horror hits me, but only for a second. I don't have the luxury of grief or shock; my only focus is escape.

I step over him.

The garage is a shrine to disorder: half storage space, half graveyard of abandoned DIY projects. The only light comes from a single flickering bulb overhead, throwing everything into jerky shadows.

Behind me, Pete kicks the door open, rage boiled down to something feral.

"You should've just loved me, Tom!"

All I can do is stop and hold up my hands.

He points the gun at me. "We could have all been happy together."

I shake my head, scanning the room for an escape, but I'm acutely aware that my time is coming to an end.

I pause and breathe.

"You know I would have given you everything," I say.

Pete, chest heaving, pauses.

"I wanted to be with you, get you away from James and start a proper life with you," I say earnestly. "I would have done anything for you, given you everything. You wouldn't have needed to blackmail me into staying."

Pete shakes his head. "That's what they all say. They promise me the world at first, before they take it away! They never stay! Nobody ever stays."

"I would have!" I cry, and part of me believes that completely.

"Well, it's nice that you look back on our time so fondly," Pete says, focusing the gun on me. "But it's too late for that."

The gun clicks.

Empty.

He looks at it like it's betrayed him. He throws it to the floor with a scream, and then he comes at me fast, faster than I'm ready for.

We crash into the metal shelving, paint tins fall, tools slam to the ground, and something sharp slices my arm. He's on me with fists, nails, teeth, all desperation and fury. I shove him back, but he's relentless. The sweet, charming boy who once held my face in his hands is gone, replaced by something vicious and animal.

He lunges again, and we tumble, knees and elbows cracking against concrete. I try to get up, but he tackles me, hands clawing for my eyes, my throat.

He wants to kill me with his bare hands.

I manage to flip him just long enough to crawl away. My fingers scrape cold metal — a wrench — but he kicks it away before I can grab it.

I back up wildly, scanning for anything, anything, and then I see it —

A coil of rope hanging from a hook.

I snatch it down just as Pete slams into me again. We land awkwardly in a heap, and before I can respond, his hands are around my throat. He squeezes hard, and my vision sparks white. My legs kick uselessly. He's stronger than he looks. His weight is crushing my chest.

The world is fading, the air disappearing, my heartbeat a wild drum in my skull—

And I swing the rope.

It hits him across the face. He flinches just long enough for me to loop it around his neck, choking his airway. He claws at it, eyes wide, but I pull. I pull with every ounce of terror and fury and grief left in me.

He thrashes. He makes these awful, desperate choking sounds, but I don't let go.

I can't.

Not after Emma.

Not after Phil.

Not after Guy.

Not after everything.

His face goes red, then purple, then slack. His body twitches once, twice. Then drops still.

When I finally let go, my arms are shaking, my fingers numb. I stumble backwards, gasping, coughing, the rope still in my hands like a dead snake.

Pete's body lies crumpled on the concrete, eyes open but empty, tongue swollen, rope mark embedded deep into his skin.

The silence that follows is too big.

Five bodies.

Five lives gone in one night.

And I am still breathing.

My chest heaves. The rest of me is a blur. I'm covered in blood that isn't mine. My heart isn't beating normally: it's vibrating, like it's trying to break its way out.

I look at Daniel.

I look at Pete.

And I think:

What have I done?

And more terrifying:

What do I do now?

EPILOGUE

TOM

The kettle clicks on and fills the kitchen with a low mechanical hum. I take out two mugs and place them on the counter.

Buster sits at my feet, nosing at the edge of his bowl, oblivious. Lucky him. Two days have passed since I walked out of that house. Two days of silence, sleep in short bursts, and the constant feeling that I'm standing on a frozen lake and the ice is whispering warnings.

I look out the window over the sink at the grey sky and breathe in slowly, as if air will steady me.

I keep replaying the night, frame by frame. Not just the violence, but the aftermath. I thought about calling the police, confessing everything. How could I explain this all, everything that happened, my role in James's death and not walk away from it unscathed?

I thought about calling Craig, but then I remembered about Phil and how getting him involved in something as insane as this was not a viable plan.

So, in a moment of potential insanity, I decided not to call the police.

I hung Pete's body in the garage with the rope I strangled him with, as a staged suicide. I placed the memory stick in his pocket with the footage of James hitting him, of Sam and James having sex, and of James killing Chris. A selection of videos that were the foundation of a story that fueled a narrative away from me.

After unlocking his phone with FaceID, I typed the message. A suicide note, remorseful and vague enough to sound believable, but with enough detail to answer questions:

James was abusive. He killed Chris. He was cheating on me with Sam. Emma came to help. Things escalated. James killed Emma. I killed James and Sam. I can't live with what I've done.

A far-fetched story, but with the video evidence of continued abuse, it would be believable, right? My brain, fuelled with adrenaline and panic, decided that the answer would be yes.

After that, it was about the cover-up. I searched the house for Pete's Apple Watch and found it in the drawer. I entered the laptop, stopped the CCTV system, then deleted everything. Every file. Every backup. Then cleaned the house. Every last bit of evidence I could find that could tie me to the house.

In the moment, it all felt logical, like I was covering my tracks.

Except for Daniel's body.

His corpse didn't fit the narrative.

But now I'm here. Making tea.

Waiting.

Waiting for the police to knock and say the one sentence I can't unhear: *We know what you did.*

I try to convince myself that I've covered every base, every hole in the story, but doubt keeps seeping into my thoughts. A hair James or skin under Sam's nails. Did I leave a footprint in the garden? My phone was in the car. Did it ping off a nearby cell tower? The kind of stuff I swear I hear every time I watch an episode of CSI.

Then, there were the texts on Pete's phone: there weren't many; he was always more of a caller. That in itself should have pointed towards him being a psychopath. I couldn't delete my texts that would scream guilt. And my Facebook conversations with Emma, those were more incriminating,but would they be looked at?

All those pieces of evidence I hadn't considered in the moment, but now it's too late.

I just have to hope no one looks too closely.

I move to the fridge to get the milk, and I wince. My leg is still sore from where Sam stabbed me with a biro. I couldn't risk going to the hospital, so I cleaned it up at home. It wasn't deep, and I'm hoping it leaves no lasting damage, although it still twinges when I put weight on it.

Grabbing the milk, I set it on the counter. It had been another morning of checking the house again for cameras after Sam's admission. I'd found five so far in various rooms. The one in the corner of my bedroom distressed me the most, but anything Sam saw in there was the least of my worries. I disposed of them earlier, not that that gives me any peace.

With a tremble, the kettle clicks off, and before I can pour, there's a knock at the door.

Buster looks up.

I freeze. I already know who it is.

I open the door, and two detectives in coats stand there, badges out and pointing at me.

"Can we come in?"

I step aside. My pulse tries to punch its way through my throat.

In the hallway, they ask about Pete. They say they've seen the texts between us. The late-night calls. They ask how we knew each other.

I keep my voice as small and harmless as possible.

"We met a couple of months ago. He gave the impression he and his husband were in an open relationship, but I didn't want to get involved in that. We talked sometimes. We'd meet for coffee occasionally. As friends."

They don't react. They don't write anything down. That's worse.

"Sorry, what's this about?" I ask. Playing dumb is the only tactic I have right now.

Then: "He called you late Saturday night. What was that about?"

I swallow hard.

"He sounded… upset. He said he and James were fighting. I got the impression it wasn't the first time. But I didn't want to get involved. I told him to get help, or call someone."

One of them watches me like he's waiting for the lie to twitch on my face.

Then the other asks: "Where were you Saturday night?"

There it is. The question.

I open my mouth—

—and Craig's voice comes from behind me.

"He was with me."

I turn. Craig calmly steps into view from the living room, where he had been waiting for his tea. He gives the detectives a polite nod.

"Oh, hello, Sir," the taller detective says.

Sir.

They recognise him. DCI Craig Hollis. Their superior. That softens something in them. A tiny shift. "Sorry, we didn't know you were…friends."

Craig doesn't acknowledge this comment. "He was at the hospital with me. In A&E. My husband was knocked down in an accident the same night, you may have heard. Tom has been a great support."

I don't breathe.

"Right, yes, we heard," the shorter detective says nervously. "I'm sorry to hear that. I hope he's doing ok, Sir?"

Craig nods. "Yes, it was touch and go initially, but they're confident he's going to make a full recovery."

Both detectives seem genuinely relieved. "Well, that's excellent news," one of them says.

There's a pause.

"Um, I'm afraid we have some bad news," the other detective says. "Pete Harris is dead. He took his own life two days ago."

I let the shock hit my face like a slap.

"Oh my god," I whisper, hand to my mouth. "No. I… I had no idea."

They nod. They give me a sympathetic look. They say they may need to speak to me again. They may need me to come in and make a statement. Standard procedure.

"Let me see you out," Craig says, leading them to the door.

Through the window, I watch him stand at the front gate with the two detectives. They talk. Craig gestures once, twice, like the calm professional he is, completely in control. For five long minutes, they talk. It feels like an hour.

And then, they leave.

Silence sinks back into the house, thick and heavy. The only sound is Buster drinking from his bowl, the slow lap-lap-lap like nothing in the world is wrong.

I turn back to the counter.

Two mugs. Kettle cold.

Tea. I was making tea for us, like this was any other quiet morning, before that knock on the door.

I switch the kettle back on and watch the water come to a boil, keeping my hands busy so my mind doesn't spiral.

Craig comes back in and closes the door softly, like he's afraid even the latch might expose the truth.

"Well?" I ask. I hear the need in my own voice.

"They're satisfied," Craig says. "They've seen the videos on the memory stick. The texts between Emma and Pete back up the 'domestic incident gone wrong' narrative. They're calling it a murder–suicide for now. They haven't dug into Emma's background yet. And I've already congratulated them on 'quick work', so they'll be keen to close it down swiftly now."

He gives a half-smile. "Truth is, it *is* sloppy policing. But for once, sloppy works in our favour."

I exhale. I didn't realise I'd been holding my breath.

I hadn't wanted Craig involved, after everything. But the second I learned Phil survived, instinct took over. I ran straight to him, and the whole truth spilt out. Craig did what Craig always does: stepped between me and the fire.

He hasn't been to work since Phil was taken to the hospital. But he's been listening and asking questions.

"Thank you for…" I start, but can't quite say *lying to the police for me*. "For what you said."

Craig nods, no pride in it, just certainty. "Let's hope things stay quiet now."

We stand there, not quite looking at each other. Our last conversation ended with me hanging up on him, accusing him, and not trusting him. And yet, here he is again, doing what he always does: protecting me, even when I make it near impossible to want to.

"You never told me," I say finally. "Why did you lie about James? About the police investigations. You made it sound like he was dangerous."

"I just needed you to keep your distance," Craig says. "When you showed me that picture, I recognised him. I'd seen him with Phil. I didn't know what was going on with them, but I didn't want you anywhere near it."

"So, you knew Phil and James were meeting?"

"Only because I followed them. Phil never said a word. I know what it looks like when someone's hiding something." He pauses, breathes. "He kept sneaking off, so I followed him one time and saw them together. I thought maybe they were… involved."

"You didn't ask him? I thought the whole point of your open relationship was honesty and communication. All that 'emotional maturity' stuff you always preach."

Craig huffs an almost laugh. "Yeah, well. I'm also human. And jealous. And completely capable of being an idiot."

He looks at me then, properly. "I didn't talk to him because I didn't want to hear an answer I couldn't handle yet. So instead, I tried to control everything else. Including you."

I nod slowly. I do understand. More than I want to admit.

"I should've known. Phil was just trying to be Phil. Save the day, play the hero like always. I know what connections he has. Getting a new identity, new accounts, and helping him start afresh. All illegal and all things I would have disapproved of, which is why he kept it from me. They were old school friends. He just wanted to help James. I know that now."

"Well, thank God he's going to be okay," I say, drifting toward the back doors, letting my eyes settle on the garden.

"Speaking of which, I need to get back to the hospital," Craig says, grabbing his coat. "I'll stay with him tonight."

I nod. He pauses, turns to me.

"Just lie low now. Especially with the whole Daniel situation."

"Right," I say, keeping it flat, harmless.

Craig sighs. "I'm sorry I didn't call the police like I said I would after Daniel attacked you. Phil was on the phone straight after, then he got hit, and… I just ran to the hospital."

"No, I get it. Everything was chaos. I went straight over to Pete's after it happened, so I didn't really think about Daniel," I lie, easily.

"And I'm sorry about sending Daniel those videos. Of you and Guy," he says, and I know he means it.

"It doesn't matter anymore," I reply.

Craig studies me for a second, then lowers his voice. "It might not be smart to involve the police about Daniel now. We don't want more attention on you. We'll work out a plan to protect you if he turns up again. Just make sure you get those locks changed. Today."

I look back out into the garden, hands resting on the cool glass of the door.

"I don't think he's going to bother me again," I say quietly.

Outside, at the very back of the garden, the borders are tidy, freshly planted after a night of furious digging.

Foxgloves and lavender stand upright, still damp from yesterday's watering. The soil is turned, rich, dark.

Anyone looking out would see a freshly planted bed, looking pleasant and unremarkable.

They'd never know what really lies beneath.

If you enjoyed **OPEN**,
why not delve into another mystery…

DEATH AT THE YUMBO CENTRE

What happens in Gran Canaria…. Won't stay buried.

Dan just wanted sun, cocktails, and a break from real life. What he got instead? A blood-soaked body count and one very messy mystery.

On holiday in Gran Canaria with his old university friend Hugo, introverted millennial Dan expects drag queens, drunken flings, and debaucherous nights at the Yumbo Centre. But after a date with a dangerously charming local, a tragic death turns the holiday into something more sinister.

Secrets unravel. Tempers ignite. And as more bodies fall, Dan starts to realise—the island's darkest stories are refusing to stay buried.

OUT NOW

ACKNOWLEDGEMENTS

Writing this book has been many things: fun, deranged, enlightening, emotionally expensive, occasionally therapeutic and wildly sleep-depriving. Mostly, it reminded me that stories don't happen in isolation, even if most of the writing does (in my bedroom, alone, eating biscuits).

The year after *Death at the Yumbo Centre* was wild in the best possible way. I met readers, writers, book people, creative chaos gremlins and extremely enthusiastic strangers from the internet. Some of you became friends. Some of you became accomplices. And somewhere along the way, I accidentally built a small community that made me feel less like a man yelling into a Word document and more like I'm at the beginning of something exciting.

This is my second Bristol book (after *Followers*), and it turns out Bristol becomes even more fun to write about once you add gay chaos and caffeine. The LGBTQ+ community here has been one of the great joys of my adult life: messy, brilliant, supportive, political, creative, chaotic and constantly reinventing itself. Being part of it, however loosely defined, has made Bristol feel not just like a city I live in, but somewhere I call home.

A huge part of this book came from my fascination with open relationships and non-monogamy. It seems everyone is in one these days, or at least they claim they're "exploring the concept." The more I learned, the more I realised it isn't one thing at all, but a buffet of emotional configurations. This book only dips its toe in. There's so much more I want to explore on this topic in the future; the tangle of love, boundaries and connections. Thank you to the people who were incredibly generous in talking to me about their relationships: you made the book richer, stranger, and more human.

Now for Thank You Corner:

Mike — for reading drafts, giving feedback, and helping me work out what stories I actually want to tell (and how to structure them without crying). Book Three would be a bin fire without your input.

Patrick — for the deep-dive conversations on open relationships, polyamory and murder logistics, and for reading the earliest versions of Book Three before it resembled a book.

Anthony — for reading all the dross I've sent over the last year, and for the IKEA days out, which were either a bonding exercise or a test of endurance. We need to go again. I still need that mirror.

Ally — for being a brilliant friend, a brilliant reader, and for being my Spanish learning pal, even when *mi abuela es elegante* is the main thing Duolingo keeps making me say.

Jacks — for listening to my endless whining about the struggles of being a wannabe writer. Not saying there's a correlation between your recent hearing loss and that, but the timing is impeccable. Thank you.

Richie at More Visual — for another incredible cover, making the book look sexy enough to be judged entirely by its exterior.

For legal and emotional clarity: I once had a real cat called Buster about twenty years ago. He was significantly friendlier than the fictional Buster and far less judgmental.

To everyone who picked up one of my books, messaged about them, recommended them to a friend, posted about them, reviewed them, or used them as a coaster (which I'm fine with) — thank you. Your enthusiasm, curiosity and sheer chaos have made this whole journey feel worth it.

There's a lot more I want to write. A lot more I want to explore. I hope I'm just getting started.

ABOUT THE AUTHOR

D. M. Pickersgill is a gay Bristol-based author who writes about messy relationships, morally ambiguous life choices and the sort of gay drama that would give most therapists job security for years.

His previous novels include *Death at the Yumbo Centre*, an ultra-gay murder mystery set in Gran Canaria's homo nightlife, and *Followers*, a domestic suspense novel that proved Bristol is an excellent backdrop for both gay chaos and murder.

Open continues his fascination with modern relationships — particularly the bit where everyone insists they're "fine with being open" moments before someone ends up crying in the kitchen. He writes fiction full of sex, lies, emotional landmines and the occasional corpse, while insisting it's not autobiographical (ish).

He lives with his two cats, Erin and Nelson, who contribute nothing to the writing process except sitting on his keyboard and leaving "chocolate kisses" on his cushions.

In daylight hours, he works as a web analyst for a large online retailer, which is exactly as glamorous as it sounds and involves playing with Excel and staring at graphs until meaning appears — kind of like tarot reading for capitalism, except the crystal ball is a pivot table.

When he's not staring at data or a manuscript, he can usually be found at the gym or in the swimming pool, attempting to make the goggles-and-swim-cap look happen.

He is a cinema enthusiast with a fondness for reclining seats and film tastes split evenly between twisty mysteries and big gay musicals, a TV-binge professional, a lapsed language student currently attempting to learn Spanish, and a mediocre chess player still baffled by the concept of checkmate.

He is technically single and hypothetically dateable, but a potent combination of social anxiety, overthinking and chronic failure to reply to dating app notifications has resulted in a thriving romantic life almost entirely in his own head.

He maintains that the juiciest stories sit squarely between romance, humour and complete catastrophe, and he plans to keep writing them until someone stages an intervention.

Please keep buying his books so he can fulfil his dream of being a full-time author, stop talking about himself in the third person and finally afford the standard of living his cats believe they are entitled to.

www.ingramcontent.com/pod-product-compliance
Lightning Source LLC
LaVergne TN
LVHW091033080826
845145LV00002B/476

* 9 7 8 1 0 6 8 4 2 8 0 4 3 *